"You know what I realized tonight, Sly?"

"What?"

Laura sighed. "That I don't love Zane anymore. It's really over."

Sly closed his eyes. "Laura, you know how I feel about you."

As if she didn't need to hear the words, she kissed him, so sweetly and eloquently that he knew everything that was in her heart. She loved him, too. It was in her breath, in the velvety feel of her tongue against his, in her touch....

He swallowed and broke the kiss. "I love you, Laura. I've loved you for a long time."

"Then show me," she whispered as a tear slid down her cheek.

"I will," he promised. "I'll show you what real love is like...."

ABOUT THE AUTHOR

Catch a Falling Star is prolific author Tracy Hughes's thirty-second novel. She's fascinated by the city of Nashville and its preoccupation with the music industry. That, and her desire to write a story with a "different, down-home kind of glitz," led her to frame her tale of a young woman's hunger for family within a popular country-and-western setting. The author, who lives with her husband and children in Clinton, Mississippi, is the winner of several publishing industry honors, including a *Romantic Times* Lifetime Achievement Award for her work in the Calloway Corners series. She also writes mainstream women's fiction under the name of Terri Herrington.

Tracy Hughes

Catch a
Falling Star

Harlequin Books

TORONTO • NEW YORK • LONDON
AMSTERDAM • PARIS • SYDNEY • HAMBURG
STOCKHOLM • ATHENS • TOKYO • MILAN
MADRID • WARSAW • BUDAPEST • AUCKLAND

ISBN 0-373-70623-5

CATCH A FALLING STAR

Catch a
Falling Star

PROLOGUE

"THERE'S SOMETHING liberating about failure." The words were tough ones, but accepting their truth was harder still. They were growth words, words that gave her a new direction. Taking a deep, shaky breath, Laura Rockford scribbled her signature on the divorce papers her attorney had prepared for her and wished such a private, intimate act didn't have to take place in front of a virtual stranger and two witnesses.

But it wasn't just those in the room who made her feel violated. Dozens of reporters waited outside the conference room for her to make a statement, as if she would spill her guts to the world in time for their evening deadlines. As calm as she'd tried to appear coming in here today, she was sure they all knew what this divorce was costing her. Everyone in Nashville who kept up with who was divorcing whom—after setting up betting pools on the lengths of those marriages—knew that she'd done everything in her power to make her husband happy.

With the divorce, she was finally succeeding.

"There you go," she said to the attorney, shoving the papers back across his desk. "In triplicate. A copy for my husband and one for my mother. Why don't we laminate them? He can frame his and hang it next to the picture of him with Elvis, and my mother can prop hers in her trophy case."

"And where are you putting your copy?" Lane West asked, playing along.

He expected her to name a part of someone's anatomy, she suspected, but as deep as she reached, she couldn't quite find her sense of humor. "Do I have to keep one?" she asked in a weaker voice.

"It's your divorce, Laura."

She breathed a laugh, then let her smile fade as the two secretaries signed their names as witnesses. Under the fluorescent lights, she knew she must look as pale as porcelain. Although her rich brown hair had been pulled back in a loose chignon, more to get it out of the way than to foster the sophisticated image the media liked to slap on her, her makeup was flawed. It was hard to keep it looking perfect when she'd broken into tears three times already this morning. Her eyes glistened in the aftermath of those tears, and her nose shone pink, a look that would have appalled her mother. But Laura was beyond caring.

"I spoke to your mother, and she told me she had wired the money to your account yesterday," Lane said, gesturing for the secretaries to leave. "I verified the deposit with the bank. It's all there. Ten million dollars."

"Of course it is. My mother always does what she says she's going to do."

He hesitated for a moment, as if weighing the irony of that statement. "Yes, well...an agent from the IRS is waiting in my office. You can just write a check from your account...."

Laura took her checkbook and scrawled out the amount, signed the check, then tore it out. For a moment, she stared down at it, trying to comprehend everything this would mean. With this check came the end of almost every significant relationship she had had in her life. It was the termination of her hope...the death of her dream.

Sliding the check across the table, she blinked back the tears stinging her eyes again. "It's all so easy," she said. "But selling my soul to my mother ought to get me a little more than broke and alone."

"Are you sure it won't, Laura?" he asked carefully.

Laura smiled and lifted her chin. "Absolutely," she said. "My mother knows exactly what she's doing. But it's about time she found out what her little girl is made of."

CHAPTER ONE

LAURA ROCKFORD HATED the phrase "poor little rich girl," but she'd spent most of her life painfully aware that it applied to her. Old Philadelphia money didn't often breed happiness, as was evident in the lives of the people around her as she grew. She remembered her father—a fourth generation financier who accumulated wealth the way he accumulated World War I paraphernalia—as a distant, crotchety man much too old for her mother. He taught her nothing during the years that she knew him except to stay in whatever wing of the huge house that he didn't occupy at any given time and to remain as silent as the servants when their paths did cross.

His greatest gift to her came at his death. Laura had never forgotten that the first time in her life she had got down on her knees and prayed, just as she had seen her Hispanic nanny do so many times, it was to thank God for removing her father from their home. She hadn't wasted any time praying for another one.

As she'd pointed out to God on that cold, quiet night, her mother was still quite beautiful. She had a trophy case full of the awards she'd won for that beauty, and any man would be proud to be seen with her. In her four-year-old way, however, Laura had indicated to God that her mother's personality might need a few adjustments. "Don't let her get mad at him, God. She gets mad easy. And don't let her have a mood when she meets him. If he's nice, maybe he'll keep her in a good mood all the time." She had considered the possibility of that, then, as an afterthought, added, "Maybe she's just always in a bad mood because of Father. But he's gone now, so nobody has to feel bad.''

The idea of death at that moment had seemed like an unwarranted blessing, one that she hadn't known to pray for but that delighted her nonetheless. And it was a good thing that no one in the household had paid much attention to her for most of that week, because her joviality might have offended them.

That joviality soon faded, however, when man after man was sent to her mother—proper candidates for her new father, in Laura's opinion—but each was quickly spurned. It wasn't until years later that Laura realized her mother had inherited billions at her father's passing, and that rather than making her happier, it only empowered her. Exactly *what* it empowered her to do was something Catrina Rockford had never quite defined in her own mind, so she increasingly used her power to subjugate everyone around her. The more men she chose to step on along the way, the merrier. Any relationships that might have sprouted were quickly squelched when Catrina's dollar signs became the screen through which she regarded them. The money her mother had expected would make her happy only made her more and more miserable.

Those next few years were just as lonely for Laura as her first four had been, for her mother never sought an intimacy with her child. More and more, the child fell to her knees and prayed for a father who would be like the television fathers she adored—Cliff Huxtable and Jason Seaver types, the kind who ate meals with his child and spent Saturdays playing in the park, the kind who would check her homework and know her friends and take her to movies. Her mother never figured much into the fantasy she had of such a man, for Laura had begun to discount her mother as part of any happy portrait she had painted for herself.

Catrina was never meant to mother. She was only meant to be beautiful and run corporations. And that was a fact that even Laura could never dispute.

Her prayer was answered when she was eight years old and Catrina brought home the first man who had ever objected when her mother told her to "run along." When Michael insisted that she dine with them, Laura knew he was the man she had been waiting for.

He had carefully explained to Laura that he owned a chain of radio stations and published several popular magazines that she had often seen her mother reading. The fact that he had altered her mother's mood completely, and that she had smiled more that night than Laura had ever seen her, told Laura that he traveled in similar financial circles as she. If he hadn't, she would have been exerting her power over him. But that night it seemed to be Michael who wielded the power.

Michael further established his footing in Laura's heart when he talked her mother out of sending her to the boarding school Laura had feared since she'd first heard of it. He told her that a child needed to be raised at home and that a mother should never turn her parental responsibility over to an institution.

Laura was never sure if it was her mother's love for her or her deep desire to impress Michael that had caused her to change her plans for Laura's future. But she did know that, without Michael, she would have been disposed of within the year.

Her mother married Michael within three months of that first dinner, then promptly lost interest in him. It was a phenomenon Laura was to see repeated many times over her life, but this first time, she found it astounding.

Laura's desperate attempts to keep Michael happy only bonded her more closely to him. When she made brownies and told him her mother had baked them, he had smiled sadly. "Your mother thinks getting chocolate on her fingers automatically constitutes a hundred calories. And just walking into the kitchen, well, she's certain that inhaling food is just as detrimental as eating it. I don't think your mother made these."

"Okay," Laura had confessed, disappointed. "I made them. But you can still eat them. Cook checked to make sure I did everything right."

He had smiled like a kid and taken the one she held in her damp palm. "You always do everything right, little Laura. Let's go to the kitchen and get some milk and eat until they're all gone."

Laura had felt downright decadent as she put her hand in his and followed him.

Though she'd had a stomachache for hours afterward, she wouldn't have traded that time with Michael for anything. Late that night as she lay in bed clutching her stomach, he had knocked at her door. "Come in," she said.

Michael came in and sat down on her bed, brandishing a bottle of pink stuff and a spoon. "Since I have a killer stomachache, I figured you did, too. I thought maybe you could use some of this."

Laura sat up and obediently took the antacid. "It's okay, though. It was fun, wasn't it?"

"Yeah, it was," he said. "I have a weakness for brownies, and little girls with big brown eyes." Messing up her hair, he got up and tucked her back in. "Hey, what do you say you and I get a kite and see if we can fly it this weekend?"

"Really?" she asked.

"Sure. I never see you playing outside, and you've got all that room to run and play. Have you ever flown a kite before?"

"No."

"Then I'd say it's time. Saturday, okay?"

"Okay."

When he'd leaned over and pressed a kiss on her forehead, she had beamed. "Good night, Michael."

"Good night, kiddo."

That weekend, they sent the kite so high that they almost lost sight of it, and Laura began to believe that Michael could do just about anything. When her mother didn't make it home from her fund-raising project in time for dinner, Michael, as though trying to cheer himself up, announced that they were going out.

"Out where?" Laura asked.

"Have you ever been to McDonald's?"

She smiled. "No. Mother says we have no business eating food that will kill us."

Michael rolled his eyes. "Your mother has some funny ideas. What fun is it to be rich, if you don't enjoy it?"

Laura considered that for a moment. "You weren't always rich, were you, Michael?"

"Nope," he said. "I worked hard for what I've made. I was raised in a regular, middle-class home. How did you know?"

"Because you're so happy," she said simply.

For a moment, she thought she'd said the wrong thing, because Michael looked at her with a new melancholy in his eyes. "Come on, kiddo," he said. "We're gonna get you one of those Happy Meals with the plastic toy inside. What do you think about that?"

"I think that'll be fine," she said.

Just as Michael knew it would, that inexpensive plastic toy had brought her more joy than the piano her mother had given her last Christmas or the electric car she'd given her the year before. When they were about to leave, a clown brought her a helium balloon.

"Can I let it go when we go outside, and watch it go up to heaven?" she asked him.

"Sure," he said, "if that's what you want."

"Okay. Will you hold it for me for a minute while I write a note?"

"A note? To whom?"

"To God," she said matter-of-factly. "It's real important."

Michael had smiled poignantly as she covered a napkin with one hand and meticulously wrote her note with the other, and he never pressed her to show it to him.

CATCH A FALLING STAR 15

When they went outside, they sat on the hood of his car and watched as the balloon disappeared into the sky, the note attached by a ribbon.

The note said, "Thank you for Michael. Love, Laura."

ONLY ONE YEAR LATER, Catrina announced that she was divorcing Michael and that he would be moving out within the week. No heed was paid to Laura's devastation over the news or her sudden withdrawal. And no explanation was ever granted.

At least, not by her mother.

Michael, however, tried to explain in the gentlest way he could. "Your mother and I have drifted apart. It's the best thing for everyone."

Laura had buried her face in her pillow and refused to look at him.

"Say something, kiddo."

"I hate her," Laura whispered.

Michael pulled her up and held her as she cried, and finally, he whispered, "Don't hate her, Laura. Your mother's hurting herself worst of all. She's the one who'll always be lonely."

"Take me with you," she sobbed, looking up at him with round, tearful eyes that broke his heart. "Please, Michael. I'll be good. I'll cook you brownies all the time. I've gotten real good at it . . . and I won't get in the way. . . ."

She saw the tears welling in his eyes as he eased her back and forced her to look at him. "I can't take you with me, sweetheart. You're not mine. They don't give custody to stepfathers."

"Why not? Mother won't care!"

When he shook his head, her eyes grew more desperate. "I could just go, and maybe she wouldn't notice. You could pay the staff to keep quiet, and I could live with you, and Mother would think I still live here!"

It was then that Michael had let her go and got up, rubbing his face as he paced across the floor. It wasn't until years later that she would learn how much that last desperate plea had anguished him. "Your mother loves you, sweetheart. She would notice."

"Michael, please don't go!" Her voice was a cracked whisper, but the words were uttered in vain.

Stooping down next to her bed, he looked into her eyes and gently pushed the hair back from her wet face. "I have to, kiddo. But we're still friends, okay? Whenever you need me, you can call. I'll always be there for you."

Laura knew it was as hard for him to walk out that day as it had been for her to see him go. But that didn't change anything. Things happened whether you wanted them to or not.

Her mother didn't notice that she brooded around for weeks afterward, and her obligatory stops by her room to say good-night were met with coolness. One night, when Laura was feeling particularly angry, she asked the question that she hadn't dared ask before. "Why did you divorce him, Mother?"

Catrina seemed uncomfortable with the question. "What a question for a nine-year-old to ask."

"Why, Mother?"

"Because we didn't love each other anymore."

"What difference did that make?" Laura asked. "You don't love anybody."

Catrina's face had reddened, and she'd stood up and stared down at her daughter with compressed lips. "How dare you speak to me that way?"

Innocent, Laura gazed up at her. "What way?"

"I think it's time you went away to school, Laura," her mother returned. "Maybe they can succeed where I've failed."

"If you want to get rid of me, why can't I just go live with Michael?"

Catrina gaped at her as if she'd just blasphemed her whole existence. "Michael is out of our lives, Laura. You'd better get used to that. He was nothing more than a brief mistake.''

Laura had been mortified when her tears overcame her. She never liked to cry in front of her mother. ''He was not a mistake! Michael loves me.''

''Michael tolerated you, Laura. That's all. But he's gone now.''

Later that night, Laura had lain awake in bed, sobbing with a nine-year-old's fervor. And in the deepest darkness of the night, she felt just as alone as a homeless orphan yearning hopelessly for a miracle.

The idea that Michael had only tolerated her festered inside her over the next few weeks, until she honestly couldn't remember if the affection he had shown her was real. It wasn't until he called her to say good-bye, before she left for school, that she realized her mother was wrong. She hadn't imagined his affection.

''Are you scared?'' he asked her.

Laura shrugged. ''A little.''

''It'll be fun, you know. There'll always be someone around to talk to, or play with, and you'll make a lot of new friends. I want you to write me, okay?''

''If you'll write me.''

''And write your mother, too.''

''They'll make me,'' Laura said. ''It's one of the rules. You have to write your mother once a week. But friends are optional.''

''Exercise that option, okay?''

''I will.''

When they said goodbye, Laura hung on until she heard Michael's click, and then the dial tone humming its finality in her ear.

Laura was silent all the way to Connecticut, while Catrina waxed poetic about the glories of her own alma mater. ''A lot will be expected of you there, darling. I was quite an achiever at Rumsey Hall, and your father was a respected member of the board of directors years ago. Don't let us down."

"I won't, Mother."

"And no tears. I hate melodramatic goodbyes. People watch us, darling, and we mustn't entertain them with our emotions." She had stared at Laura, and when the girl met her mother's eyes, she saw the faintest trace of tears there. Her mother reached over and stroked her hair out of her eyes. "It's going to be good for you, darling. It really is."

Laura let her eyes drift out the window and wondered why her mother went to such lengths to keep from growing close to her.

It was a question she would ask herself many times over the years.

CHAPTER TWO

HAVEN BERRINGER was to Princeton University what Elly May Clampett had been to Beverly Hills. That she didn't fit in was an understatement, though it didn't disturb Haven in the least, for she didn't *really* fit in anywhere. She was a self-contained enigma who had taken a vow of poverty for the sake of her art.

The problem was, Princeton didn't foster the image of poverty, and neither did the fact that her father had long been considered one of America's richest and most success-ful country music stars. But Haven fancied herself a poet— a poet of the common people, just as her father had been in his early days—and in her mind, "cush" wasn't conducive to art.

So, instead of the designer clothes that her peers pa-raded, Haven owned only two pairs of jeans and five T-shirts—three army green and two brown—which she wore every day. She kept her sandy hair cut carelessly short, for vanity was something she deplored. She wore her modesty the way Queen Elizabeth wore royalty.

And though her eccentricities made it difficult for her to keep a roommate, Haven barely noticed. Her mind was too occupied with ethereal things to worry about pettiness and worldliness.

So on the first day of her senior year, when she was paired to room with Laura Rockford, daughter of the practically famous Catrina Rockford, Haven was too distracted to worry about good impressions.

Laura, on the other hand, dreaded getting to know a new bunkmate with every bone in her body. She had lost her last roommate to marriage and had never been comfortable making new friends. Even at boarding school, her circle of comrades had been very small, and none of them had been lasting-enough friends to have kept in touch since graduation.

When she walked in, loaded with three suitcases and more on the way, she found Haven sitting on a corner of a bare mattress and playing an acoustic guitar, staring off into space with casual abandon.

"Hi," she said, dropping her suitcase and holding out a hand to Haven. "I'm Laura Rockford. Your new roommate."

Haven stopped strumming and regarded her for a moment, then shook her hand. "Haven Berringer. You can have your pick of the beds."

Laura shrugged and glanced at the empty one. "That one's fine."

"This one's by the window," Haven said in her slow, Southern accent. "It has a nicer view."

Laura hesitated. "Well . . . okay. If you want the other one."

"I don't. I mean, I don't care. I won't be sleeping here that much."

Laura sat down slowly and tried not to look disappointed. "Where will you be?"

"Around. Sometimes I pitch a tent and sleep outside."

Laura frowned. "Why?"

"Why not? It's really pretty, sleepin' under the stars." Haven started strumming again, and her eyes seemed to focus on some distant nothing across the room.

Laura decided not to pursue the subject any further, so she opened her suit bag and slid open the door to the closet. "You haven't unpacked yet?" she asked, looking over her shoulder.

"Sure I have," Haven said. "But I don't have that much. It all fit in a drawer."

"Oh." This didn't surprise Laura, for she had seen Haven on campus many times over the last three years and knew that she had a limited wardrobe. And she had heard rumors that the girl was spacey, and that she had barely escaped suspension several times over the years because her grades were below Princeton's acceptable average.

Laura began hanging up her clothes as Haven continued to strum her guitar. Finally, she turned around. "That's pretty good. Do you sing like your father?"

"His voice is deeper."

Laura smiled, and she saw the beginnings of a grin creeping across Haven's mouth. Shaking out a blouse and slipping it on a hanger, she said, "I should probably tell you up front, I don't know much about country music."

"No problem. I don't know much about finance. That is what your mama's into, isn't it?"

Laura regarded her for a long moment, then shrugged and turned back around. "That's what they tell me. So what's your major?"

"Philosophy. Yours?"

"Business."

Haven stopped strumming. "You don't look much like a business major."

Laura smiled. "I don't *feel* much like a business major."

"Well, it's only one more year."

"Not for me." Laura closed the closet and opened a suitcase. "I have to come back for an MBA, and probably a doctorate before it's all over."

"What do you mean, you have to?"

Laura tried to smile. "I mean, it's predestined. Written in the stars. My mother has sealed my fate, and I'm powerless to stop it."

"Nobody's powerless," Haven said, beginning to strum again. "Not unless they want to be."

Something about her certainty in that statement bothered Laura. "Then why are you here?"

Haven smiled. "Because my daddy informed me that he brought me into this world and he could take me out. He has this thing about me gettin' the education he never got. But I wasn't powerless. I had the choice whether to risk his threats or not."

Laura laughed. "Yeah, right. Well, I guess I had the choice, too. Given the alternatives, I think a decade in college is a small price. My mother almost always gets her way."

Haven began to laugh, and Laura turned back to her. "What's funny?"

"Won't your mama love it when she finds out you're roomin' with Zane Berringer's daughter? That's like puttin' Princess Di with Minnie Pearl."

"You have a little more class than Minnie Pearl," Laura assured her.

"Yeah," Haven conceded. "I do dress better, don't I?"

The two women erupted into laughter, and Laura knew then that it was going to turn out all right. She and Haven Berringer were going to get along just fine.

"IT'S ONE THING to be thrown together in the room with her," Catrina Rockford said the first time she visited her daughter during her senior year. The two sat lunching on lobster in a restaurant of Catrina's choice. "It's quite another to be seen with her when you don't have to be. It isn't good for your image, dear."

"My image?" Laura laughed. "Mother, I don't need an image."

"Of course you do. You're my daughter. You're a Rockford. Heiress to a fortune, and everybody knows it."

"A lot of good it does me."

"And what do you mean by that?"

Laura sighed and shifted in her chair. "I mean that if I can't choose my own friends, none of it is worth anything."

"Friends," Catrina said, as if the word were distasteful. "Darling, friends are not what count in life. They only distort your vision. You have to set your mind on your goal and decide how you want to accomplish it. Then get rid of everything in your way. Tell me, Laura. What are your goals?"

"I don't need any, Mother. You have so many for me already."

Catrina sat back and brought her martini to her lips. "I only want what's best for you."

"And you think a lonely life without friends, in hot pursuit of more money, is what's best for me? I already have more money than I could ever spend in a lifetime."

Catrina's face reddened, a rare occurrence, since she prided herself so on never giving away an emotion. "I won't tolerate that attitude, Laura. I'm warning you."

It was enough to shut Laura up, though she couldn't say exactly what her mother was warning her of. All she did know was that she hadn't yet learned to cross her mother without shrinking within seconds afterward. The subsequent chill was almost more than she could bear.

"I was thinking that perhaps I should get you your own apartment. Maybe it's time you got out of that dorm. There are some lovely little condos on the other side of town. We could get it decorated just the way you like."

"I told you, Mother. I like the dorm. There are people there. Besides, it would be a waste to buy something when I'm not even here all year. Unless, of course, you don't mean to work me as hard this summer. If I had a free weekend now and then, I could come back . . ."

Her mother was shaking her head even before she could finish. "You're going to work, darling, just as you always have. If you ever hope to take over the business, you have an awful lot to learn. You already have twice the business acumen I had when your father died, and by the time you have your MBA, you'll be able to give any of the other executives in the company a run for their money." She took a sip of her drink. "No, darling. The condo wouldn't get you off the hook. It would just remove you from the influences of people who can pull you down."

Laura shrugged. "I like living with Haven."

"Why?" Catrina asked. "What about that hick could you possibly like?"

"She's not a hick."

"And above that she sounds crazy. I wouldn't be surprised if she was addicted to some kind of drug...."

"She doesn't even drink, Mother. Haven's a very spiritual person."

"Well, of course she is, with a name like that. Have you met her father?"

"No, but I've seen pictures."

"Does he wear that Elvis suit around the house?"

Laura smiled. "She hasn't mentioned it if he does. But frankly, I think he's very sexy."

"Wonderful," Catrina said, throwing up her manicured hands. "I allow you to stay in the dorm, and the next thing I know you're hooked on Conway Twitty."

"Not Conway Twitty, Mother. Zane Berringer. He's more along the lines of Kris Kristofferson than Conway Twitty."

"Don't tell me you're listening to his records."

"I've heard some. I was planning to give you one of his CDs for Christmas." She was goading her mother, and Catrina knew it.

Changing the subject, Catrina gestured for the waiter to refill her glass. "So, tell me about the men in your life. There haven't been any photos in the tabloids lately. You do date, don't you?"

"Sometimes." Sobering, Laura let her gaze drift over the diners seated around them.

"Well, who are they? Where are they from?"

"Nobody you know, Mother. But as soon as I start to get serious, I'll be sure to get you his vital statistics so you can do a proper search."

"Don't be ridiculous."

"Have you seen Michael?" Laura asked, changing the subject.

"Of course not. Why would I?"

"I got a letter from him last week. He said he might come visit me next month."

"What on earth for?" Catrina asked.

"We're friends, Mother. Michael's a great person. He's getting married again, you know."

"Bully for him. It's about time."

"Yeah, well, some people don't go through mates like they go through light bulbs."

"Excuse me?"

The spear had been skillfully thrown and painfully received. It was enough for Laura.

"So, how's Pierre?"

Pierre was Catrina's fourth husband, a French film producer who crossed the ocean several times a year to visit his wife. Had they ever lived together, Laura doubted the marriage would have lasted the two years it had.

"He's very well, thank you."

Haven would have loved it, Laura thought. She would have been snickering at Catrina's airs and mentally composing a song about her fingernails percussing the marble tabletop and her intimate response to Laura's non-probing questions. It would have been filled with irony and caustic wit, and would have got closer to the truth about Laura's relationship with Catrina than either of them had ever been able to articulate.

As her mother's limousine dropped her back at the dormitory, Laura saw Haven sitting on the steps playing her guitar. Her brown T-shirt was wrinkled and her jeans were faded with a hole in the knee, and in spite of the laced black boots on her small feet, she had a feminine look to her. Her short hair shone in the sunshine, and her nose and cheeks were tinged with pink sunburn. "Let me get Haven," she told Catrina. "I want you to meet her."

"Must I? Laura, I really have to get back to Philadelphia."

"It'll only take a minute." Stepping out of the car, she called to Haven, and the girl stopped playing and got to her feet.

"Come meet my mother!"

As if she'd been summoned to meet anyone off the street, rather than the richest woman in America, the one that paparazzi often hid behind bushes to photograph, Haven ambled, unimpressed, down the dorm steps and came to the door of the limo. Leaning in, she extended a hand. "Hey. How's it goin'?"

"Hello." Catrina withdrew her hand as quickly as possible.

"I was vaccinated when I was five," Haven assured her.

Catrina shot her a look. "Excuse me?"

"All right, since you asked so nice."

Haven backed away from the limo, and fighting the grin on her face, Laura leaned back in. "Thank you for lunch, Mother. I'll see you at Thanksgiving."

It took a moment for Catrina to stop gaping at Haven, but finally, she rallied. "Oh, yes. I meant to tell you. I'm meeting Pierre in France for Thanksgiving this year, and we're taking a cruise. You'll have to make other plans."

"Oh." Laura didn't know why it still surprised her when these things happened, but she always seemed to get that lump in her throat that was so hard to swallow. "Well, have a wonderful time."

"I'll see you for Christmas instead," Catrina said.

"Yes. All right." She offered her mother a spurious kiss, then watched quietly as the limo drove away.

"Interestin', huh?" Haven observed.

"What?"

"That all that money still can't buy good manners."

The observation struck Laura as funny, for manners of any kind were usually the last thing on Haven's mind.

"So, you want to come home with me for Thanksgivin'? We do it up big."

"Really?" Laura considered it for a moment. "To your father's or your mother's?"

"Well, both. Just because they're divorced doesn't mean they're separated."

Laura struggled to follow her. "What?"

"Well, you know. Daddy lives in the big house, and Mama lives in the guest cottage. As much as she's in and out of the big house, it's almost like they're still married, except for their lovers that come and go. We still celebrate holidays together, though."

"And they wouldn't mind if I came along?"

"Heck, no. One more wouldn't make any difference."

Laura glanced after her mother's limousine and realized Catrina would have a fit—might even cancel her plans—if she knew what they were talking about. "I don't know. I'll probably just go on home, anyway, and spend the week reading or something."

"Yeah, that ought to make her happy."

"Who?"

Haven smiled and started up the stairs.

"Haven, what are you implying?"

"Nothin'. If she wants you to spend Thanksgivin' all by yourself, then you'd better do it."

Laura watched her reach the top of the stairs and sling her guitar over her shoulder. It was true. She was letting Catrina control her, and Catrina's prejudices were infiltrating her reasoning powers. "Haven!"

Haven turned around with a smug smile on her face, and Laura hurried up the steps behind her. When she reached her, she said, "All right, I'll go home with you. But don't expect me to ever like country music, no matter how much I like your family. And by the way, I know *you've* been vaccinated, but have they?"

"Yeah, and we'll make sure we pick all the ticks out of your pillow and fumigate your room before we put you there."

"All right then," Laura said, laughing. "We've got a deal."

CHAPTER THREE

LAURA DIDN'T KNOW why she expected Haven's home to be less opulent than her own. Perhaps it was the five T-shirts her roommate owned, and the rusted, leaky VW she drove, and the fact that she was more comfortable sleeping in a sleeping bag than she was on satin sheets.

But when they arrived at the Berringer estate in Laura's BMW—she had refused to ride in Haven's beat-up bug—she found that the mansion was as large and meandering as the Rockford house.

"I didn't quite expect this," Laura said, gaping at Haven's home before they got out.

"Why?" Haven drawled. "Did you expect a tar paper shack and clothes hanging out on the line?"

"No," Laura said. "I knew your father was successful. I just didn't think..."

"There's a lot of money in country music," Haven said with a slight note of resignation. "Common people write songs about common problems, and they make a zillion dollars. Then they buy a big mansion and fancy cars, and they forget where they came from."

"Did your dad forget?"

Haven sighed and considered that for a moment. "He forgot long before I came along. Brace yourself, Laura. My family is generally more materialistic than I am."

"Darn," Laura said. "And I was so sure that this was just for show, and that there was a line of pup tents on the back lawn where all of the Berringers really sleep."

"Don't tell my folks I do that, okay?" Haven said seriously. "They don't like it."

"I can't imagine why."

Haven smiled slightly in spite of herself, then grabbed her bag out of Laura's trunk. "I hope you're ready for this. The noise level is usually pretty high around here."

"I thought you were the youngest. Do you have brothers and sisters still at home?"

"Still at home?" Haven laughed. "My brothers all built houses on Daddy's land. They're always here with their wives and children, in and out, in and out, all the time. It's like a bus station. And my sisters come home whenever they have fights with their husbands. They've actually started synchronizing their fights so they can be here at the same time."

"You're kidding."

Haven smiled. "Yeah, but it's not so far from the truth. Ford and Rally run Daddy's publishin' company, and Blue is Daddy's manager, and Choral and Angel work wherever they're needed whenever they feel like it, so everybody's with everybody else all the time."

Grinning, Laura pulled her luggage from the trunk and set it on the sidewalk. "Where did your parents come up with these names?"

Haven laughed. "Mine's kind of obvious. They figured I was heaven sent, which, of course, I was. Blue was named after one of Daddy's first hit songs. Rally got his name after Daddy took a shot at racin' cars. And Ford—the oldest—was named for the place he was conceived."

"Not in the car."

"The back seat," Haven confirmed. "Of course, Choral's and Angel's names are as obvious as mine. It's an occupational hazard, I guess, bein' the children of a music star. At least we weren't named Moon Unit and Dweezil. Come on. I'll get somebody to come back for your suitcases."

Slinging her duffel bag over her shoulder, Haven led Laura up the steps and through the front door.

"Anybody home?" Haven shouted as she kicked the door shut behind her.

A chorus of shouts came from some other place in the house, and in moments they were surrounded by people who were laughing and hugging Haven as if they'd assembled just to greet her.

It was a different Haven, this woman who stood surrounded by her siblings, laughing like a kid while they hugged her and mussed her hair and teased her.

"You look great, Haven. Is this a new T-shirt?"

"Did those boots come with that hole in the toe, or did you have to pay extra for it?"

"Haven, honey, please let me take you to my hairdresser. He can give you the cutest cut, put a little highlightin' in..."

"Hush, Cille. My baby sister is allergic to hairdressers. They make her limbs go so stiff that you can't even get her through the door."

"How's your writin' comin'?" her oldest brother whispered, sweeping her into a hug and kissing her cheek.

"I've got a bunch of new songs," Haven whispered back. "I'll play 'em for you later. Everybody, this is my roommate, Laura Rockford."

But Laura hadn't been ignored. After greeting Haven, each of the family members had turned to Laura and hugged her with just as much warmth, reiterating how glad they were that she had come.

She heard something like a growl at the top of the opulent staircase, and Laura jumped. Zane Berringer stood there, grinning down at his daughter like a wolf about to pounce, and said, "Is that my little Haven? Come here, girl!"

"Hey, Daddy." She started toward the stairs, but Zane was all the way down in an instant, crushing her in a giddy embrace and shouting over her, "You must be Laura. Welcome to the craziest household you've ever seen. You'll have to excuse us, 'cause we haven't seen Haven since August."

Haven pulled out of her father's embrace. "Where's Mama?"

"She'll be up in a minute." He turned back to Laura and took her under his arm. "Say, Laura, haven't you been able to improve her wardrobe any? When she told me she'd moved in with you, I thought, 'Thank you, Lord. Hallelujah.' I thought maybe some of your style might rub off."

"Actually," Laura said, smiling at Haven, "I've been considering wearing nothing but T-shirts and jeans myself."

"Don't believe her, Daddy," Haven said. "If she did, it'd be designer jeans and Liz Claiborne tees. Simplicity has to come from the inside out, you know."

Laura didn't take offense any more than Haven did. "There's style, and then there's style. But it's nice to meet you, Mr. Berringer."

Zane winced. "Honey, if you don't mind, I'd prefer that you call me Zane. I feel old enough without you constantly remindin' me."

"All right, Zane."

A shriek came from another room, and Haven turned around and caught the embrace of a woman who Laura assumed was her mother. "Look at you! Baby, it's so good to see you!"

Haven looked back over her shoulder. "Laura, this is my mama. Rosy Berringer."

"Laura!" Rosy threw her arms around Laura, too. "It's so good to finally meet you. Tell me, now. Do you like country music?"

Laura shot Haven an eloquent look. "Well, uh...I haven't been exposed to it that much."

"Guys, we got work to do," Zane said.

"How can you call yourself an American and not listen to country music?"

"Well...uh..."

"She's not hopeless yet, Mama. Laura's not sure what she likes. I'm still workin' on her."

"Haven's stuff is great," Laura piped up, hoping to redeem herself.

Zane's smile seemed to fall as he looked down at his daughter. "Haven's stuff?"

She had apparently messed up, for she saw Haven's face close up. "It's no big deal, Daddy. Just a couple of songs."

But Laura knew there were many, many songs to Haven's credit. As the family moved from the foyer into the kitchen, she couldn't help wondering why Haven's music was such a touchy issue for one of country music's most legendary performers.

THAT NIGHT, Haven stopped by her room to say good-night and plunked down on her bed. "So, what do you think of this crazy crew?"

"I love it," Laura said. "It's what I've always imagined a family to be." She sighed and said, "Haven, I don't know if you realize how lucky you are."

"I guess." She got up and pulled her socked feet beneath her. "Listen, about my music . . . You probably noticed my daddy's chill every time somebody mentioned it."

"Yeah. I hope I didn't start any trouble. I didn't know."

"It's all right. Daddy's just goin' through a bad time right now. You know, he's had twenty-three albums go platinum, and he's won awards, and there was a time when he was the hottest thing in country music. His concerts would sell out in the first couple of hours. People camped out to get tickets."

"I thought they only did that for Springsteen."

"Well, things aren't so great anymore. I think Daddy's feelin' the pressure of all these new acts catchin' up to him. Billy Ray Cyrus and Dwight Yoakam and Jerry Joe Wagner. He's started to turn a little bitter about the business, and he's pretty much laid the law down. We can work in the business as long as we're not artists. He'd rather have us join cults than record songs."

"That's really sweet," Laura said softly. "That he'd care about you like that, I mean."

"Well, personally, I think it has more to do with him not wantin' our competition. Truth is, I'd rather he supported me just a little. I can take care of myself."

"He'll come around."

Haven pulled herself up and stretched. "Well, whether he does or not, I've made up my mind. He's not gonna stop me. See ya in the mornin'."

"Night, Haven."

Laura sat in the quiet room after Haven had left, thinking about the fact that Haven's father had expressed his concerns about her getting her heart broken, had given her advice, had *cared*. There was something so very sweet about that, even if none of it was what Haven wanted to hear. And from what she had seen, Laura doubted very much that there was any mercenary motive behind it.

This house was alive with love and warmth, unlike the cold, quiet mansion that Laura called home. This was what family was supposed to be like, what she had yearned for all her life. Her mother had asked her about goals, but Laura hadn't had an answer. Now she did. If Catrina ever asked her that question again, Laura knew what she would say.

"My goal is to have a family like the Berringers, Mother. And I intend to reach it."

ZANE FINISHED his last repetition of bench presses, then with a herculean effort dropped the 250 pounds of weights into their supports. Glistening with perspiration, he sat up, braced his elbows on his thighs and hung his head as he tried to catch his breath.

At fifty-five, bench presses weren't as easy as they had been twenty years ago, but then nothing was. Keeping his body fit was a constant struggle, just as maintaining his career was. And his finances. But in the last two areas, he embraced the philosophy that if you ignored the problems, they'd go away. So far, his competition in the music arena hadn't cooperated with that line of thinking. And neither had the IRS.

The cordless phone he had placed on the floor rang. Zane grabbed a towel to throw around his neck and snatched it up. "Hello?"

"Zane, it's Bill. I just got the notice you forwarded over from the IRS. Why didn't you let me know the minute you got it?"

Zane took the end of the towel and rubbed his face. "Well, blazes, we had thirty days. What was the hurry?"

"Every day counts, if I'm supposed to get you another extension. Unless you've just had a windfall and had ten million dollars drop out of the sky."

Zane heaved a sigh, wishing he could have done without this phone call tonight. "No, I haven't come up with it. I told you I could pay them as soon as I get royalties on my last album."

There was silence on the other end, and finally Bill cleared his throat. "With all due respect, Zane, you haven't exactly been sweeping in the profits for the last few years. What makes you think this album will do it?"

There was nothing Zane hated worse than the idea that his music couldn't hold its own. "Because it will, that's why. It has to. Just get me another extension and try to negotiate it down."

"They're not going to keep giving you time, Zane, and I've already gotten them to settle for half of what you owed. We've got to put our heads together and find some way of coming up with this money."

"I told you how I'm gonna come up with it," he said. "Just do it!"

With that, he cut the phone off and flung it across the room, then dropped his head down again and clasped his hands behind his neck.

"Is everything all right?"

Zane looked up and saw Laura standing in the doorway. She was a beauty, that one . . . the hair of a two-thousand-dollar-an-hour model, the almond-shaped eyes of a pageant queen, the mouth of a seductress and the body of a twenty-one-year-old girl. "Yeah, sorry," he said with a self-deprecating grin. "Hope I didn't wake you."

"No. I was going down because I left my purse in the kitchen. I heard something fall."

"It was the phone," he said, nodding toward it. "They generally do fall whenever somebody throws them."

Laura winced. "You threw it?"

He laughed softly and took the towel off his lap. "Yeah, I threw it."

"Oh."

He couldn't help grinning at the way she refused to pry, and crooking a finger, he invited her in. "Care to keep an old man company?"

She came in, and something stirred inside him. She was wearing a Japanese floral robe, all silk and flowing, and through the fabric he could see the faint outline of a negligee. Did she sleep like that every night, or was she just trying to drive him crazy?

"You're not old," Laura said, coming in and taking a seat on the rowing machine across from him. Looking around, she said, "You must work out every day."

He knew better than to bait her, but he wasn't able to stop himself. "Why do you say that?"

"Because you're in such good shape. What do you bench?"

"Oh, about three hundred," he lied.

Her eyebrows shot up. "That's pretty good."

He grinned. "What do you know about it?"

"I had a brief relationship with a football player last year," she said. "That's all he talked about."

"It didn't work out, I gather."

She laughed. "No. It was tough having to hide all the mirrors whenever he came over."

Zane chuckled, letting his eyes linger on her, and suddenly he realized that he felt better. There was nothing like a beautiful young woman to breathe life back into a man. Especially when she was sitting right in his own home in nothing but a negligee and a robe that made his mouth water. It didn't hurt that her name happened to be Rockford.

He wondered what she was worth. One, two billion? The possibilities began to excite him even more than her presence did.

"So you don't listen to country music, huh?"

She looked embarrassed. "Only because I haven't been exposed to it that much."

"Haven doesn't play it at school?"

"Haven?" Laura laughed. "The stereo in our room is mine, and so are all the CDs. Haven hasn't got any."

"She's got plenty," Zane said, standing up and reaching for a barbell. "Why she refuses to take any with her is a mystery her mama and I will never understand."

"It's materialism," Laura said. "She doesn't want any part of it."

Zane snorted. "What's the deal with her, anyway? You live with her. You see her every day. Is she trying to create some kind of image or what?"

"I don't think so," Laura said. "Haven doesn't care what anyone thinks about her. I think she's just trying to experience commonality. She's a gifted poet, you know, and she feels she can't write for the common people if she's lived a cushy life."

"Sue me," Zane said, pumping the barbell until his biceps bulged. "I provided a nice life for my daughter. I have no apologies."

"Well, you shouldn't. Haven's just . . . Haven. She's her own person, and she's a real treat to have around."

"So, have you heard any of these . . .*songs* . . . she's been writing?"

"Some," she said. "I mean, she's never performed them for me or anything. But I hear her strumming, and now and then I find lyrics written on paper sacks or napkins."

"You're kidding." Zane started to laugh. "That girl."

"They're pretty good, though, from what I can tell."

Zane's smile faded, and he shot her a sidelong look. "Have you heard her sing?"

"Well, no, not really."

Zane nodded as if he'd suspected as much. "Haven fancies herself a performer, like me. Problem is, the kid can't sing."

Laura couldn't believe it. "Are you sure? She's *your* daughter."

"Yeah, well, she inherited her mama's vocal cords."

He switched the barbell to his other hand and pumped again.

"Is that why you're discouraging her?"

Zane counted ten repetitions, then said, "You got it. I don't want to see her trampled in this business. It's bad enough when you have talent. But Haven has zip."

"Oh, no." Laura wasn't sure why that disturbed her so. It was something about the injustice of Haven having such a strong dream and working so hard for it, and it all being in vain. "That's too bad."

Zane finished his curls, then set the weight back down. "I sent Haven to Princeton, hoping she'd come back with a degree in engineering or law. It took me four years to realize that would be as easy as turning Lassie into a brain surgeon."

The idea made Laura smile. "Poor Haven."

"She'll be all right," he said. "I have five other kids I've successfully steered away from being entertainers, which isn't easy to do in Nashville. I'll steer her out of it, too." He threw the towel back over his shoulder and said, "Are you in a hurry to get back to bed?"

She shook her head. "No. I was having trouble sleeping."

His grin was as sexy as his pictures indicated, and his body, glistening with the slightest sheen of perspiration, was downright seductive. "Then come downstairs with me, and I'll acquaint you with a little country music. Some really good stuff. Mine."

"I'd love to."

"Good," he said, setting his arm around her shoulders. He escorted her down the stairs and into the living room, which had been so full of family today. But tonight only a single small lamp glowed in the corner, and a comforting quiet filled the room.

Zane got out one of his CDs, popped it into the stereo, then turned back to Laura. "There's only one condition. You have to say you love it whether you do or not, and you have to dance with me."

"Dance?" she asked, looking up at him. "Can you dance to your songs?"

Zane chuckled softly as the music began to play. "Darlin', you can dance and cry and make love and do anything else you can think of to my music. I can see I've got a lot of educating to do tonight."

She took his hand and allowed him to pull her against him as his voice began to work its magic, the deep, gravelly tones wrapping around her, titillating her, disturbing her. And along with the music came the warmth of his body against hers, the gentle way he touched her and spun her around the room, the sweet way he occasionally dipped her, then grinned with the charm of a gifted child who was well aware of his power.

She smiled up at him, no longer feeling awkward, no longer feeling awed by the image she had had of him.

"You know, I've seen pictures of you in magazines with your mama," Zane whispered, "but I never knew your eyes were quite that blue."

"Funny," she said, "I was just thinking the same thing about you."

He grinned. "My eyes aren't blue."

"No, but they're silver. More silver than they are in your pictures." Smiling, she said, "I love your voice. It's very . . . virile."

It was the perfect description to keep Zane awake all night. "Thank you," he said. "I hoped your first foray into country music would be pleasant."

She almost blushed. "That's an understatement."

"And you can dance, too. You're easy to lead. You follow like a feather."

"I took lessons at school. It was required. Besides, it's easy when the music is so sweet."

His smile faded. "Do you really mean it? You're not just saying it because I told you to?"

"No," she insisted. "I like it. I really do."

"Enough to go home and throw out all your classic rock CDs?"

"Well . . ."

He laughed then and dipped her again. "Okay, it was a lot to ask," he said, pulling her back up and spinning her. "But I thought I'd try."

"But I'll definitely add it to my collection," she said.

The song came to an end, and Zane spun her against him and dipped her one last time, until she hung her head back and laughed. "That was fun."

"You're fun," he said, pulling her back upright and letting her go. "No wonder Haven likes you so much. She doesn't have a lot of friends, you know."

"Haven doesn't *need* a lot of friends. She's very self-contained."

"She is that." He went to the stereo and turned the music off, and Laura felt a surge of disappointment. She could have stayed here and listened to the songs all night, dancing with her best friend's father and laughing as if they were both kids.

But it was a ridiculous fantasy, and it was getting late. Sighing, she said, "Well, I guess I'll go turn in."

"I enjoyed getting to know you," he said, leaning back against a table and crossing his muscular arms in front of him.

"Yeah," she said. "We'll have to do it again sometime."

"How about tomorrow night?" he asked, and from the smile in his eyes, she didn't know if he was serious or not. "After everybody goes to bed."

She smiled. "I'd like that."

"Good night."

"Good night."

He watched her float back up the stairs with a million-dollar smile on her face. It wasn't until she was gone that Zane realized she hadn't got the purse she had come down for.

CHAPTER FOUR

ROSY BERRINGER hummed an off-key chorus to a song Laura didn't know and bustled around the kitchen as though she belonged there. She looked up when Laura came in and said, "Good mornin', honey. Did you sleep well?"

"Yes, thank you," Laura said. "Is that coffee?"

"Help yourself," Rosy said. "I just made it. I guess Haven's still sleepin'."

"Must be." She poured a cup, then sipped it black. "Sure is quiet around here this morning, after yesterday."

Rosy got her cup and sat down across from Laura. "Well, you know, everybody has their own lives. Nobody but Zane actually lives in this house anymore, and Haven when she's home. But there's always somebody else here. The kids are in and out, *I'm* in and out. It's a madhouse, sometimes. Later on today it'll be Grand Central Station again, bein' Thanksgivin' and all. But I guess everybody's house is like that on Thanksgivin'."

Laura shook her head. "Not mine. My house is more like a mausoleum than a home. It's very quiet, even on the holidays. I'm really glad Haven invited me here."

Rosy patted her hand. "I'm glad she did, too, honey. And I hope you brought your appetite. The girls and I are cookin' up a storm today."

"You do your own cooking?" she asked.

"Usually. Oh, Zane has a couple of housekeepers, and one of them does most of his cookin', but I gave them the day off. I'm takin' care of things today."

Laura smiled at the fact that Rosy still ran Zane's house as if it were her own. "I finally heard one of Zane's songs yesterday. I was surprised. I didn't expect to like it."

"Oh, yeah. He can sing, all right. Not like he used to, though. He used to just melt your toenails off. Had that gritty kind of bedroom voice. But he's lost his edge."

Laura looked up at her as she stood and went back to the stove. "What do you mean?"

"Oh, you know. The business has changed. There are a lot of younger stars movin' up. He's a little bitter sometimes."

"Well, they couldn't have anything on him."

Rosy laughed. "Well, for heaven's sake, don't tell him that. You start feedin' that man's ego and you'd better prepare for the worst."

Rosy opened the oven to check the turkey and the aroma escaped, filling the room. "So, are you and Haven goin' to see her daddy play Saturday night?"

"Play? Where?"

"At the Opry. You didn't think you were comin' to Nashville without going to the Grand Ole Opry, did you?"

"Well, I didn't know. I'd love to go, even if Haven doesn't."

"Oh, Haven'll be there. She can't get enough of it."

"Enough of what?"

They both turned and saw a sleepy Haven standing in the kitchen doorway. "The Opry, baby. Laura wants to go."

"Mm-kay," Haven said simply. Pouring her coffee, she clutched the mug and sat down, pulling one foot up into her chair. "How long have you been up?"

"Just a little while. I was talking to your mother."

"Oh, no. Not about me, I hope."

Rosy and Laura laughed. "Sure we were, baby. I was asking Laura how I could get you to wear somethin' besides T-shirts and jeans."

"I hope she told you it was hopeless."

Laura smiled.

"What about when you dress up, Haven honey? Don't you ever go anywhere where you need to look a little better?"

"Sure I do," Haven said. "And on those occasions, I tuck my shirt in."

Laura smiled. "She does, it's true."

They heard a buzz on the intercom by the door, and Rosy went and pushed the button. "Hello?"

"That you, Rosy?"

"Yeah, baby, it's me." She grinned like a schoolgirl, then winked back at them over her shoulder. Pushing another button, she said, "The gate's unlatched. Come on in and head over to my place. I'll be there in a minute."

Turning around, she took off her apron. "I've gotta go."

"Who is that?" Haven asked.

"Barry Michaels. You know the fiddler."

"Is that who you're seein' now?"

Rosy laughed. "That's who I'm seein' this mornin'. Can you look after the turkey?"

Haven frowned. "Mama, you know I can't cook."

"I didn't ask you to cook it. Just look after it. Laura, you know how to look after a turkey, don't you?"

"Well, uh..."

"Good. Just keep checkin' on it."

"Checkin' for what?" Haven persisted.

Rosy rolled her eyes. "Oh, never mind. I'll be back to check on it myself. Just don't let the kitchen burn down."

"So, who's Barry Michaels?" Laura asked after Rosy had buzzed out the door.

"He's a studio musician. Not much older than me. Mama likes 'em young."

"Well, apparently they like her. She's really cute."

Haven smiled. "She's a mess. You really want to go to the Opry? It's an awful lot of country for somebody who doesn't like country music."

"It'll be fun," she said. "Besides, I'd kind of like to see your dad perform. I came back down to get my purse last night, and I ran into him. He played one of his songs for me. I really liked it."

Haven eyed her for a moment, then glanced at the purse lying on the floor. "That purse over there?"

Laura saw it and got up to pour another cup of coffee. "I guess I forgot what I came down for."

"Guess so."

Heavy silence followed, and Laura realized that Haven didn't like the idea of her fraternizing with her father. "What did your mother say to do about the turkey?"

"Check on it," Haven said.

"Oh, yeah." She went to the oven, peered in through the glass and said, "Looks pretty good to me."

"Me, too," Haven said. "No flames, no charred flesh. I think we're doin' a pretty good job."

The two wilted in laughter.

THE TURKEY SURVIVED Laura and Haven's vigil over it, but it didn't survive the pillaging by Haven's five brothers and sisters, their four spouses and twelve nieces and nephews.

Content after a meal that could have fed an army, Zane sat on the porch swing on the back of the house and watched his children and grandchildren engage in a game of touch football.

Laura was right at the center of things, playing and laughing as though she had known them all her life. He never would have figured that about her. From the articles he occasionally ran across in *People* or *The Enquirer*—not that he read them, but he was always on the lookout for what they were saying about *him*—she seemed aloof and above it all, like her mother. But that wasn't the Laura he'd spent time with last night.

He smiled as she ran for a touchdown and celebrated with a little dance as her team cheered her. Man, she was beautiful. He'd known lots of beautiful women before—in the biblical sense, even—but he couldn't remember ever being quite as bowled over by any of them as he was by her. Her rich brown hair shone like satin in the sunlight, and her dark eyes gave a look of innocent vulnerability. But those same eyes also had a sexy, seductive quality that he couldn't seem to ignore. She had the lips of a temptress, as well, and when she smiled or pouted or grew pensive, they underscored her moods. She was the kind of woman hit songs were written about.

And the icing on the cake was the fact that she was about as rich as anybody in the country. Her mother was worth a fortune, and Laura probably had never wanted for anything in her life. Ten million dollars would be a drop in the bucket for someone like her. And he doubted if the IRS had ever given the Rockfords one moment's trouble.

He watched her toss the ball to Ford, then prance toward him, where she'd left a bottle of water. "Come on, Zane. Help us out."

"You don't need my help," he teased. "You're doin' fine on your own."

She brought the bottle to her lips, and he watched the way her young breasts seemed to perk up under her shirt. When she stopped drinking, she screwed the top back on and smiled up at him.

He leaned forward, elbows on his knees, his face too close to hers. "Are we still on for tonight?"

Her smile faded somewhat, and he saw a pink hue spread across her cheeks. "Well, yeah."

"I'll play you some more Zane Berringer CDs."

"I'd rather you play them live."

He laughed. "I could do that."

"Okay, then," she said. "I'll see you tonight."

Zane watched her bounce back into the game, then leaned back in the swing, wishing time didn't creep by so slowly.

"She's too young for you."

He looked over his shoulder and saw that Rosy had come to stand in the doorway. "You ought to know about robbing cradles," he said.

Rosy smiled and strolled out onto the porch. "None of mine are young enough to live in a dorm, Zane. 'Course, it wouldn't be the first time for you. Remember that seven-teen-year-old I caught you with down in Houston?"

"It was Dallas, and she told me she was twenty-three."

Snickering, Rosy pulled a cigarette out and began to light it. "You're hopeless, Zane."

"She's Haven's best friend, Rose. There's nothing going on."

Rosy smiled down at him, and he knew she could see straight through him. "Is that why she asked you to play a few songs for her...live?"

"So she's interested in my music."

"It's not her interest that surprises me, sweet thing. It's the fact that you would do it. The last time *I* asked you to play me somethin', you said, 'I only play for money.'"

"Things change, darlin'."

Rosy wasn't buying. "Not you, Zane. You never change." She started back into the house, then stopped and caught him staring out at Laura again. "Be careful, huh?"

"I'm a big boy," Zane said.

"It's not you I'm worried about. She's a nice kid. I hate to see her turn into another of your casualties."

"That could be a song, Rosy. Write it down, and maybe you can start earnin' your keep around here."

Rosy laughed under her breath and went back into the house.

LAURA HAD SPENT a lifetime wishing for the family love and affection she experienced that day. She found herself laughing with Haven's brothers and sisters, playing with their children and feeling more at home than she'd ever felt in her mother's house.

That night, while Zane was in another part of the house, Haven's brothers urged her to play some of her songs for them. Laura sat curled up on the living room couch, watching her friend stick her neck out for the people she loved most in the world.

All of her siblings listened with rapt attention until Zane came in, stayed for all of ten seconds, then left with a distasteful look on his face. Haven let her song die, and she stared after him with eyes that betrayed more emotion than Laura had ever seen in her.

"Don't mind him, Haven," Blue said. "He'll come around. The songs are terrific."

"I'll bet I can get 'em published for you, Haven," her brother Rally said. "And I could show 'em to Emmylou. She's been lookin' for some new stuff. They sound like her."

Haven sighed. "I think I'll just hang on to them for a while."

"Don't waste 'em, Haven," Choral said, flipping her hair back over her shoulder. "They're too good. Somebody'll want to record 'em."

"That's just it," Haven said. "*I'm* gonna record 'em."

With that, she started playing again, and Laura saw the telling looks being passed around the room. No one here had any more faith in Haven than her father had. And while she had to admit that Haven's voice lacked the usual flair that most singers boasted, there was something about it that Laura liked. Something that she couldn't put her finger on.

And she figured that if people like Willie Nelson and Bob Dylan and Carole King had been able to forge careers with their offbeat, sometimes off-key voices, Haven had a shot.

When everyone had gone home, leaving only the two of them in the living room, Haven put her guitar back in its case. "They didn't think much of my songs."

"That's not true," Laura said. "They loved them."

"Well...I guess it was just my singin' they hated. But they go together. They're a package deal."

"Why are you so adamant about that?"

Haven shrugged. "I want to sing. My songs are my ace. Why should somebody else get famous singin' them?" Sighing, she got up and said, "Well, I'm gonna hit the hay."

"I think I'll stay up a little longer," Laura said. "I'm not tired yet."

"All right." Haven found the remote control and tossed it to her. "I'll see you in the mornin'."

Laura watched her friend slough out of the room and fought the shiver of anticipation that shot through her. Would Zane remember that they'd promised to meet? Would he come back from wherever he had gone?

Flicking on the television, she found the Nashville Network and tried to get a feel for the music video playing there. It was a Jerry Joe Wagner tune, one that she had heard before, with a beat that made a person want to get up and dance. That kind of music was reminiscent of the Eagles and other crossover bands of the seventies, and it was the kind that she would like to have in her collection.

"You don't listen to *that* crap, do you?"

Laura jumped and saw Zane standing in the doorway. "Uh . . . well, I just turned it on and there it was."

He went to the television and shut it off. "I can't believe they call that music. That guy ought to be arrested for fraud."

She didn't want to tell him that she had liked it, so she dropped the remote control on the cushion and asked, "Do you know him?"

Zane laughed without mirth and went to the stereo. "Yeah, I know him. He's a wannabe, hanging on everybody's coattails and trying to brownnose his way to the top. There're a lot of folks in Nashville like that, Laura." He popped a CD into the player, then turned back to her. "This is what real talent sounds like."

Just as she expected, it was his voice that filled the room. He had an ego, no doubt about it, yet there was something about that cocky, unapologetic confidence that amused her. His voice was like warm syrup oozing down bark, seducing her, and when he reached for her hand and pulled her to her feet, she went willingly.

He hummed along as he danced her around the room, and something about his strong, comfortable embrace and his mature self-possession made her wish he wasn't her best friend's father.

The song ended just before Laura had fallen completely under his spell. Smiling up at him, she said, "That was beautiful. Did you write it?"

"Long time ago," he said. "I used to write all my own material."

"No more?"

He shrugged. "My creative well ran dry. Either that or I just got lazy. Doesn't matter, though. There're plenty of good songs out there."

"Maybe Haven would let you record some of hers."

He snickered and turned the stereo down, even though his voice had already launched onto another guitar-picking, hand-clapping cut. "I don't think I have any use for any of her stuff."

"Why not? Didn't you think they were good?"

"I couldn't tell. Her voice kinda got in the way."

So Haven had been right. "But a lot of great stars haven't had classic voices," Laura said, supporting her friend. "Look at Bob Dylan. Yet he was a world-class writer."

"Well, I never liked him, either," Zane informed her. "I don't think there's any reason to encourage Haven to go into a line of work that's going to chew her up and spit her out."

"What would you like to see her do?"

"I don't know," he said. "She's not conventional enough to go into business. She's too spacey to teach. There's not much calling for nonconformists who can play a little guitar but can't carry a tune in a bucket."

"I kind of like her voice," Laura said quietly. "And frankly, I can't see Haven doing anything *but* performing. I think her songs are wonderful, and as stubborn as she plans to be about selling them, she might just make it. But if she doesn't, at least she doesn't need a lot to live on. Haven gets by on next to nothing."

"She does at that," Zane agreed. When Laura sat down, he sat next to her and settled his arm comfortably across the back of the sofa. "Tell me something. How did you and my Haven get to be such good friends when you're so different?"

Laura laughed. "Haven's real easy. She doesn't judge, she doesn't have an envious bone in her body, she doesn't have any hidden motives. What you see is what you get. Why she likes me, I'm not really sure. But she doesn't have that many close friends, so I'm glad I'm one of them."

"Why *wouldn't* she like you?" Those laugh lines around his eyes crinkled, and he touched her hair and slid his finger along the silky strands. "You're as sweet as an angel, which is a real surprise considering all the stuff I've read about your mama. And you have the face and body of a..." His voice trailed off, and he cleared his throat and grinned. "Well, let's just say I've wished more than once over the last day that I was a little younger... or that you were a little older."

Laura's face reddened with the heat of understanding, and she met his eyes. When she started to speak, she found that her throat was dry. "Age doesn't matter so much."

His smile was absolutely disarming, and his voice was no more than a whisper when he asked, "You think?"

Quietly, she shook her head.

"Then, if I were to, say, lean over and...maybe kiss you, real soft, you wouldn't slap my face?"

Her gaze dropped to his lips, then moved back to his eyes. Slowly, she shook her head.

Her heart sprinted to an unnatural pace as he lowered his lips to hers and, just as he'd promised, kissed her softly, sweetly, with only the slightest brush of his tongue next to hers.

When they parted, he stroked her hair again and whispered, "You're just about the sweetest little thing I've ever seen."

She swallowed and looked up at him, wishing she didn't appear so innocent, wishing she had at least some of the experience that Zane probably had.

He trailed his knuckles down her cheek, then took a deep breath and got to his feet. "Blazes."

"What?" she asked.

He looked down at her and smiled, as if the frustration were more than he could stand. "You don't even know what you do to me, do you?"

She couldn't answer.

"Haven would probably shoot us both."

Smiling, she looked down at her clammy hands. "Maybe I should just say good-night."

He rubbed the back of his neck, then said, "Yeah. That would probably be a good thing."

Disappointed, yet a little relieved at the same time, Laura got up and started for the door.

"Hey, Laura?"

She turned back.

"You wouldn't be interested in coming to the studio tomorrow, would you? I'm cutting a track, and I could use a little good luck."

"I'd like that a lot," she said, her smile blossoming again.

"I'll get Haven to come, too, just so we don't start a scandal."

"Okay," she said. "Good night, Zane."

"Good night, little Laura."

Something about the endearment wrapped itself around her heart and was still with her when she fell asleep that night.

CHAPTER FIVE

"Now, THAT WAS PERFECT." Zane slid back the stool he'd been sitting on in the vocal booth and peered through the glass to Sly Hancock, the producer of this album.

"We need another take, Zane."

"Well, what did you do wrong?" the singer blared back into the mike.

Sly wasn't fazed by Zane's retort. He had only one goal in mind, and that was to make the best album he could with the talent he had to work with. "I didn't do anything wrong. But you were flat on the bridge."

"I wasn't flat," Zane argued. "Maybe what you're hearing is the guitar. It sounded a little off to me."

"That guitar player is Jeff Knight, the best studio musician we've got. It wasn't him."

"All right, play it back for me," Zane challenged.

Sly sighed and rewound the tape, and started the song from the beginning. When it got to the bridge, Sly signaled to him, but Zane pretended he couldn't hear the problem.

"It was perfect. You need to have your ears checked."

"Fine, Zane. I will. But just for the sake of perfection, can we do it one more time?"

"No," Zane said. "I'm tired of that song. I'm ready to move on to the next cut."

"Zane, I've worked with people who've spent weeks perfecting one cut."

"And I've worked with people who could finish a cut in thirty minutes."

"And they produced third-rate tracks that didn't sell worth a dime. That's why you dragged me all the way to Nashville."

"Dragged you." Zane sneered. "It was the best chance you'll ever get in your life."

"Right," Sly said sarcastically. "Now, can we get on with this? One more take, since my name's going on this album, too?"

When Zane didn't object again, Sly made a few adjustments to the board, then started the music, which had been recorded days earlier without Zane. That day he'd worked with five musicians—professionals whose only interest was in creating the best sounds they could, people with ideas and creative input, people who didn't fight him every step of the way—and things had gone much smoother. He'd be glad when this day was over.

Zane started to sing, but as he did, the door to the control room opened, and Zane's daughter Haven stuck her head in. "Okay to come in?" she asked.

"Sure, come on in," Sly said irritably. "He told me you'd be coming."

Turning his head back to the console, he made a few more adjustments.

Laura slipped in behind Haven and closed the door quietly, as if any noise would be heard on the tape. Through the glass she saw Zane in a booth, singing his heart out. She smiled.

His eyes caught hers, and he forgot the words.

Sly stopped the music and, rubbing his forehead, spoke into the mike. "Let's try it again, Zane."

But Zane wasn't listening. "Hey, darlin'. Glad y'all came."

Haven assumed he was talking to her. Leaning toward the mike, she said, "That sounded great, Daddy. Sorry we distracted you."

"No problem." He leaned closer to the mike. "Laura, you sure look pretty today."

She blushed slightly and mouthed "Thanks."

It was only then that Sly looked up from the board and saw her. Getting up, he stretched to his full six feet two inches and grinned at her, the laugh lines around his eyes telling her it was a common expression for him. "I'm sorry, I didn't see you come in. I'm Sly Hancock, Zane's producer."

"Laura Rockford."

He was taller than Zane by at least two inches and couldn't have been older than thirty-one or thirty-two. His black hair played havoc with his playful blue eyes, and he tilted his head and considered her name. "Rockford, huh? As in daughter of Catrina?"

"The same," she said. "I'm Haven's roommate."

He turned back to Haven then and gave her a squeeze. "It's good to see you, babe. You don't come home enough."

"Yeah, well, I've been busy."

"Written any songs lately?"

She smiled as though he had validated her. "Yeah, as a matter of fact. If you're really good, I might let you hear 'em later."

"Don't tease me with them if you won't let me sell them for you."

Haven laughed and shot Laura a look. "Sly's the best engineer in the country. Daddy got him here from Los Angeles to help him make his comeback a couple of years ago."

"Comeback?" Laura asked. "I thought he'd always been popular."

Sly eyed the artist in the studio, and Laura sensed a hint of contempt there. "Let's just say he needed a major boost. We brought him back with the first album I produced for him, but the last one didn't do so well."

Across the speaker, Zane bellowed, "Are you gonna shoot the breeze all day, Sly, or are we gonna do business?"

Sly bent over the mike and in a carefully restrained voice said, "Are you ready, Zane?"

"I'm always ready."

He started the music again, and Zane started to sing—not in the soft, clear, unadorned tone that Sly had suggested, but in the same dragging, lazy, yet almost pretentious voice that had doomed his last album. But despite what Sly heard, Laura Rockford heard something else entirely.

Sly glanced back at her and saw the telltale stars in her eyes as she watched the fabricated passion on Zane's face as he belted out the sad lyrics. To someone who didn't know Zane, Sly supposed his oversentimentality could be mistaken for sincerity and genuine pain. The song was about broken hearts and empty beds and getting used to being alone. When he had first heard it on the demo an aspiring songwriter-valet had slipped into his cassette deck while parking his car, Sly had known that he wanted it on this album. It had all the elements of a hit—presuming Zane could get it right, which was becoming a more remote possibility with every take.

When Zane reached the final chorus, he opened his eyes and sang right to Laura. Sly quit listening from a professional standpoint. He'd seen this happen too many times before. There was nothing the star loved more than a teary-eyed female and the possibility of singing his way right into her pants. Sly only hoped that Laura was more savvy than she looked.

When the song was over, there was absolute silence for several seconds. Finally, Haven started to laugh.

"Laura, you've got tears. I thought you didn't like country music."

"I guess I've never heard it sung like that before," she whispered.

Haven leaned down toward the mike. "Daddy, you've gone and made Laura cry."

"Then I'd say I got it right that time."

Sly wasn't sure he agreed, but he did know that Zane would refuse another take. Whatever was wrong with the cut, he'd just have to fix it in the mix. "We'll see, Zane," he said. "I'll get the backup vocals laid down tomorrow. If everything doesn't come together, I might need everybody to put their heads together and come up with a plan."

But Zane wasn't listening. Instead, he was intent on watching Laura as Sly played the tape back.

Something twisted in Sly's stomach as he watched the singer skillfully lure his prey. But there was nothing he could do to intervene.

This was business, he told himself. He wasn't paid to head off heartbreak in Zane's relationships. All he was supposed to do was keep his career afloat.

The problem was, one was becoming as impossible as the other.

HAVEN WANDERED out of the studio before Zane had finished a rough run-through of his next song, but Laura stayed in the control room, watching, mesmerized by the process. As they listened to a playback, Sly smiled over at her. "How long are you going to be here?"

Laura's eyes were transfixed on Zane, but shaking herself, she glanced at him. "Uh... we drive back Sunday."

"How have you liked Nashville so far?"

"I like it," she said, "but I can't say I've seen a lot of it yet."

"Been staying close to the Berringers, huh?"

She smiled. "We're getting out this afternoon. Haven's taking me to the Country Music Hall of Fame so I can see Zane's exhibit. And tomorrow night we're going to hear him play at the Opry."

"What about tonight?" he asked.

She glanced back at Zane, who winked at her. Grinning, she almost lost her train of thought. "Tonight? I don't think we've made plans."

"Then there's only one thing to do," he said, leaning back in his chair and crossing an ankle over his knee. "What do you say I take you for a tour of the Nashville night spots?"

She forced herself to turn away from Zane and looked at Sly. His eyes were bluer than she'd noticed before, and his smile was hard to resist. If she'd met him a week ago, she might have jumped at his invitation. But she had hoped that tonight she and Zane...

"I really can't make plans without Haven. It would be rude."

"She can come along. Haven and I are pals."

"But I'm not sure what...or if..."

"Let's do it again," Zane said into the microphone as the playback ended. "Laura's not crying."

Laura laughed, and her eyes sparkled as she leaned toward the mike. "It was still wonderful."

Sly saw that her mind had switched gears again and she was tuned into Zane now, forgetting that he'd even asked.

But he wasn't easily dismissed. "Should I take that to be a no?"

Laura smiled. "Not tonight, Sly."

The laugh lines at the corners of his eyes crinkled, and he shrugged. "A word of advice, Laura. Zane's a charmer, but getting involved with him might be the worst thing you ever do."

She shot him a look that said she didn't appreciate his directness. "I can take care of myself."

She hadn't noticed that Zane had left the vocal booth until the control room door opened and he walked in.

"So what are you two talking about that makes Sly forget what he's being paid for?"

Laura tried to smile. "We were just—"

"I was trying to get her to go out with me," Sly cut in. "But I didn't have any luck."

Zane's smile suddenly revived. "So what else is new? Your harem must be boring you, Sly, to start hitting on my house guests."

Laura grinned and lifted her eyebrows. "Harem?"

Sly shot him a murderous look, but Zane winked. "He's got more women vying for him than any nonperformer I know. I wouldn't exactly call him a womanizer, but—"

"Thanks, Zane," Sly said. "I appreciate that."

"Let's just say Sly doesn't have to spend too many nights alone."

Sly hated the teasing way Laura's eyes danced up at him, as if she'd been told the truth just in time. "I may not have to, Zane," he said with his own slight grin, "but just because I get offered a banquet doesn't mean I partake. There's a thing called self-control. You should try it sometime."

"Yeah, and I've got some swamp land for sale," Zane threw back.

Laura eyed Sly again, as though seeing him in a new light, and Sly knew it would be hard to dispel the image of him as a womanizer. He only hoped he'd get the chance to set the record straight.

THAT NIGHT Haven was getting restless, and she decided that they had to go to Sludmuster's Guitar Pit, a bar near the Ryman theatre, the first home of the Grand Ole Opry, to hear some friends of hers play. "They're thinkin' about startin' a band with me," she said. "I want to hear 'em, and see if they're good enough."

Laura hesitated, wondering what Zane would be doing that night. "Sludmuster's Guitar Pit? Sounds elegant."

"Well, they don't sell caviar with their beer, if that's what you want." Haven cocked her head playfully. "Come on, you don't want to sit around here all night."

Laura realized that staying home would look suspicious, and it was crazy besides. Zane was at least thirty years older than she, and he was the father of her best friend. She couldn't be infatuated with him. Besides, he probably had plans of his own.

"All right, I'll come," she said. "But I've warned you. I'm not really into country music."

"You sure didn't mind it today at the studio," Haven pointed out. "If Daddy isn't country, I don't know what is."

"Yeah, but his isn't as nasal and twangy as I've always thought, and he doesn't have all those steel guitar sounds."

"That was the first thing Sly got rid of. But if you like Daddy's music, you'll love Tommy and the Bad Boys. They're more contemporary."

"The Bad Boys?" Laura chuckled. "I don't know, Haven."

Haven grinned. "You think that's bad. You should see what they suggested I call my band."

"I can't wait."

"Haven and the Hellions," she said. "Priceless, huh?"

"More like worthless."

"Yeah, well. I personally am leanin' toward Haven Berringer, period. The band's just gonna be incidental. I could use some percussion, a bass player and maybe a keyboard, but I could do it without 'em. I'm an acoustic artist, after all. I just want to check 'em out, see what they can do."

"All right," Laura said with a sigh. "I'll go. But if I break out in hives or something, you'll bring me home, won't you?"

LAURA DIDN'T BREAK OUT in hives, and she found herself enjoying the earthy music. It brought with it a sense of reality, and she began realizing how foolish it was of her to think romantically about a man who could have been her father.

It was just that the kiss . . .

But that was silly. Zane probably kissed a dozen women a day. Sly had warned her that he was a charmer, but then, Zane had warned her about Sly, as well. She was likely just taking all this too seriously.

"Hey, look who's here," Haven said, glancing toward the bar. "Sly."

"Really?" Laura wrenched her neck around and saw that he had spotted them, too.

He brought his glass up in a salute, then, grinning, pushed off from the bar and ambled through the crowd toward them.

"It must be fate," he told Laura when he reached their table. "Mind if I sit down?"

"We were savin' it for you," Haven said.

"I doubt that, but I'll take it anyway," Sly said. "I'm glad to see you got out tonight, Laura, even if you wouldn't come with me."

Haven shot Laura a surprised look, but Laura only smiled. "It's good to see you, too, Sly. Where's your harem?"

Sly laughed. "It's tough being a legend."

Haven looked confused. "Have I missed somethin'?"

"Your father was just filling Laura in on my virtues—or lack thereof—today," Sly explained.

Haven frowned at Laura. "Sly has more virtues than anybody I know."

"And more women, from what I hear," Laura teased.

"Well, yeah, but most of 'em happen to be his sisters." Haven chuckled as Sly gave Laura an I-told-you-so look.

Laura wasn't buying. "Zane didn't mention sisters."

"I have four of them," he said. "I'm the oldest, and the only son."

"That's why he's such a protector. All those little sisters probably needed a lot of savin'."

"I may have bloodied a nose or two when their boyfriends got a little too cocky," he admitted. "But mostly I learned to listen. Couldn't help it. I could hardly ever get a word in." He looked at Haven and laughed.

"It's true. I've met them." She patted his hand. "But it gave Sly some great trainin', and now he's renowned as Nashville's best listener. Whenever a relationship breaks up around here and the woman's been done wrong, whose shoulder do you think she cries on?"

Laura grinned at the discomfort on his face. "Sly Hancock."

"I wouldn't say that," he argued.

"Sure," Haven insisted. "He has some kind of radar that zooms in on ladies in distress, and when he puts those big arms around 'em, well..." She started to laugh as she saw the way Sly was eyeing the door for an escape. "I'm sorry, Sly. We can't fault you for havin' compassion."

"Is that what they call it in the paternity suits?" Laura teased.

He shook his head. "I can guarantee there are no little Hancocks running around here. And there aren't any Sly worshipers, either. In fact, I don't believe I've broken a single heart in the last four or five minutes." He winked, and Laura started to laugh.

The music stopped and the band announced a break. Haven slid her chair back. "I'm gonna go talk to Tommy for a minute and give Sly a chance to undo some of my damage." Wagging her eyebrows, she ambled off.

Laughing softly, Laura watched her approach the stage, where two of the band members waited anxiously for her critique. Being Zane Berringer's daughter carried a lot of weight in the music world, she realized.

"I'm really not such a bad guy, you know."

She looked back at Sly, enjoying the way he was still squirming. "I never thought you were. Even if you did have a harem."

His eyes looked bluer in this light than they had in the studio today. "So what do you think of the band?" he asked.

Laura glanced back at Sly and rested her chin in her palm. "They're not Meat Loaf, but they'll do."

"Meat Loaf, huh? So you prefer rock and roll?"

"Usually."

"I sure wouldn't have guessed it from the way you were getting into the session today."

"That was different. I know the singer."

"Well, I know these guys. They're all studio musicians. The drummer and bass player played on that cut we finished today. They used to play rock music in Minneapolis, but they weren't making any money. They came to Nashville to work, but you can't live in Nashville and not play country."

"Maybe that's the problem," she said. "As good as they sound, they don't look as if their hearts are in it. And they could use a little polish. A slicker image, maybe."

"You think so?"

"Yeah, I do. I don't know a lot about music, but I know about presentation."

"So did you pick that up in college, or at home?"

She smiled. "Both. I've been working summers in my mother's company since I was twelve. She was grooming me to run the business, you know. I always liked the public relations part of things best. I figure it doesn't matter how great the product is if it isn't packaged right. You have to make a major event out of the presentation. Start off with a bang, and keep it popping."

"I wish some of our promoters could see things that way. Sometimes it's an uphill battle to get my CDs marketed with any kind of creativity at all. As creative as Nashville is supposed to be, it's sometimes pretty rigid."

"I would think the promotion part of the business would be considered as much an art as the music itself."

"Yeah, well, that assumes that we're dealing with creative genius. Which we're not."

She smiled at his matter-of-factness and realized this was the first real conversation she'd had with him. He took her seriously, something that wasn't a normal occurrence in her experiences with men. Something about that stimulated her, but it was his cologne that teased her—its outdoor scent spawning images that made her uncomfortable. She wondered if he realized how virile it was. "How long have you been working with Zane?"

"Three years. Long enough to know better."

Her eyebrows rose. "You don't act as if you like him much."

"Yeah, well, my frustration level usually gets pretty high by the time we've recorded thirty or forty cuts for one album and still don't have ten good enough to use. He gets pretty tense, too, but we always survive it."

"He's been very nice to me," Laura said.

Sly laughed softly. "Yeah, I'll just bet he has."

Laura didn't like the tone of his voice. "What is that supposed to mean?"

"It means that Zane's nice to a lot of women. The younger the better."

"Sounds like you're a little jealous."

"Me?" Sly shook his head, and she could see that the accusation chagrined him. "I'm just being honest. And the fact that I think you'd be crazy to rule me out, since we're obviously so perfect for each other, has nothing to do with it."

"Who says I've ruled you out?"

He grinned and fixed those blue eyes on her. "Tell me, is it my directness that kept you from going out with me tonight? Should I have played a game or two? Should I have acted indifferent to pique your interest?"

She laughed softly. "No."

"Then did you just formulate your opinion based on the way I look? You don't *seem* quite that shallow, but looks can be deceiving."

He had a way about him...she had to give him that. Fighting her smile, she said, "If I had based my opinion on your looks, I'd have been drooling over you like every bimbo in this room."

He smiled at the offhanded compliment and glanced around the club. "Then if it wasn't my looks, it must have been my job. You're only interested in the famous and the infamous?"

"Of course not," she said, laughing.

His eyebrows arched with disarming vulnerability, and he asked, "Then what?"

"Then nothing. You've got my attention riveted on you now, don't you? Although I have to admit I'm getting a little uncomfortable about the women that are starting to circle. Some of them have very long fingernails."

He closed his hand over hers and leaned close. "You're safe as long as you're with me, babe."

"Oh, good," she replied facetiously. "My hero."

The band started to play again, and he squeezed her hand. "So, do you dance up in Philadelphia?"

"Sometimes," she said.

"What do you say we give it a whirl?"

Warily, she eyed the dance floor. "I don't know any of those line dances."

"Who needs line dances?" he asked with a wink. "What's the good in dancing if you can't touch your partner?"

It was just what she'd been thinking. "All right, let's go."

He led her to the side of the massive dance floor, where couples danced together, and pulled her close.

She laughed softly as she looked up at him. "You're tall."

"Only six-two," he said. "What are you, about five-five?"

She nodded.

"Well, I'd say that's just about perfect, wouldn't you?"

It did feel perfect as they began to move across the dance floor, laughing with each spin and dip and playful twist, falling against each other, then swinging apart. "Where'd you learn to dance like this?" she asked over the music.

"My sisters," he said. "I was the only partner in the house."

Before she replied, he swung her around him, pulled her close again, and as her arms closed around his neck, he ended the song in a deep dip, then brought her up again, her face unmercifully close to his.

"You, my friend, are a fabulous dancer."

Breathless, she let her eyes drift to his lips, wet and grinning. "That was fun," she whispered.

His face only seemed to come nearer as the next song started. "I told you we were perfect for each other."

The song was slower now, sweeter, and he didn't let her go but pressed her head against his chest and wrapped both arms around her as they swayed to the sensuous rhythm of the drums.

She could feel his heart beating against her face, and she thought how nice it would be to tip her head back and kiss the crook of his neck. If he belonged to her, if she belonged to him . . .

She felt a tap on her shoulder and stopped dancing.

"What's a nice girl like you doing in a dump like this?"

Laura swung around and saw Zane, waiting to cut in. "Zane! You didn't tell us you were coming."

"Well, blazes, I had to come make sure my little girl didn't hook up with this no-account band, didn't I?" Glancing over her head to Sly, he said, "Thanks for entertaining her, Sly, but I can take it from here."

"Oh, can you really?" Sly shot back.

"I need to sit down, anyway," she said to Sly. "Aren't you thirsty?"

He made a gesture with his hand, offering her free rein to do whatever she pleased, and feeling her spirits sinking, she led them back to the table.

Zane grabbed a chair from another table and slid it between Sly and Laura as they started to sit down. "Have I missed anything?"

Sly's smile was sarcastic. "You, Zane? You never miss a thing."

"Good." Slapping the table, he waved toward the waitress. "Bring me a Jack Daniel's, straight up, on the rocks. And whatever the lady here was drinking, and Sly can have his milquetoast malt."

Another man might have reddened or fought back, but Sly seemed undaunted. "Make it a double Milquetoast malt," he told the waitress with a wink. Smiling, she sashayed away, and Sly turned back to Zane. "Make up your mind, Zane. Am I a Milquetoast or a womanizer?"

Zane chuckled. "Well, I guess you're a little of both."

"Are you getting all this, Laura?" Sly's amused eyes met Laura's again, but she only grinned.

"So, how's the band?" Zane asked.

"Pretty good," she said.

"But are they loud enough to drown out Haven's singing?"

Laura slapped his arm playfully. "Stop that. I'm sure she'll be glad you came to help her make up her mind."

"She doesn't want my opinion," he said. "She wants me to tell her what she wants to hear, even if it means watching the business beat her to a pulp."

Sly shifted in his seat. "She has a right to try her hand, Zane."

"She also has the *right* to hitchhike across the country with every ax-murderer who can give her a ride, but I don't want her doing it!"

Laura smiled. It was heartening, somehow, to see Zane's protective instinct where Haven was concerned, even if it wasn't something she wanted. She would have given anything to have someone care like that about her.

The waitress brought their drinks, and she met Sly's eyes across the table as he lifted his to his lips. Forcing herself to look away, she asked herself how she could get into this position—attracted to two men at the same time and sharing a table with them both.

Finally, Zane got up and bent over her. "Let's show them how it's really done, honey." He pulled her to her feet, and Sly watched as she let him commandeer her toward the dance floor.

THE GRAND OLE OPRY was a pleasant surprise to Laura. Even though she knew that country music was a favorite of both upper-class and working-class acquaintances of hers, some small part of her had still pictured toothless men in overalls playing jugs and spoons, rather than the seasoned musicians and gifted composers she saw now.

Backstage, where Haven pulled her through the crowd, Grammy-calibre artists were coming and going. A few stood in the corner, engaged in intense conversation. And myriad technical people busied themselves with work of various sorts. Some four thousand people packed the geometric building in sweeping semicircles that ascended from the stage. Onstage at the moment was Jerry Joe Wagner, droning out his latest hit to the cheers and whoops of people all over the building.

She wondered if Zane provoked such a response.

"That guy's pretty good," Laura told Haven. "He reminds me of Don Henley."

"Don't tell Daddy that, for Pete's sake," Haven said. "He hates Jerry Joe with a passion."

"Why?"

Haven's laughter bordered on disgust. "Apparently Jerry Joe had a thing goin' with my mama when she and Daddy were still married. Daddy caught them in the act, and he's been lookin' for a good time to kill Jerry Joe ever since."

"Caught them in the act?" Laura stopped midstride, astounded. "Your parents told you about this?"

"Sure," Haven said. "We don't keep that many secrets in our family."

"And how did you feel about that? I mean, your mother having an affair."

Haven sighed with resignation. "Yeah, and with a man as young as Jerry Joe. He couldn't be more than twenty-four now. He was probably nineteen then. 'Course, I didn't know about it until she and Daddy were already split up. I heard 'em screamin' at each other a couple of years ago, and Daddy dragged that back up and reminded her of it, right in front of God and the family. It was pretty funny, thinkin' back. She said it was a one-night stand, though, so we all figured it wasn't worth gettin' our panties in a wad over."

"Was that the reason for their divorce?"

Haven shook her head. "They're divorced because Daddy's so hard to live with. Mama's no pussycat, either, if you get right down to it." She looked around, then gave up. "Well, I guess Daddy isn't here. We might as well go sit down and watch the show."

"Why isn't he here?"

"He plays a song or two early in the show, then another one a couple hours later. He hardly ever sticks around between acts. Come on, we'll listen to Jerry Joe."

Feeling like a traitor for enjoying Jerry Joe Wagner, Laura followed Haven to their reserved seats near the stage and watched the singer weave his magic over the crowd.

And as she watched, Laura realized that if he wasn't a big superstar already, Jerry Joe Wagner would one day become one. His original songs had a way of implanting their lyrics in the listener's mind, and he sang them with the confidence and finesse of a seasoned artist. But there was something else, too. Something about the way his hips jerked as he sang, like Elvis, something about the cocky charisma that pulsated from him along with the beat, something about the expression on his face that suggested he was having the time of his life and didn't care who knew it.

The crowd begged for an encore when his set ended, but Jerry Joe only promised to come back out later, and as Porter Wagner came on to follow him, Laura found herself getting lost in the excitement of the crowd. By the time several more acts had finished and Zane took his place on a stool in front of the famous red barn, guitar in hand, his band behind him, Laura chastised herself for feeling like a starry-eyed groupie. When the applause died down, he cleared his throat and strummed a few chords, then looked out into the audience. "I wrote a song last night, and I'd like to play it for you now," he said, his gravelly voice filling the auditorium. "I call it 'Soulful Eyes.' And the little lady I wrote it about knows who she is."

He looked down at Laura in the front row then, winked at her and left her beaming as he started to sing.

The words seeped into Laura's heart like warm honey, soothing and refreshing her.

Those soulful eyes were hers, she had no doubt in her mind. And as Zane sang, she found herself more and more mesmerized with the man whose voice had worked its way into her heart.

"Isn't that somethin'?" Haven asked in a dull monotone as she stared scathingly at her father. "He really said he wrote that last night, didn't he?"

But Laura didn't answer, for she didn't want to miss a note of the song.

CHAPTER SIX

THE WEEKEND WAS OVER all too soon, and the moment she got back to Princeton, Laura started counting the days until Christmas vacation, when she planned to return home with Haven. Her mother wouldn't like it; she was certain it would cause problems. But no matter what it cost her, she found herself determined to see Zane again.

She told her mother when she came to visit Laura two weeks before Christmas break, and Catrina made an effort to put her foot down. "Absolutely not. It's bad enough that you spent Thanksgiving with a bunch of redneck hillbillies, but you are not going there for Christmas."

"Mother, they're not rednecks. They live in a house as big as ours, and Zane has a collection of antique cars just like Father used to have. They have—"

"I don't care what they *have!* They're new money, and I won't allow you to subject yourself to their vulgar displays of it. I didn't send you to all the best schools all your life so that you could lower yourself to palling around with someone who cuts her own hair, wears nothing but green T-shirts and aspires to sing that nasal, nauseating excuse for music that's made her father more money than he ever deserved to have."

"You don't know anything about them!"

"I know that *you* are not going to spend Christmas with them."

"You'd rather I spent it alone in that cold mausoleum you call a home, while you spend your time at the office or jetting off to Europe?"

"I don't work on Christmas, and you know it."

"No, you don't, Mother. You sleep until the servants have Christmas dinner ready, and then we sit at opposite ends of a ten-foot table and dine in style. Don't you see, I'd rather sit at a table full of people who love each other, and laugh and talk about a thousand things? I'd rather say, 'Pass the potatoes,' than to have Matilda serve them to me on an antique platter."

"Then we'll invite people over this year," she said. "Pierre will be here, and we'll ask Larry and Joliet and ... we'll think of someone else."

"I'm not comfortable with them," Laura said. "They're your friends, and all they talk about is other people I don't know."

"Then we'll invite some of your friends ... the decent ones."

She caught the sting intended for Haven and bristled. "I don't know a soul who would want to come to our house for Christmas."

"Oh, you can think of *someone!*"

"All right. Can we invite Michael?" She knew before she uttered the question what her mother's reaction would be.

"Of course not!"

"Then I'm going to Nashville, Mother, and there's nothing you can do to stop me."

"I can revoke your credit cards," she said. "I can refuse to buy your airline ticket. I can take back your car and cut off your allowance."

"Fine," she said. "I can live with that."

Her mother's face reddened, and Laura thought the top of her head might explode right through her perfectly coiffed hair. "Can you? Can you really? I don't think you understand what that means, Laura."

"Yes, I do," she said. "It means you can't control me, Mother. It means that I'm going to have Christmas with the Berringers.

HAVEN AND LAURA drove from Princeton down to Nashville at Christmas break. Since Laura didn't have the money for an airline ticket, Haven didn't want to fly, either. They drove in fits and starts in Haven's beat-up VW, stopping every couple of hours to pour water into the ailing radiator. Once, after they'd stopped to eat, the bug refused to start again and had to be jump started by a traveling salesman who looked remarkably like Ted Bundy. It was right up Haven's alley, the suffering and struggling, but it was a new experience altogether for Laura, and she wasn't sure it was one she wanted to repeat.

Cold, tired and dirty, they dragged into the Berringer home at 2:00 a.m. and found Zane asleep in a recliner in front of the test pattern on the television.

"He must've been waitin' up for us," Haven said. "I guess he was worried sick."

She leaned over and kissed his cheek, and when his eyes fluttered open, she whispered, "Hey, Daddy. We're home."

"Thank God." Getting to his feet, he pulled Haven into a hug, then reached for Laura with his other arm and squeezed her so tightly that she knew the magic between them hadn't died. "It's a thirteen-hour trip, girl, and you left eighteen hours ago. You could have hitchhiked in less time. You *didn't* hitchhike, did you?"

"I wanted to, but Laura has this irrational fear of drivers with chain saws cruising America's highways lookin' for innocent women to decapitate."

Laura smiled up at him. "Call me paranoid."

"We had car trouble," Haven added. "The radiator's leakin', and the tires are bald. I'll probably take it by Jim's tire place tomorrow and buy a couple of retreads."

Zane rubbed his eyes and reached for the half-empty glass next to his chair. "No, you don't. You're either getting four new ones, or you're driving back in that Volvo I bought you."

"All right," Haven said with a disgusted sigh. "I'll take the tires, 'cause there's no way I'm drivin' that yuppie-mobile."

Laura's eyes met Zane's in a conspiratorial grin. "What's she got against Volvos?"

"They're civilized, that's what," Zane said.

"They're just not my style," Haven corrected. "I like my car." Standing on her toes, she pressed a kiss on Zane's cheek. "We'll argue later, Daddy. I'm goin' to bed. Does Laura get the same room as last time?"

His eyes locked with Laura's again. "If that's okay with her."

"Sure. I'll be up in a minute. I'm just going to warm up here for a minute."

"All right. G'night."

"'Night." Zane watched as Haven disappeared up the staircase, then turned back to Laura, who was warming her hands at the fireplace. "Well, I'll tell you what, for somebody who's probably been through Hades for the past eighteen hours, you sure do look good."

She smiled. "Your daughter thinks hardship is romantic. She probably got a dozen songs out of this trip."

Slowly, he set his drink down and came toward her. "And what do *you* think is romantic?"

She hoped he thought the pink blush on her face was generated by the fire. "I don't know."

"How about standing in front of the fire with somebody you think a lot of, and warming your hands?" He took her hands in his and rubbed them gently, his fingertips tickling the center of her palms. "You want to know something real troublesome to me, Laura Rockford?"

She swallowed and made herself meet his eyes directly. "What?"

"It's real troubling to me that you've been on my mind so much for the last month. I didn't know a man could think about a lady that much."

Her eyes sparkled. "I've thought about you a lot, too."

"I'm real glad you came back."

For a moment, he was all seriousness as he gazed down at her, drinking in the sight of her dark eyes and her full lips. When his fingers swept through her hair, her heart stumbled.

His kiss took her by surprise, and yet it didn't, for she met him halfway and rose up on her toes to plunge headfirst off the precipice of restraint she'd teetered on. There was something decadent about dallying in passion with this older man. Something forbidden and irresistibly exciting. Something that touched her deepest, darkest yearnings, ones that lurked in the empty corners of her soul, and fed them with the power of this seductive kiss.

When they separated, she caught her breath.

"Is it the worst kind of sin in the world for a man to want his daughter's best friend?"

She shook her head faintly. "I . . . I don't know."

"Well, there's no use mourning what is," he whispered.

Again he kissed her, and this time she slid her arms around his neck, her fingers through his hair, and gave back just as much as he gave to her. She felt as though she were falling, fast and dangerously, hurling toward the ground with nothing to grab on to. It was a heady, intoxicating feeling, an abandonment foreign to her.

Then suddenly, it was over.

He stepped back and looked down at her with troubled eyes. "This is crazy."

"Yes," she whispered, backing away, embarrassed. "It is. I . . . I should just go on up."

He turned his back to her then, hands on his hips, and stared down at the floor. She saw the struggle in his rigid back and sensed his apparent self-abhorrence. For a moment, she considered touching him, turning him around, throwing herself at him. But what if he rejected her? The possibility sent a lonely but familiar chill through her bones. Quietly, she started to walk away.

"Laura?"

She turned around, holding her breath.

"You're the prettiest thing I've ever seen. Do you know that?"

Her smile blossomed with the beginning of relief across her face, then spread to her eyes. "You're not so bad yourself."

He held her captive in his gaze, like a deer frozen by the sight of headlights, and finally, he stepped toward her again. "I know I should feel bad about this," he whispered, "and just let you run upstairs . . . but I feel like I've been waiting a whole lifetime for you."

Again, he kissed her, but this time there was no struggle over the morality of their desire. When he lifted her in his arms and carried her up the stairs, she knew he was taking her to his bed.

They made love for the first time in Zane's bed, and Zane treated her with gentle kindness, sweet sensuality, loving patience. He made her feel cherished . . . singled out . . . something she'd never felt before, and the emotion was so great that she wanted to cling to it, to him, for the rest of her life.

Before dawn came and she returned to her own bed, she whispered, "I love you, Zane."

Zane smiled at her and snuggled closer. "I love you, too, darlin'. I've just got to figure out what I'm gonna do about it."

LAURA WENT WITH ZANE to his recording session the next day, and Haven concluded that her sudden interest in the music business was because she had a thing for Sly and couldn't wait to see him. Laura let her believe that.

Sensing Sly's interest in Laura, Zane kept her beside him like his own special muse, as he rehearsed with the studio musicians, changed music and revised lyrics, discussed concepts and worked out the problems that inevitably came up during his sessions.

It wasn't until he said, "Honey, how about going to get me a cup of coffee," that she left the studio for the first time that day.

Obediently, she hurried down the corridor to the kitchen, where fresh coffee brewed in a pot. She got a cup and was about to pour, when she heard someone beside her. Turning around, she saw Sly leaning in the doorway, his arms crossed. He was watching her with interest that swung somewhere between disgust and fascination.

"I sure would have figured you to have more brains."

She glanced up at him, irritated. "I think you'd better be a little more specific, Sly. We dense types need things spelled out for us." She turned back to the coffee and poured Zane a cup. The hot liquid sloshed over and burned her finger, and she jumped slightly.

Sly ambled across the floor and looked down at her. "All right, Laura, I'll spell it out. You're going to get hurt, babe. It won't be pretty, and I will hate to see it."

"I know what I'm doing," she snapped.

"How could you? You're what...twenty-one years old?"

Not quite, Laura thought, but she wasn't about to admit that to Sly. Instead, she said, "The last time I checked, that was the legal age of adulthood."

"Just barely."

"So what's your point?"

He sighed and leaned back against the counter, shaking his head. "It's like watching someone I really like running toward a cliff without slowing down, without even knowing it's there, and holding my breath waiting for them to drop off the edge."

"Very dramatic," she said, turning back to the coffee. "You should write."

"I'm serious, Laura. You're headed for disaster."

"Because I'm young, or because I didn't go out with you?"

He smiled then and reached for the container of cream, handing it to her. "All right, I'll admit I'm still smarting a little. But that doesn't change what I see happening. I know Zane better than you do."

"I doubt that."

He chuckled softly. "Don't doubt it. Just because you're sleeping with him doesn't mean you know him."

Laura swung around. "How dare you?"

"How dare *you?*" he countered. "Last month you were a lady with a good head on her shoulders, and now you're letting this guy drag you around by the nose just because of your hormones."

"This is not about *hormones!*" she muttered through clenched teeth. "It's about how he makes me feel."

"How *does* he make you feel, Laura? Like another notch on his belt? Like a trophy? Like a step on the social ladder that's so important to him?"

She slammed the container of cream down and clutched her head. "No!" she said. "He's not like that! No one has ever cared about me the way Zane does. No one. And I don't care what anyone says. I've found what I've wanted all my life."

"A father? Someone to give you limits and order you around and make decisions for you?"

Her face turned crimson, and her eyes glowed. "This is none of your business. I'm not one of your little sisters, so just stay out of it!"

"The thing about my sisters is that I'm usually right about the motives of the men in their lives. They've come to trust me when I warn them."

"Well, who's going to warn me about your motives, Sly?"

He chuckled bitterly then. "I'd say Zane's doing a pretty good job of that. But even if I had no interest in you at all, Laura, I'd still tell you what I see happening. Somebody has to, because you can't see it yourself."

"I'm not stupid, Sly. You can't be raised a Rockford and never question motives. I've been hit on a thousand times by men who were out for my money or the prestige of getting their picture taken with a Rockford. This is different. Zane doesn't need my money or my name.''

"Think again, Laura. You don't know him that well.''

"I know him better than I know you! I've spent more time with him.''

"Yeah, well, maybe he has more layers to peel away. You might know him for years and never get to the real Zane Berringer.''

"And I'm supposed to believe that you don't have any layers?''

"I've got plenty of layers, baby, but none of them are there to cover up anything.''

Laura went back to the coffee, poured in too much sugar, then, frustrated, dumped it into the sink. Sly reached around her and got the coffeepot and poured it for her. Softening his voice, he said, "Look, this is not about me. Truth is, if we ever had the chance to find out, you and I might not hit it off, anyway. I might decide you're a shallow, self-centered little debutante and not have the slightest interest.''

She shook her head and said sardonically, "You've got a way about you, Sly.''

"Even if I thought you resembled a human gargoyle and had as much personality as—''

"That's right,'' she said, trying not to be amused. "Keep buttering me up.''

"I'd still feel compelled to warn you about Zane.'' He leaned onto the counter, getting too close to her, and she looked into his eyes. Suddenly, she wished they weren't quite so blue. It confused her, and she needed to keep her head clear.

"And what about Haven?'' he asked.

"She'll be happy for me,'' Laura said, tearing her eyes away and staring down at the coffee again. "All of the Berringers will.''

"Think again. I've seen their reactions to some of Zane's women. The younger they are, the more disgusted his family seems to be."

"Well, they sure don't seem disgusted by Rosy's flings. Besides, they may not have known the other women first. They all know me. They already treat me as though I'm one of the family."

"That's not a family you want to belong to, Laura. Trust me."

"I trust *Zane,*" she threw back. "He's all I need. Not you. Not my mother. Not anybody else!"

She heard people coming up the hall and grabbed the coffee. The door to the studio opened as one of the musicians came out, and she heard the playback of "Soulful Eyes." "He wrote that song for me, you know."

"Is that what he told you?"

"He didn't have to," she said, and headed back to Zane.

Sly went back into the control room and sat down. It was amazing the things Zane would do to get into bed with a woman. He'd seen him do worse, but this one was getting under his skin. Maybe it was because Laura, who seemed so sophisticated and so savvy, was really just an innocent, and she had such high hopes that Zane would be the one to fill up all the emptiness inside her.

How could he make her understand that Zane would only take more from her, leaving her with an even greater longing than when she started out?

However he managed it, Sly thought, he would have to do it without breaking her heart. That was why he couldn't tell her that Zane had written that song a year before he'd met her and just hadn't recorded it until now because it was unfinished. A few months ago Jack Ingram, one of the studio pianists, had worked all day helping Zane complete it. The truth was, the lines about the soulful eyes had been Jack's, and they referred to his little girl.

But that was the way Zane worked, and Sly supposed he should let it slide off him as usual. The trouble was, there was nothing usual about Laura, and for the life of him, he hated to see where this whole thing was headed.

It was almost Christmas, after all, and he had the feeling that she hadn't had that many good ones.

CHRISTMAS AT THE Berringers was exactly as Laura had imagined it would be. All of Zane's sons and daughters brought their families back into the homestead for Christmas Eve, so that each family member could share in the children's delight at Santa's visit. It was the kind of Christmas that Laura had experienced only in books when she was a child, the kind that had a spirit of its own that had little to do with gifts.

But there was no shortage of gifts, and Laura found herself amazed at the sweetness of the presents everyone gave her, in which more thought had been spent than money. Moved to tears, she thanked each of them with a warm hug. Haven, however, gave gifts to no one. She proclaimed that Christmas wasn't about commercialism but spiritualism, and she asked that donations be made in her name to various charities, instead.

But it was Zane's thoughtfulness that moved her the most. After everyone had gone to bed and they found themselves the last ones up, Zane brought out the small box he'd kept back tonight. In it was a gold locket with tiny diamonds that outlined a guitar, and inside the locket was a miniature key.

Tears came to her eyes as she took the little key out. "Read the inscription," he whispered.

Laura turned the locket over and read the words, *"The key to my heart, for my Soulful Eyes."* The tears rolled down her cheeks as she looked up at him.

"Hey, now, what's the matter?"

"It's so sweet," she managed to say. "So beautiful. And all I got you was a tie."

"I love that tie," he told her. "It's the best tie I've ever seen. I'm gonna sleep with that tie."

Laughing softly, she wiped away her tears. Then growing serious again, she said, "You mean so much to me."

He touched her chin and drew her face closer to his. "I was just thinking the same thing."

His kiss stirred the embers that seemed to stay hot these days, and a familiar yearning shuddered through her. "I want to be with you tonight," she whispered, breathless, "but there are too many people in the house. It's too risky. I don't even think Haven's gone to bed yet."

"Tomorrow night, then," he said.

"Okay," she whispered, getting up. "Tomorrow night you're mine. I can't wait." She gazed down at him, her emotion-filled eyes betraying every feeling in her heart. "Merry Christmas, Zane. Thank you for the best one I've ever had."

"Merry Christmas, darlin'."

She went up to her room and took the locket off so she could hold it in her hand, study it, adore it.

Someone knocked on her door, and a tiny thrill shot through her. Had Zane decided to throw caution to the wind and come to her despite the risk? Quietly, she opened the door.

It was only Haven, an amused grin on her face. "I had to give you one last thing before I hit the hay," she said, stepping into her room. "Daddy sent me by Sly's today to drop off some music, and he gave me somethin' to give you."

"Sly?" Laura asked. "What?"

"Are you ready?"

Laura frowned at the suspicious amusement on Haven's face. "I guess."

"Okay, just a minute." She slipped back out the door and reached for a box in the hall. "I had to hide it from Daddy," she said, bringing it in. "He has these rules, so I put it in the garage. Anyway, Merry Christmas."

Laura gave her one last look, then opened the box. A tiny white kitten lay curled up in a bed of shredded paper, and when it saw her, it stretched and let out a grand "Meow!"

Laura caught her breath and scooped it up. "A kitten!" she asked, awestruck. "For me? Really?"

"Yep." Haven plopped stomach-down on the bed. "Sly's got it bad for you, you know."

"No, he doesn't," Laura said. "You're wrong about that."

"Right," Haven remarked sarcastically. "This cat was from his own cat's litter, and it was his favorite. And I didn't notice him givin' *me* one. He said he thought you needed someone deservin' to give your love to."

Laura knew that had been an insult to Zane, and she almost bristled, but the kitten reached up to box with her and she started to laugh. "I've never had a pet before," she said. "My mother wouldn't let me."

"Yeah, well, we're gonna play heck hidin' it in the dorm. But I figure we can do it. What are you gonna name her?"

Laura thought for a moment. "Didn't he have any ideas?"

"Yeah. He's been callin' her Blizzard, since she's white and all. But she's only six weeks old. He said you can name her anything you want."

"I like Blizzard."

"I do, too." Haven pushed up and got to her feet. "Oh, I've got a litter box out in the hall, too. You can bring it in and keep her in here if you want. And there's a bag of food, but he said somethin' about mixin' it with water and mushin' it up. You can put it in your bathroom."

"Zane won't mind?"

"Sure, he'll mind," Haven said. "Just don't bring it up. That's how I get around things."

She meandered to the door, then turned back. "Call Sly, Laura. Thank him. It is Christmas, you know."

"I will, Haven. Thanks for the delivery."

When Haven was gone, she brought the litter box in and was amazed that the kitten already knew how to use it. Sitting on the floor, she laughed softly as she watched the kitten dig into the litter and cover what it had left there, then romp out and explore a pair of shoes parked against the wall.

She played with the kitten until it tired itself out, then scooped it up, laid it on her stomach and called information for Sly's number.

He answered on the third ring. "Uh, Sly?"

"Yeah?"

"This is Laura."

It was the first time she'd ever *heard* the sound of a smile. "Merry Christmas, Laura."

"Merry Christmas," she said. "From me, and from Blizzard."

He laughed. "I didn't know if you'd want to keep her. It's kind of presumptuous giving someone a gift with years of responsibility attached, but hey, I don't do things halfway."

"Just try getting her away from me now," she said. "I really love her, Sly. I'm just not sure why you'd send me a gift after...well, after the things we said to each other the other day."

"I said some tough things, Laura. I was out of line."

She sighed. "You were looking out for a friend. I'm going to try to appreciate that."

"Look, I don't have ulterior motives, okay? You just looked like somebody who could use a little furry pal, and I thought you might have something she needed, too."

That he saw anything of worth in her was a surprise, for she had given nothing back to him. Stroking her hand across the tiny animal, she felt it purr. "I think you're right on both counts."

"There was never a question about it." For a moment, there was silence between them. Finally, she said, "So, why would a man like you be all alone on Christmas Eve?"

"I'm not alone. My sister and her husband and my mother are here from California. We never miss a Christmas together. We like to keep our traditions."

She smiled. "Sounds nice. Well, I won't keep you. I just wanted to say thank-you."

"You're very welcome," he whispered.

She almost hated to hang up, but then her eyes fell on the locket that lay open on her bed, and an uneasy feeling of unfaithfulness stirred within her. "Good night, Sly."

"Merry Christmas," he said again, and then he hung up.

She set the phone back in its cradle, still moved by Sly's gift, a gift that would give back so much love. Then she picked up the locket that had been so thoughtfully designed, so carefully inscribed. She was a lucky woman, she realized, to have two wonderful men who cared about her. But she could only be true to one of them.

And that one had to be Zane.

She fell asleep that night and dreamed of both Zane and Sly, of kittens and diamond lockets, of guitars, cowboy hats, and blizzards, of clear sterling eyes and haunting blue ones.

But it had to be Zane, her subconscious seemed to tell her. She needed what he could give her. Experience, confidence, security, wisdom, family... Things that she lacked, things that few others had ever had to offer her. But most of all, he gave her love, and that, she realized, was his greatest gift. It was the one thing that could fill up the empty wells of her soul.

CHAPTER SEVEN

"WHERE AM I SUPPOSED to get that kind of money?" Zane sat somberly in his dark study the night after Christmas, telephone thrust between his chin and shoulder as he massaged his eyebrows with his thumb and forefinger. "It's been a long time since I've had ten million dollars lying around."

His CPA knew that all too well. He was the one who'd been juggling Zane's books for the last few years, trying to make some sense out of them. But there was no getting around the fact that Zane had failed to pay all that he owed the IRS, and now they had caught up with him. "I don't know how you'll get it, Zane, but you'll have to do it soon. They've been held off long enough, and if we don't pay them off before the deadline, they'll freeze all of your accounts, evict you from your own home and sell it and everything in it. Oh, and they'll garnishee your royalties until they're paid off. There's got to be somebody you can borrow from or some kind of advance you can get from your label."

Zane covered his face with his big hand and shook his head. "I've tried already. The records haven't exactly been flying off the shelves lately. Nobody's selling much."

But Bill knew better than that. He had clients, in fact, who were doing better than they'd ever done. It wasn't the market . . . it was Zane.

"Maybe you need to try a different approach. Update your image."

"When I want your advice on my image, I'll ask for it," Zane quipped. "Until then, stick to the numbers, why don't you?"

"All right." The frustration in Bill's voice reminded Zane that it wouldn't do to have his only mediator with the feds angry with him.

Still, he couldn't make himself apologize. "Look, I'm doing what I can. I have a few ideas. Just make sure they don't take any action until my deadline. Let them know I'm working on getting them the money."

He hung up the phone and sat in the dark quiet, staring at the four-foot poster of himself on the wall across from him. He had aged since he'd started his career—there was no way around admitting that—but he had aged well. His stomach was still flat, not something every man his age could boast, and he hadn't yet turned gray. And he could still carry his own in bed with a young little thing like Laura.

He smiled and propped his feet on the desk. She had it bad for him, and there was nothing wrong with that. It was good for a man's image to be seen with an adoring little beauty, especially when her last name was Rockford. She was no ordinary girl. She was one of the richest young women in the country. And she just might be the answer to the prayers he'd been meaning to pray.

When he heard the knock, he dropped his feet to the floor. "Come in."

Laura opened the door slightly and stuck her head in. "Zane? Are you all right? Why are you sitting in the dark?"

"Thinking," he said.

"About what?"

He turned the desk lamp on then, illuminating his face in a yellow glow. "You."

She smiled. "Me? Really?" She closed the door behind her, and when he reached for her, she allowed him to pull her onto his lap. "And what about me?"

"Oh..." He sighed, as if the words didn't come easily. "I was thinking how much I'm gonna hate it when you go back to school. We only have a couple more days."

She was quiet then. "I was thinking...maybe when I graduate...I could come to Nashville and look for a job."

"Yeah?" he asked with a hopeful smile.

"Yeah."

He kissed her softly, then drew back and gazed up at her with a stricken look. "Too bad you have to wait until then. What's a girl like you need a job for, or a college degree, for that matter?"

"My mother is adamant about my getting an education."

"You have one," he whispered. "And your name is Rockford. That carries a lot more weight than the silly piece of paper the college is gonna give you."

"Then why are you making Haven stay?"

"Haven doesn't have everything going for her that you have," Zane said. "Besides, it's more her mama that's big on degrees than me. I believe in life experiences, not book learning."

She frowned down at him, trying to follow his reasoning. "Are you asking me to stay here?"

"It's a thought," he whispered. "A real nice one."

She gazed at him for a moment, thoroughly confused, and when he reached up to kiss her, she felt all her reasons for needing that degree flutter out the window and disappear on the wind. She lost herself in his kiss, lost herself in the sense of belonging that his arms around her always represented.

Neither of them noticed when the door opened, spilling a bright triangle of light into the dimly lit study.

But the moment the kiss broke, they both saw her.

Haven stood in the doorway, staring at them with her mouth open, not saying a word.

Laura jumped. "Haven!"

Haven didn't say anything, but she turned and ran up the staircase and was in her room before Laura could catch her.

"She'll be all right," Zane said from behind her, halfway up the stairs. "She had to find out sooner or later."

"But that wasn't the way I wanted her to find out," Laura cried. "She's my best friend in the world. I don't want her to hate me."

"She'll be over it by morning," Zane assured her. "Trust me, darlin'. My little girl doesn't run deep enough to hold grudges."

On some level, Laura recognized the injustice in that statement, for she believed Haven ran deeper than anyone else she knew. It was easy to mistake her sweet, simple spirit for naiveté, but she hadn't expected Haven's own father to do so.

Still, when Zane kissed her again, she felt all her reservations and regrets flying away. And when he lifted her and carried her into his room, she forgot all about Haven.

HAVEN COULDN'T STAND the four walls anymore or the ceiling, which seemed to smother her. She needed fresh air and the stars above her. What she didn't need was the constant hum of central heating, the television and radio blaring from different rooms in the house, and her father making love to her ex-best friend.

Pulling her sleeping bag from the top of her closet, she reached for the green parka she had bought at the army surplus store. It was warm enough for a night like this.

Making sure there was no one in the hallway, Haven stole down the stairs and went out into the cold night. She traipsed across the lawn, past the pool and the wet bar, past the cottage where her mother lived, past the garden that her father rarely walked through.

When she was far enough out on the acreage to feel she was alone, she unzipped the sleeping bag, got into it and stared up at the stars.

Laura with her father? There was something disgusting about the whole thing. She tried to blink the image out of her mind but found that it was the betrayal that hurt worst of all. They had both betrayed her.

She wondered how long it had been going on, when it had started, if that was the real reason Laura had come back with her for Christmas. She wondered if her father really had been anxious to get Haven safely home or if his concerns had been for Laura. She wondered if anyone else had known about this and not told her.

She should have known better than to get so close to a roommate. She'd never done it before. But Laura had seemed to need a friend, and Haven hadn't wanted to reject her.

Now she wished she had. This changed everything. She could request a new roommate, but it was unlikely that she'd get one in the middle of the year. Or she could just make sure that her path never crossed with Laura's. She could sleep every night out in her tent, take showers after Laura had left for class and make sure that she didn't hang around in the room when Laura might be there. It was doable. She just didn't relish the idea.

The bald truth was that she was going to miss Laura. Her eyes filled with tears and she wiped them away, angry at their assault. This shouldn't have happened, but it had, and she would just have to vent the pain by writing about it. Maybe she could get a good song out of it.

It wouldn't be a fair exchange, a song for a friend, when she had so many of the former and so few of the latter. But that was the way it was, and she couldn't help it. She couldn't be Laura's friend if Laura was Zane's lover. One automatically precluded the other, and she didn't like being used by Laura as a stepping-stone to get to Zane.

Those tears rushed forward again, and she closed her eyes and tried to shut out the image of Laura anxious to spend Christmas with her, willing to drive for hours in a broken-down car to get there. She didn't want to face the fact that it wasn't their friendship that had brought her but a lust for a man old enough to be her father.

Maybe that was the appeal, Haven thought with sad resolution. Zane was the closest thing to a father Laura had ever had. She just wished Laura had found one other than her own.

ZANE FELL ASLEEP holding Laura that night, but sleep wouldn't come as easily for her. Haven was angry at her, and that haunted her like a restless ghost in the smothering darkness around her.

She had to go to Haven and explain that she hadn't meant to fall in love with Zane, that it had just happened. She had to tell her that she'd never met anyone like him before, and that they had struggled over their attraction but it had overwhelmed them. And they had kept it a secret to spare her the pain she was suffering right now.

But it all seemed so lame, so sleazy, and Laura didn't like herself much anymore.

Slipping out of Zane's arms without waking him, she slid off the bed and groped for her clothes. As she dressed, she looked down at him and felt a warm burst of emotion flood through her. He was the best thing that had ever happened to her. The best and the worst.

And as determined as she was to make up with Haven, it wouldn't be at the expense of her relationship with Zane. She loved him as she had never loved anyone, and no matter what it cost her, she was going to be with him.

HAVEN JUMPED WHEN SHE heard footsteps in the grass behind her, and she sat up and peered into the darkness.

"What am I gonna do with you, girl?"

She let out a breath of relief at the sound of Rosy's voice. "What's wrong, Mama?"

"You, that's what. You sleepin' out here in the dirt when it's gotta be freezin'. You'll get pneumonia."

"No, I won't. I do it all the time. How did you know where I was?"

"Laura called lookin' for you, and when she said you weren't in your room and the car was still home, I knew right where to find you."

Getting down on her knees, she dropped the pile of twigs and branches she'd been carrying. "I brought you some stuff for a fire, in case I couldn't talk you into comin' in."

"Who's with you, Mama?"

"At the house? Oh, just Stevie. But I'll send him on his way if you want me to."

Haven sighed. "No, that's okay. I'll stay here."

She took the lighter her mother proffered and arranged the sticks and twigs to catch the flame. As the fire began to burn, Rosy shivered and sat down on the ground next to her. "So, what's wrong? What sent you runnin' out here when you know how your daddy and I feel about it?"

"Did you know about them?" She looked at her mother, pinning her with the question. "Daddy and Laura?"

Rosy moaned. "Well, I suspected that if somethin' hadn't happened yet, it would soon. What did you do? Catch 'em?"

"You might say that," Haven said. "I feel like a stupid fool."

"Why, honey?"

"Because I thought Laura was here because of me. I thought she had eyes for Sly."

"Well, she's crazy if she didn't. What she sees in your father is beyond me. And I'm sure she *is* here because of you. One thing has nothin' to do with the other."

Haven didn't want to talk about it anymore. Her mother didn't understand. A roll in the hay was just that to her. It meant nothing but a night of cheap entertainment. There was no soul or heart involved. But it wasn't that simple to Haven. And she couldn't believe it was to Laura or her father, either.

Her mother sensed that Haven wasn't going to say anymore, so she took her hand and patted it. "It'll be okay, sweetie. The two of you will make up tomorrow and be the best of friends again. Your daddy doesn't care anything about her. It's strictly physical, and maybe he's a little star struck, seein' how she's got that famous name and all. You know, she's supposed to be so classy and everything, and Lord knows your daddy could use a little class. It'll blow over like the smell of yesterday's fish, and you'll forget all about it. Your daddy's libido is not worth losin' a friendship over."

But as her mother left Haven alone there on the dark outskirts of their property, Haven couldn't help thinking that the friendship was indeed over. She had nothing more to say to Laura, and she would never trust her again.

LAURA WAS WAITING in the kitchen early the next morning when Haven came back in, smelling of campfire smoke and morning dew. She got up and confronted her rumpled friend.

"Haven, I'm so sorry..."

Haven pushed past her toward the hall.

"Haven, please. Talk to me."

"There's nothin' to say, Laura. It's your life."

"Then you're not mad at me?"

Haven turned around, clutching her sleeping bag around her like a sleepy little girl wrapped in her favorite blankie. "I don't like bein' used, Laura."

"Used? How did I use you?"

"A lot of people have used me to get to my daddy. They still do. Usually I can see it or it doesn't make any difference. But you really pulled one over on me this time."

"Haven, I wasn't trying to deceive you. I didn't mean for it to happen. I worried about you the whole time..."

"Spare me," her friend said. "I have an empty stomach." She started out of the kitchen, and Laura followed after her.

"Haven, why can't you be happy that two people you care about have fallen in love? If it's the age difference, people get around that all the time. Your own mother goes out with guys younger than me."

"You leave my mother out of this!" Haven said, dropping the sleeping bag and bolting back into the kitchen. "This is about you and my father, and the fact that I don't play pimp for anybody!"

"Haven, you've got it all wrong!"

Through her tears, Laura saw that Haven was crying, too, something she had never seen her friend do. Torn with compassion, she wanted to go to her, put her arms around her and comfort her, but the only way to do that would be to vow never to see Zane again.

And that was something she couldn't do.

Haven jerked her sleeping bag off the floor. "Since I'm not the kinda person who leaves people stranded, I'll still take you back to Princeton. But it's the last time you and I'll be doin' anything together."

Laura sank down into a chair at the table and covered her face as a great sob rose in her throat. A profound sense of loss came over her, and she whispered in a raspy voice, "Haven? Don't be mad at him, okay? He's the only father you've got."

"Oh, I'm not mad at him," Haven said. "I blame you for the whole thing."

CHAPTER EIGHT

LAURA HAD HOPED that when she went to the studio to meet Zane she could go a couple of rounds with Sly and boost her spirits. Something about his wit always did her good, even when he was saying what she didn't want to hear.

But her heart jolted when she caught sight of him through the open door of the mixing room. Serendipity Chance was sitting on a table gazing at him, her fingers hooked into his jeans pockets.

She would have expected him to choose his women more carefully, Laura thought, stepping away from the door and leaning wearily back against the wall. When she'd first been introduced to the starlet, she'd asked if that was, indeed, her real name. Haven told her that her real name was Jane Brown, but that she had gone by her stage name ever since the studio had changed it. "Don't ever call her by her old name," Haven warned her. "She has a demon's temper and won't put up with it."

From the looks of things, she had a demon's lust, as well, and Laura found herself listening to a conversation that was none of her business.

"Go home, Serendipity," Sly said, and she wondered how he kept a straight face using that name. "You need to relax in a hot bath, drink a cup of herbal tea and just chill out for a while. Then tomorrow, come back up here and make a few demands of those jackals who are mismanaging your career."

"What about you, Sly?" she asked seductively. "When do I get to make some demands of you?"

Laura stuck her finger in her mouth and pretended to gag.

"Me?" He laughed softly. "I wouldn't dream of taking advantage of you in this state."

"What if I wanted you to?"

"I'd say you don't know what you want. You've been upset all afternoon."

"This has nothin' to do with my fight with the execs, Sly. I've been tryin' to get you to come home with me forever."

"But I'm not your type," he said, grinning. "I don't wear big belt buckles or boots, I've never been in a barroom brawl, and I've never owned a pickup truck in my life. If you and I got together, what would you ever have to write about?"

Laura couldn't help stealing a look again, and she saw Serendipity start to slide her arms around Sly's neck, but he stopped her and put her hands at her sides. "I'd have a whole new wellspring to write from," she insisted. "Come on, Sly. One more rejection today might just push me over the edge."

"You're tough, Serendipity," he assured her. "You can take it."

Laura backed away again and waited as she heard the girl's heels click on the floor. "You're gonna be sorry you passed this up. I may not offer you the opportunity again."

"I'll have to take that chance," he said.

Finally, the singer breezed out of the room and shot Laura a haughty look.

"Hello, Jane," Laura said.

Serendipity's eyes darkened, and without a word, she whizzed down the hall.

Laughing to herself, Laura stepped toward the door. Sly was already eating a ham sandwich with one hand and jotting a couple of notes with the other.

She smiled. "I think I came at a bad time, no matter how you look at it."

She wondered if she just imagined the way his face lit up when he saw her. "Why do you say that?"

"Either I came when you were on the brink of ravenous passion or ravenous hunger. I'm not sure which."

He laughed. "Oh, you saw? She just needed a shoulder."

"I don't think it was your shoulder she was interested in."

Grinning, he set down the sandwich and laced his hands behind his head. "So, what brings you here? Zane hasn't got a session today."

"He said he was coming to see how the mixing was going, and he asked me to meet him here. We've been having to kind of avoid each other at home."

"Oh, yeah?" Again she saw the disapproval on his face. "Why's that?"

Laura lowered her head and resisted the urge to use that same shoulder Serendipity had allegedly needed.

Taking a deep breath, she forced back the tears and looked up at him. "Haven sort of...walked in on us. It was just a kiss, but she went off the deep end."

"Oh."

Getting up, Sly leaned back on the table behind him and crossed his arms. "And you're going to keep seeing him?"

"I can't help myself."

"You can always help yourself, Laura."

Sighing, she sat down. "You don't understand," she said so softly that he had to strain to hear her. "I've never felt like this before. No one's ever treated me this way. I had hoped that the family would understand, especially Haven, but—it doesn't change how I feel."

"Well," he said, staring at the floor as though he could see her life mapped out on the patterned carpet, "I guess it's a good thing you're going back to school in a couple of days. Maybe the distance will help you clear your head."

"I'm not going back."

His head snapped up. "What? Why not?"

"I'm staying here," she said. "I've been looking for an apartment this morning. Zane doesn't want me to go, and

Haven isn't speaking to me, so the choice looks pretty simple."

"You would throw away your last semester of college for him?"

"Yes," she said. "I can always go back later if I want, but right now, this is where I've got to be."

He moaned. "I wish I could talk you out of this."

"What's the matter? You don't like the idea of having Blizzard and me in Nashville?"

His eyes locked on hers. "I love the idea, Laura, and if it were just your decision to stay here, that would be great. But it's the way Zane fits into this equation that bothers me. You've got a cloudy picture of him, babe."

"I know everything I need to know."

Sitting down in his own chair, he leaned forward, his elbows braced on his knees, and covered his face with his big hands. "Well, I guess the only thing left for me to do is help you look for an apartment."

Light came back into her dark eyes. "Do you know of any?"

"I own a condo in a pretty nice area, and occasionally there's one for rent. But what are you going to do about a job?"

"I haven't gotten that far yet," she said. "There must be something for an almost-graduate."

"Almost won't get you very far," he said.

"It'll work out, Sly. I know it will."

"What will?" Zane's voice thundered into the room behind her, and she got up suddenly. Something about the way she dashed to him with that ever-loving smile on her face made Sly want to throw something.

"What were you two talking about?"

"Serendipity Chance's career," Laura lied, and Sly realized that she hadn't told Zane her plans yet. She was intending to give up her life, her friends and her family and move into a strange place, without a job, just to be with a man who was going to rip her to shreds before he was through with her.

And all Sly could do was watch.

LAURA SIGNED A LEASE on a furnished apartment that afternoon in the condominium complex where Sly lived. Though she didn't have a cent for a deposit, the condo's owner gave her two months' grace to get it, for she was, after all, Laura Rockford. It wasn't as if she didn't have the money.

But of course her landlady didn't know that Laura had only a few dollars and some change, and in light of her recent decision, she doubted her mother would be coming to her aid.

But Zane was a different story. The minute he heard she was staying, he was the happiest man in the world. His only reservation was about the apartment. Why couldn't she just live in the house with him? When Haven went back to Princeton, there would be no reason for them not to be together.

"We're not married," Laura said innocently. "I don't think it would be a good idea to live together."

"We could call it a prenuptial arrangement," he said.

She smiled, noting the half proposal. "I can't, Zane. I have to get my own place."

"All right. I guess it won't hurt to have the apartment for a while. As long as it's temporary."

HER CHOICES HIT THE FAN a few days later when her mother tried to reach her at school, only to be told by Haven—rather bluntly—that Laura had decided to stay in Nashville with Zane. By the time she was able to locate Laura by phone, Catrina was livid.

"He's old enough to be your father, and he's nothing but a low-class redneck who wouldn't have a dime to his name if anyone down there had any culture at all!"

"Mother, he's nothing like you think."

"I don't *care* what he's like! I don't want this getting around. If you don't come home within the week, I'm coming to bring you home myself!"

"I'm a grown woman, Mother. I can live wherever I choose."

"How will you support yourself, Laura? I swear I won't give you another penny!"

"I don't need your money, Mother. I can work like everybody else."

"Do you *hear* yourself?" She moaned into the receiver. "I didn't raise you this way, Laura. I'll say it one more time. If you aren't back at school within a week, I'll come get you and bring you back myself."

With that, Catrina slammed down the phone.

Laura sat in her small living room, looking around at furnishings that would have been comfortable by most standards but were miles below what she'd grown used to. But it was all hers, for now. It felt good to be out of her mother's control. And it felt good to have someone who loved her.

Blizzard scurried across the floor like a snow-covered tumbleweed and jumped into her lap. The moment she began to pet her, the kitten purred like a dial tone. It made her smile.

And she knew that things were going to be just fine.

CHAPTER NINE

THE STUDIO WAS ABUZZ with activity when Sly came in the next morning, sleepy-eyed and weary from an all-night mixing session. He'd tried every trick he knew to punch up Zane's latest cuts, but there was only so much you could do with technology. After two hours' sleep, he was back to keep trying. Bebe, the secretary and would-be starlet who usually sat preening at the front desk, was riffling through a file cabinet and handing things to Suzannah, assistant to the studio president.

Sly looked up the hall and saw three "suits" standing in a cluster, then heard Zane's voice bellowing over them all. "What's going on?" Sly asked.

Bebe threw him a glance but kept digging through the files. "It's the IRS. They're auditing Zane's royalties."

"Why?"

She shook her head. "Got me. It wouldn't be a big deal, except Zane keeps getting in the way. Geez, you'd think he was *trying* to antagonize them."

That didn't surprise Sly. Down the hall, he saw Zane's accountant taking him aside and telling him in a whisper to shut up. Good luck, he thought.

"Is this the producer?" someone asked, spotting Sly.

"Yeah, that's him."

Sly started toward them, wondering exactly how he fit into this ordeal, and wishing he had followed his instincts and slept later. "Sly Hancock," he said, reaching for the hand of the first agent he came to.

"Alex Murray, Internal Revenue Service," the man said. "Are you the one producing Zane Berringer's latest album?"

"Yes. Why?"

"We'd like to talk to you about it."

Sly glanced at Zane but saw no hint of what this was about. "All right," he said. "We could go in here." He headed toward a conference room, but Alex Murray stopped him. "No, we'd rather do it in one of the rooms where we can hear what he's working on."

"We're not finished. I'm still mixing and we haven't decided for sure which cuts are going on the album."

"We don't expect perfection. We just want an idea."

Again, he looked questioningly at Zane. "Just go with them," Zane said impatiently. "Let 'em hear, so we can get this crap over with."

Gesturing in the direction of one of the mixing rooms, Sly led them into the room he'd been working in just three hours ago. When they had shut the door behind them, he dropped into a chair and said, "You guys are going to have to forgive me. It's a little early for such high drama after two hours' sleep."

"We understand you were here all night."

"That's right."

"Do you usually keep such long hours?"

"It depends. I do when I have a deadline closing in. You guys know about deadlines."

Ignoring the stab at sarcasm, Alex pulled out a chair and sat down. The other man remained standing at the door, arms crossed like a sentinel. "We'd like to hear some of the album Zane's been working on. Play us the best you've got."

Sly cringed and wished he could have one more day to get things right, but he suspected they wouldn't give it to him. Why were they interested in Zane's cuts, anyway?

Deciding that he was too tired to argue with them, he snapped a tape on its reel and turned it on. "Like I said, it's not finished."

The song began to play, and Sly wished he'd added a little more reverb at the chorus. He should probably go back and redo the percussion track, and maybe give Zane one more shot at the vocals. It was far from perfect, and Sly didn't like putting his name on anything that wasn't.

Halfway through, the two men shot each other eloquent looks, then asked him to turn it off.

"You're considered something of an expert in this business," Alex said. "How do you feel this album's going to do?"

"As well as any of his others," Sly said honestly. "He has a pretty steady following."

"That following is getting smaller with each album. We were hoping he was right about this one. That it had something different. Something to breathe life back into his career."

Sly's brows knitted together as he regarded them. "I'm a little confused. Since when has the IRS gotten involved in career management?"

"When someone's ten million dollars in arrears, we consider everything they do our business. And since Zane is trying to convince us to wait for the release of this album and attach to its royalties, we've got to make a judgment as to whether it has a chance."

"Ten million dollars?" Sly looked back at the stack of cuts Zane had recorded and told himself that there was no way on earth that Zane was going to earn ten million on this record. There wasn't a potential hit in the bunch, and he was just lucky the label kept him on. If Zane took any of Sly's advice about updating his sound or his image...maybe. But Zane didn't like taking advice from anyone. That was why his career was heading down the toilet.

"His last three albums have done poorly. One of those didn't even earn out the advance they paid him."

"It's a funny business," Sly said, noncommittally. "You never know which song might take off. A person can be selling plasma one day and be a country star the next. Zane used to be the biggest name in Nashville."

"Well, he's not anymore." Alex Murray stood up, and the other man opened the door. "Thanks for your time."

"No problem," Sly said. At least he hoped there wasn't a problem. Ten million dollars in back taxes could have serious repercussions. If they started selling off Zane's possessions, the media would have a field day with it. It wouldn't help the sale of this album any, and Sly's success rested on the success of the people he worked for.

He put on his headphones and decided that, no matter what, he'd have to take the mediocre material that Zane had given him to work with and mold it into a technological marvel that would fly off the shelves.

Fat chance, he mused as he started the song again. Something told him that Zane's heydays were long gone.

ZANE WAS IN a reflective mood that night as they drove to the Grand Ole Opry. His melancholy disturbed Laura, but she suspected that it had something to do with the fact that they had cut his time on the show and allotted more time to Jerry Joe Wagner. It was clear that Zane wasn't happy about it.

She tried to work around his mood and hoped her own cheeriness would bring him up. "Are you sure we're doing the right thing, Zane? I mean, if we show up there together, and I'm hanging around backstage and all, people will know we're an item. It'll be all over the papers by tomorrow."

Zane finally smiled. "That can only help my image, darlin'." Putting his arm around her and pulling her close, he said, "I want people to know we're a couple. I want them to get used to us, because I have a feeling they're gonna be seeing us together for a long time."

Words had never made such an impact on her, and these sent a stream of warmth coursing through her. Nervously, she straightened her clothes, wishing she'd had something more Western-looking to wear. Haven had sent by express all the clothes she'd had in the dorm, at Zane's rather insistent request, and now Laura wished she'd had the chance to pack the things she had at home in Philadelphia. She didn't have money to buy anything, and so far her job search had gotten her nowhere. She could have borrowed money from Zane, she supposed, but she didn't want him to think less of her. She was a grown woman, after all, and somehow she could make a living.

And so she had dressed in her usual sleek, expensive style—a short skirt that accented the shape of her legs, a silky tunic that came midhip, and the full-length mink her mother had given her a couple of Christmases ago. She felt out of place next to Zane's rhinestone-studded cowboy shirt and alligator-skin boots.

And when they got backstage and pushed through the crowd, none of whom seemed the least abashed about staring at her, she felt even more awkward. The first thing she'd do when she got some money, she told herself, was to buy some Western clothes.

She saw Rosy standing in a crowd of musicians, laughing as though she'd known them all for years, and Laura smiled at her. She wasn't sure whether Rosy was speaking to her or not. Two of the brothers, Blue and Ford, had already lambasted Zane about his affair with her, but she hadn't heard yet how Rosy was taking it.

Rosy saw them and her laughter faded into a tight smile. Leaving the cluster, she crossed her arms and sashayed toward them.

Laura's mouth fell open when she saw that Rosy was dressed exactly like Zane, from the bolo tie at his throat and the arrangement of the rhinestones across the front of his shirt to the style of black jeans and the very boots he had on his feet.

"Aw, blazes," he muttered. He grabbed Rosy's arm when she was in reaching distance and said under his breath, "I told you to stop dressing like me! It's embarrassing!"

Laughing, she looked up and straightened his collar. "Well, honey, since when did I do anything you told me to do?"

"I'm serious, Rosy. How did you know what I was wearing?"

She laughed again. "I know everything you do," she said, then threw Laura a glance. "Every little thing."

Laura wasn't sure if Rosy was goading her or just being her usual sassy self, but the whole scene stung her. "The color's nice on you, Rosy," she said.

"Why, thank you, darlin'. I can see right now that we're gonna have to take you shoppin', though. You look like a debutante at a rodeo, for heaven's sake. Zane, wouldn't she look perfect in a tight pair of jeans with some high-heeled boots and maybe a Stetson hat on her head?"

"Why don't you just copy my wardrobe again and we can all three dress alike?" Zane suggested sarcastically.

"Great idea," Rosy said with an overbright laugh. "Let's do it."

Laura bristled. "I don't think so."

"Oh, spoilsport." Rosy waved a hand, dismissing them, then sashayed back to the men she had left.

"Does she always dress like you?"

"Every blasted time," he said. "And how she knows what I'm gonna wear is a mystery to me. It's like she's psychic or something."

"Or has a key to your house." It was all she was going to say on the subject, for she knew that she had no right to start making changes in Zane's life. Still, Rosy was going to be a little hard to bear.

"She just does it to embarrass me. Call attention to us. It's some big joke to her, and she really gets a kick out of it."

Laura's eyes drifted to Zane's ex-wife, who now had her arms around the neck of a young guitar player. She could let it get her down, she thought, or she could lift her head high and enjoy the evening. Looping her arm through Zane's, she smiled up at him. "Well, it's not going to ruin my evening. I can't wait to hear you perform tonight."

But instead of lifting him up, those words seemed to restore his earlier melancholy.

SHE HADN'T EXPECTED any surprises from Zane tonight, in light of his mood after his short performance at the Opry. He'd stopped at a liquor store on the way home, stocked up on the sustenance he would need for the night and stewed all the way home. When they got back to her apartment, he'd poured a drink, belted it down, then poured another.

"I've got a surprise for you," he said when he seemed reasonably calmer. He smiled, but she wasn't sure if it was the liquor or the surprise that had made that possible.

"A surprise? What?"

He sat down, his hand still in his coat pocket, and pulled out a small velvet box. "I've been thinking a lot about you and me, Laura, and how I'd feel if you'd gone back to Princeton, and how I feel with you over here in this little place every night, and me way over there...."

She knew what was in the box even before he opened it, and something in her heart leapt.

"I was just thinking about that today, and it came to me all of a sudden that you and I...that we...really ought to do something about it. So this is what I want to do."

He opened the box, and she looked down at the two-carat diamond ring, sparkling like white fire against its black velvet casing. "Oh, Zane, it's beautiful."

"Nothing but the best for my darlin'." He didn't tell her that it wasn't quite the best, or that he had gotten it on credit. But after he married her, he suspected he'd have plenty to pay it off.

"I want to marry you, Laura. I want you to be my wife."

The tears flooding her eyes surprised her, and as she threw her arms around him, she realized that her life had become totally complete. Someone loved her enough to make a commitment to her, something that no one, including her mother, had ever done. "Yes, Zane," she whispered. "I'll marry you."

SLY HEARD ABOUT the engagement on CNN the next afternoon, when he ran home for lunch and a shower after being at the studio all night. It hit him like a fist in the gut, and he sank down onto the edge of his bed and stared at the screen. A picture of Laura and Zane backstage at the Opry the previous night flashed across it, and once again, he was stricken by Laura's beauty and class and Zane's rode-hard-and-put-up-wet image. The two just didn't fit together.

And that was only the outside. It was the inside that bugged him the most. Laura, for all her sophistication and worldliness, was an innocent in matters of the heart. He suspected that she'd never really felt love in her life, and now she clung to the first person who had offered it to her.

He had hoped that he would have the opportunity to get to know her better, now that they were neighbors. But she was constantly with Zane, and now it was too late.

Or was it?

He started to dress and went to the window as he buttoned his shirt. Across the courtyard he could see her apartment. A plume of smoke rose from her fireplace, so he assumed she was home. He hadn't seen Zane's ostentatious car parked in the lot when he'd come home, so, taking a chance, he decided to go over there.

She answered the door seconds after he knocked, holding the kitten.

"Sly! I thought you were Zane."

He came inside and turned back to her as she shut the door. His eyes strayed to her left hand, and he took it in his. "I was hoping it was just a nasty rumor."

"Where did you hear it?"

"On CNN," he said. "I'd like to think Zane's name warranted that kind of coverage, but I have a hunch it was you they were interested in."

She smiled and looked at the ring herself. "Or the combination of the two of us. We'll complement each other well, I think."

Sly's lack of response was more eloquent than Laura wanted to admit, so she turned away. "Do you want something to drink?"

"No thanks. I have to get back to the studio." He sat down in an easy chair in the corner and crossed an ankle over his knee. "So, when's the big day?"

"We haven't set a date yet. I think it's best to take it kind of slowly. My mother's going to hit the ceiling. She'll probably be calling any minute."

"Does your mother's opinion carry any weight with you?"

"None."

"That's too bad." He leaned forward and set his regretful eyes on her. He thought of telling her that she could come to him if she ever needed a shoulder, but he knew that would imply that Zane was going to hurt her. She wouldn't believe that in a million years. She was going to have to find out for herself.

And then he thought of telling her about the IRS. Had Zane told her that they were bearing down on him, that he was in hock for ten million dollars?

Before he could open his mouth, the door swung open, and she turned around, her face lighting up at the sight of the star barging inside.

Blizzard hissed.

Instantly, she set the cat down and had her arms around him. "Sly came by to congratulate us."

Zane couldn't quite meet his eye. "I thought you were at the studio. I've got to get that album out on time, you know."

"It'll be done," Sly said, getting to his feet. "I haven't been late yet. Are you coming to the studio today? I want to go over some stuff with you."

"Yeah, I'll be there shortly."

"Fine." Sly's gaze swept back over Laura, standing there as if she were on top of the world, not knowing that she stood over the trapdoor of a volcano. "Well, I'll be going."

He saw the hurt on her face when he didn't offer best wishes or congratulations, but he couldn't bring himself to say the words. She watched him as he walked across the courtyard, not looking back.

I DON'T KNOW what you told them, but it sure didn't help me any," Zane ranted hours later when he came back into the studio.

"Told who?" Sly didn't have the stomach for this today, not after hearing the constant flow of gossip about Laura and Zane all afternoon.

"The IRS, that's who! You were supposed to tell them how much confidence you have in my new album, and how we were gonna be raking the cash in...."

"Sorry, Zane. I didn't get the script in time, so I had to wing it."

"Well, what *did* you say? They were considering extending my deadline to pay them and attaching the royalties from the album. But when they came out of here after talking to you, they said they'd decided it wouldn't work out, and the deadline had to stay."

"When is the deadline?"

"February 1, if you must know! That gives me a little over three weeks to come up with ten million dollars, and I don't have that kind of cash lying around."

"You should have paid your taxes."

"I did, some of them," he said, dropping into the chair next to Sly. "I thought they were being paid. I never paid that much attention. And now..." Defeated, he rubbed his forehead. "So, what did you tell them?"

"I didn't tell them much of anything, Zane," Sly admitted. "I just played them the best cut. 'Soulful Eyes' was the closest to being finished."

He sat up and leaned forward. "They liked it, didn't they? I mean, they said they did, didn't they?"

Sly rubbed a finger across his half-grinning lips. "I didn't get the idea they were big fans of yours."

"Fans or not, it's good music. And if it's not good music, it's because you're not doing your job!"

"Give me a break!" Sly pushed his chair back and shot up. Setting his hands on his hips, he glared down at Zane. "You're not putting this off on me. If this album bombs, it's not because I didn't give everything I had to save it!"

"Everything but talent!"

"Then why did you beg me to come here from L.A.? You thought I had talent then! And I'll tell you something, Zane. I do have talent. But what I need working with you are miracles, because you don't take any of my advice or suggestions, anything creative I offer gets thrown out, you insult my musicians and test my patience, and then you have the gall to blame me when the fans don't go wild. Fine! If you want another producer to finish up this album, find one. If you think there's anyone in this town—no, in this country—better than me, then have at him."

"Did I say I wanted another one?"

Sly wanted to knock his head off. "No, Zane. You didn't. And I didn't think you would."

Zane picked a piece of lint off his sleeve and looked down at the floor. "I was just asking what the IRS said." He got up to leave the room, but Sly stepped in his way and stopped him.

"One more thing."

Zane had to look up at Sly, something he never liked to do with anyone. "What?"

"Have you told Laura about your trouble with the IRS?"

"I don't think that's any of your business."

"It's going to become my business, Zane, if you don't tell her today. I think she needs to know that your proposal came on the same day that the IRS cracked down on you."

Zane's face reddened. "One thing has nothing to do with the other."

"Fine. Then there won't be any harm in telling her. Tell her tonight, Zane. Or I'll tell her tomorrow."

CHAPTER TEN

"I DON'T WANT to wait to get married."

Laura frowned, not sure what Zane was suggesting. He'd been anxious, restless, since he'd come to get her tonight, and then he'd had trouble deciding where they were going to have dinner. Now he seemed to have given up on the matter entirely, and she felt a tiny shiver of apprehension. "You don't want to wait until when? We haven't set a date yet."

"I don't want to wait at all." He got to his feet as though he'd made his mind up as he spoke, and taking her hand, he pulled her up. "We're getting married now. Tonight. We'll fly to Las Vegas and elope before anybody can stop us."

Laura laughed out loud. "What! Who's going to stop us?"

"Nobody. Because nobody will know about it. What do you say, Laura? Will you marry me in Las Vegas tonight?"

Her smile faded as she realized he was serious. "I don't know, Zane. That's not exactly how I pictured it."

"It'll be beautiful. We'll buy you a dress when we get there, and we'll find one of those sweet little chapels . . ."

She sank down onto the couch, trying to stop the whirling in her head. "But I always thought I'd get married in a real church, and that I'd have bridesmaids and groomsmen, and a huge reception with lots of friends, and Michael would give me away . . ."

He didn't know who Michael was, but he didn't take the time to find out. "But that's how everybody does it. Think about it, Laura. Just you and me, jetting off into the night without telling a soul. It would be a story to tell, a lot more romantic than some stuffed-shirt wedding with the paparazzi flying overhead to get pictures."

She thought for a moment and felt the panic beginning to rise inside her. "Couldn't I even call my mother and just warn her? At least offer her the opportunity to meet us there? And I'd like for Michael to be there, and Sly, and your family. I'd hoped to make up with Haven first. Don't you think that would be best?"

"Do you want to marry me or not?"

"Well, yes. Of course I do. I've never wanted anything more in my life, but..."

"But nothing, darlin'. When it comes right down to it, this is about you and me. Nobody else matters, and I don't want my wedding day tainted with the ill feelings of the people who claim to love us. Let's just fly there on pure joy, spend the night in an elegant hotel and come home to announce that it's a done deal. The press and all those others can just find out later. What do you say?"

Laura leaned over and scooped up Blizzard, who'd been sleeping on her feet. "I'll have to tell Sly, so I can ask him to keep Blizzard for me."

"No," Zane said a little too quickly. "Sly's not too good at keeping secrets, darlin'. We'll just leave her plenty of food and water. She'll be fine."

"But she's so little." Stroking the kitten, she tried to sort the plans out in her mind. "If we were just gone for one night, I guess it would be all right. I could leave the light on...."

"She's a cat, Laura. Just a cat. She won't even know you're gone."

"Of course she'll know. She loves me. She sleeps next to me every night."

"That's not love," he said. "She only does that to keep warm. You're not gonna put off our wedding for the sake of a cat, are you?"

For a moment, she looked at Blizzard, searching for the answer somewhere in the kitten's thick coat. Then she looked up at Zane, and finally, a tentative smile scurried across her face. "Okay, Zane," she said softly. "Let's go get married."

SLY WATCHED FROM his window as they drove away and wondered where Zane was taking her tonight. He could tell he hadn't told her about the IRS yet. She'd seemed too happy as they'd crossed the courtyard toward his car.

But he hadn't missed the overnight bag Zane carried. She was probably going to spend the night at his house. Why that bothered him so, he wasn't sure. He should have given up on her by now. But that was hard to do.

He dropped back into his chair and stared at the ceiling, wondering if his obsession with her had to do with some kind of emotional entanglement or was just that familiar protective instinct that had so often gotten him into trouble. He could see her headed for disaster. It was just a matter of time, and it was so unnecessary. But lovers never listened. They just acted, and by the time the stars blurred and the clouds faded, there was only pain left behind.

He rubbed his hand across his face and told himself that he'd have to get over it. He wasn't going to divert her; she was going to have to learn this lesson for herself.

THEY GOT MARRIED in a chapel attached to a casino in Las Vegas, and though Laura refused to wear the white-veiled cowboy hat and white satin jumpsuit and boots that Zane saw in the window of an all-night store, she did abide by his wishes on everything else. A little disappointed that she hadn't been given the time to find a wedding gown, she kept on what she'd planned to wear to dinner that night, and they got married by a preacher who, thankfully, looked nothing like Elvis.

Feeling elated and bubbling with the champagne they had in the rented limousine on the way back to the hotel, they stumbled into their suite in the wee hours of morning and spent the rest of the night in romantic bliss, fulfilling each other's fantasies and convincing one another that nothing could ever come between them.

Before dawn even collided with the night, word of Laura Rockford's marriage to the waning star would fly across the AP wires and appear in small articles in almost every paper in America.

THEY WERE ALL WAITING when Zane and Laura came home the next afternoon. Blue and his wife, Cille, and Rally and Anna stood against the wall, arms crossed, as they walked into the foyer. And from the door they could see into the living room, where Choral sat with her husband, Bobby, and Angel perched on the arm of the couch next to Lenny. Ford leaned in the doorway. And on the staircase, sitting alone, was Haven.

There wasn't a smile among them, and Laura was struck suddenly by the contrast between this welcome and the one she'd received the first time she'd come into this home. Then, she and Haven had been showered with hugs and greetings warmer than she'd ever known. Now she felt the hatred in their stares and wished she could shrink back and hide until they all went away.

"Well, well. I guess y'all heard the news." Zane tossed his coat to Blue, who caught it and held it in front of him, as though it disgusted him. "Boys and girls, say hello to your new stepmother."

That wasn't what Laura had wanted to say, and she felt her cheeks stinging as her eyes meshed with Haven's. She had never seen so much emotion in her friend's eyes, and the emotion was pure abhorrence.

Tears filled her own eyes, and she tried to blink them back.

"I can't believe you did it," Ford said. "How could you?"

"Didn't it occur to you that we might want to know our daddy was gettin' married?" Choral asked.

"She's younger than your youngest child, Daddy," Blue said. "It's embarrassing."

Zane set his hands on his hips. "You wanna know why I didn't tell you?" He pointed to his oldest son. "That's why. Because of remarks like that. You all married who you wanted, and by God, I can marry who I want. I don't need the permission of any of you. So if you don't have anything nice to say, then get out."

One by one, they left. First Blue and Cille, and then Angel and Choral, and finally the others, all without saying a word. Only Haven remained.

Laura couldn't hold the tears back, and she wiped her face as she looked up at her friend, daring to hope that maybe Haven had stayed to offer her blessings, that maybe all wasn't lost.

But when Haven stood up, she said in a quiet voice, "Mama wanted to make you a cake."

"A cake?" repeated Zane, disgusted.

"Yeah," Haven said. "She's real depressed that she didn't get to do it. You know how she gets when she's left out. I think I'll go stay with her tonight."

She started down the stairs, and Laura searched for something to say, something that would break the ice and restore her in Haven's good graces. "Haven?"

Haven stopped, keeping her back to them.

"Tell her . . . tell her we'd love for her to make us one. Tomorrow, maybe."

Zane breathed an expletive, but Haven gave no reaction at all. Instead, she just kept walking until they heard the back door close.

Laura spun around to Zane. "I told you we should have waited and invited them," she cried. "Now they'll never accept me. They'll just all hate me, like Haven does!"

"They'll come around, darlin'," he said, pulling her against him and holding her. "This isn't the kind of family that holds grudges."

THE COMMOTION DOWNSTAIRS woke Laura the next morning, and she glanced over at Zane, who was beginning to wake himself. She could hear a woman's voice shouting and the housekeeper shouting back. Someone was hurrying up the stairs and the shouting grew louder and closer, and suddenly she realized whose voice it was.

Catrina's.

Sucking in a breath, she got out of bed and groped for her robe. "Zane, it's my mother. Get up!"

Zane sat up, letting the sheet fall around his hips. "Your what?"

"My mother!" The door burst open, and Laura caught her breath as Catrina stormed in.

"Pack your bags, Laura. You're coming home with me."

"No, Mother." Fastening her robe, Laura faced Catrina. "I'm not."

"Laura, I'm giving you ten minutes. I'll be waiting downstairs."

With the command of an admiral, the famous Catrina Rockford strode out of the room to wait for her daughter to follow orders.

Laura turned to Zane, who was getting out of bed with a look of disbelief on his face. "This is my house, and you're my wife, and if anybody is gonna order you around, I am."

Already, Laura was changing clothes in a fury. "I'll go down and talk to her, and explain that I'm not going anywhere. Maybe in a little while she'll calm down, and the two of you can meet...." Her voice trailed off as that possibility made her even more nervous, and running a brush quickly through her hair, she said, "Maybe you should just stay here until she leaves."

"It's my house," he said again. "I'll go anywhere I want!"

She sighed. "Okay. Well, I'll just do what I can."

In moments she was down the stairs, and she found the housekeeper, red-faced and pacing, ready to pounce on her. "I don't run this house this way, Miss Laura. I can't have folks burstin' in and screamin' at me. It's enough to give an old woman a heart attack."

"I'm sorry, Eugenia," Laura said. "But that's my mother. Would you mind getting us some tea?"

Eugenia started toward the kitchen. "You ask me, she needs a good strong belt of Jack Daniel's to calm her down. You should have told your mama you were gettin' married, child."

Laura swallowed back her consternation as the housekeeper scurried off, then finally, she went into the sitting room and faced her mother squarely. "All right, Mother. Here I am. Have at me."

"What are you *doing?*" Catrina demanded. "What are you thinking? Are you out of your mind?"

Laura thought for a moment. "I assume you're referring to my marriage?"

"Do you know how I found out? Ivana called from New York. *She* had heard it on the news network. Can you imagine how I felt having someone like that telling me my own child had gotten married?"

"We thought it would be romantic to elope," she said quietly. "And besides, I knew how you'd react. I didn't want you to try to stop us."

"Are you pregnant?"

Laura almost laughed. "No, Mother."

"Thank God." Catrina dug through her purse for a tissue, but Laura knew she wouldn't need it. Catrina rarely showed emotion. This was the biggest rise she'd ever got out of her. She should have done it sooner, she mused.

"He's a wonderful man, Mother. I love him."

"You haven't got a clue what love is."

Laura sat down then, facing her mother across the glass coffee table. "Before I met him, I didn't. I'd never really experienced it before."

"Lots of men will love you, Laura, because you're a Rockford, and that name is spelled with dollar signs. You're not mature enough yet to distinguish between those after your money and the ones who really love you."

"Well, I have a choice," Laura said calmly. "I can go through life like you, suspecting everyone and never loving anyone, or I can take a chance with someone who makes me feel wonderful. It is my choice."

"How dare you?" Catrina's words sizzled across the room, and she got up and went to the fireplace, where a clutter of family pictures in various shapes and sizes on the mantel caught her attention for a moment. Laura knew what she was thinking. It was bad taste to put family pictures in the sitting room but either the Berringers didn't know that or they didn't care. Probably both. That was why she liked them so much. Swinging around, Catrina lifted her head high. "It's not too late. I can still have the marriage annulled. We can chalk it up to teenage rebellion, and soon everyone will have forgotten."

Laura gaped at her, astonished. "I'm not a teenager. I'm a grown woman, and I'm not getting my marriage annulled, Mother. You'd better get used to it. I'm staying right here with my husband."

With a controlled rage, Catrina moved closer to her daughter and pinned her with fiery eyes. "Then you'd better forget you were ever a Rockford. Because nothing associated with that name is yours anymore. I'm not releasing your trust fund, and I'm not paying any of your bills. And when your *husband* starts trying to bilk you out of the Rockford money, you can tell him that he's out of luck."

The words chiseled at Laura's spirit, but she told herself that her mother was wrong. She'd never understood love, so she never trusted it. How could she know what Laura had with Zane?

"Zane doesn't need the Rockford money, Mother."

Catrina laughed then, and picking up her mink from where she'd tossed it, she pulled it on. "They always need it, Laura. You'll see. But don't come to me when that happens. As long as you're married to that hillbilly, you won't get a cent out of me."

She pushed past Laura and headed for the door, just as Eugenia came around the corner with a tray of coffee and tea. When she slammed out of the house, the housekeeper looked at Laura. "I declare, that's the rudest woman I've ever seen in my life!"

Laura only started back up the stairs, to find solace in her husband's arms.

CHAPTER ELEVEN

ORDINARILY, SLY WOULD have considered it heaven to be lying on the floor with two of his nephews and a niece, who were capsizing in giggles as they tried to bury him in kittens. But he'd been in a foul mood since he'd heard the news about Zane and Laura.

Sharon, the oldest of his sisters, rescued a kitten from her two-year-old, then, getting up on her knees, gazed at him upside down. "All right, Sly. What's wrong?"

"Nothing," he said. "I just got some bad news about a friend yesterday." He pulled a kitten off his neck and pretended to stuff it down his nephew's shirt. The child squealed until he realized it was just Sly's hand.

Melia, his youngest, pregnant sister, asked, "Anybody we know?"

He shook his head. "Nope. Quit rubbing your belly. You're gonna rub a hole there."

"Don't want to talk about it, huh?" Sharon asked.

"Nope." Sly sat up and disentangled himself from the kittens, giving one to each child. "You're gonna have to take all of them, Sharon," he said, slumping into a chair. "The kids are getting attached."

Sharon shot Melia a look. "Listen to him. We have a problem and he hounds it out of us, but when *he* has one, it's none of our business."

"I never said it was none of your business."

"You implied it," Melia said.

"And we inferred it," Sharon added.

He leaned his head back on the chair and let out a long, labored sigh. "I just don't see any point in boring you to death."

"I knew it," Sharon said, her eyes lighting up. "It's a woman."

Melia sprang up and went to sit on the arm of his chair. "All right, Sly. Let's hear it."

For a moment, he only looked at her, and finally, he said, "It's not what you think. I mean, I'm not involved with her or anything."

"Yeah, right." Melia glanced at her sister.

"No, really. She's a...a good friend, and I've been watching her dive headfirst into the biggest mistake of her life."

"What else is new? You do that all the time." Smiling, Melia rubbed her belly again, then grabbed Sly's hand and placed it where the baby had last kicked.

"Yeah," Sharon agreed. "You've sure watched plenty of mine."

The baby chose not to kick, but Sly kept his hand on his sister's stomach, waiting. "Why do you think that is?"

"That you keep watching people you care about make mistakes? I don't know. Maybe it's like passing a car accident. You know it's gonna be bad, but you can't make yourself look away."

"Profound analogy, Sharon. I feel so much better."

Melia let go of his hand and got up. "Maybe you're just choosing the wrong people to care about. Maybe you have bad taste in friends."

"Actually," he said with a grin, "I have very *good* taste in friends. But my friends' friends..."

"Well, you know what they say."

"No, Sharon, what do they say?"

Sharon winked at her six-year-old son. "Tell him, Davy."

"You can pick your friends," the boy said, "and you can pick your nose, but you can't pick your friend's nose..."

Sly dived off the chair and wrestled the giggling boy to the floor, and immediately, the other two started covering him with kittens again.

When the giggling died down, Sly sat up again. "So which ones do you guys want?"

Sharon chose two calicos off of him. "I think I'm gonna have to take these two. We can't decide between them, can we, kids?"

A chorus of no's followed.

"I call them Rolo and Dexter," he said. "But you can change it if you want."

"Rolo's mine!" Sharon's four-year-old daughter shouted.

"I get Dexter!" Davy said.

Sammy, the two-year-old, stuck his thumb in his mouth as though trying to decide how to challenge either one of them.

"It's not fair, Sis. You should really take three."

"We'll take two," she said with a thank-you-very-much smile.

Sly scooped up a kitten and got to his feet. "What about you, Melia? Don't you want one?" He held the kitten up and made a pouty face, but she shook her head.

"I'm pregnant. I can't."

"What's that got to do with anything?"

She laughed. "I read something about pregnant women being advised not to handle kitty litter!"

The doorbell rang, and Melia got up. "Expecting company?"

"No," he said, but that wasn't unusual, because most of his company was unexpected. "Get it, will you?"

Melia opened the door, and Sly saw Laura. Something jolted inside him, and he got to his feet. "I didn't expect to see you," he said.

She blushed slightly, something he found refreshing, and glanced around him at the mess of kittens and kids. "I'm sorry. I'm interrupting, aren't I?"

"No, no," Sharon said, pushing past Sly and extending a hand. "I'm Sharon, Sly's sister. And this is Melia. . . ."

Davy rushed forward. "And I'm Davy, and this is Rolo and Dexter. . . ."

Laura smiled. "Sly's names, right?"

"Yeah," Sharon said, "but we like them."

"Me, too," she said, pulling Blizzard out of her coat. "Meet Miss Blizzard."

Sharon and Melia crooned over the kitten for a moment, both confirming that it had been the prettiest of the litter, and then rounding up the kids, they herded them outside and down the sidewalk.

Laura felt strange walking into his apartment, with the fire going and the two remaining kittens scurrying around their mother. The warmth of Sly's home was too inviting, and she worried that married women weren't supposed to feel this way with other men. "How did your sisters come to live in Nashville?" she asked.

"Well, Sharon's husband is a mixing engineer, and I convinced them that Nashville was a better place to raise kids than the West Coast. And I sort of fixed Melia up with a friend of mine here. They've been married a little over a year now. I'm slowly working on getting the whole gang here."

"That's nice. I envy you."

An awkward silence settled over them, and finally, he sobered. "I hear you've got a new family of your own. Are the rumors true?"

She smiled, but he noted right away that it was a weak attempt. Something was wrong. "Yeah, they are. We thought it would be romantic to elope. Zane just came over to get me for dinner the other night and suggested we do it, so we did. Everybody's furious at us for not telling them. I thought I'd come by and see if you were, too."

Sly's smile faded, and he got to his feet and went to the fireplace to stir the fire. "I can't say I was jumping for joy.

But I wasn't surprised, either. In fact, I don't know why I didn't expect it.''

Laura frowned. "Really? Did Zane tell you we were going to do it?''

Sly turned the log over, making the flames pop and wave around it. As he did, he felt his own anger licking up inside him, yellow-hot and destructive, not because he'd been bested, but because she had. When he set the poker down, he turned back and went to sit on the edge of the coffee table, facing her. "Laura, something happened that day. Zane and I got into an argument, because I warned him to tell you the truth about something or else I would. The next thing I knew, he'd whisked you off. And I'll bet everything I own that he hasn't told you yet.''

He saw the dread on her face and realized what she must have been through since they'd come home. This wasn't how marriage was supposed to be for her. She was supposed to be glowing, basking in congratulations, flying. But she couldn't fake that.

"Told me what?''

"About the IRS.'' He waited, gauging her reaction for a sign that she knew, but he saw nothing pass across her face.

"What about them?''

Sly knew how easy it would be to drop the whole story in her lap. But that could make him the villain—the last thing he wanted to be to her. "Ask him, Laura. Ask him the real reason he was in such a rush to marry you.''

Livid, Laura backed away and shook her head. "Why are you doing this? Why is everybody so determined to ruin my happiness? First my mother, and then you....''

"I'm not trying to ruin you, Laura! I'm just trying to open your eyes!''

"Is it so hard to believe that he could just love *me?* That I make him feel good, that he likes having me around, that he's been happier than he's ever been before since I've been in his life? Is that so farfetched?''

Sly hated to see a woman cry. It touched him in a way that made him almost helpless, and he took in a deep breath and stepped closer to her, his voice dropping to a gentler level. "Of course it's not farfetched, Laura. That's easy to believe. And maybe on some level, that is how he feels."

"You don't believe that," she accused. "You think he was after my mother's money, even though that would be ridiculous, since he has plenty of his own."

"Laura, Zane's not exactly at the top of his career. His CDs aren't selling. They're just not working anymore, and he's a stubborn man. He's not willing to change his style or update his image. This is the last of his records I'll be working on. In fact, when I'm through with him, I may wash my hands of Nashville entirely."

"Good," she said bitterly. "Zane doesn't need turncoats like you in his camp. Making up lies and interfering...."

"They're not lies, Laura. Ask him. You have to find out sooner or later."

Her sobs came harder, and she covered her face again, but this time, Sly pulled her into his arms and held her tightly. She knew she shouldn't seek comfort there. She was a married woman now. But she couldn't bear the pain she felt at Sly's suggestion that a lie stood between her and Zane, and the feeling that had haunted her all her life—that she really wasn't worthy of anyone's love.

Sucking in a deep breath, she tried to calm herself. "I have to go."

Easing out of his arms, she picked up her kitten and started for the door.

"Laura," he said, setting a hand on her shoulder before she touched the knob. "I want you to know that if you need to talk, you can come to me. I'll listen."

"You're a little biased," she said bitterly. "You hate my husband."

"I don't hate him. I couldn't work with him if I hated him. I just don't like the things he does."

"Well, I happen to love the things he does. And I'm going to make him happy. Nothing is going to change my feelings for him."

Sly dropped his hand to his side. "I hope so, Laura," he said. "I hope you have the chance to prove all of us wrong."

ZANE COULD SEE that she'd been crying the moment she came home, and he pulled her onto his lap. "What's wrong, darlin'. You're supposed to be happy, not teary-eyed."

She had thought about what Sly had said all the way home, and as angry as she was with him, she didn't want him completely out of her life just yet. If Zane knew that Sly had even suggested he was keeping something from her, he'd fire him, and that wouldn't help anyone. All the work on the album would be jeopardized, and Sly would likely go back to California.

No, she had to keep that part to herself and act as though she'd heard it from some other source. "I was just thinking about my mother," she lied, "and all the things she said. And I was wondering which parts are true."

"What?" He frowned and made her look down at him. "Honey, you can ask me anything."

She sniffed and tried to control her tears, but they kept coming. "She said that she'd heard a rumor that...that you were in trouble with the IRS."

He moaned, as if he'd rather it had been anything else, and holding her, he let her cry against his shirt. "Listen to me," he said after a moment. She looked up at him, hoping beyond hope that he would set her mind to rest and tell her it was all a lie, that no part of it was true.

"I was brought up in a real conservative family," he said, "the kind of family where a man's not a man if he can't handle his problems himself. I may keep a lot of my business problems to myself, but it's not because I'm hiding anything."

"But, Zane, I need to know if it had anything to do with our eloping. You should know that I don't have any money.

My mother has control of my trust fund, and she's very angry at me right now.''

"Shh," he said, stroking her hair back from her face. "You and your mama will make up. Mothers don't stay mad for long. But I don't want your money, darlin'. All I want is you. You just let me worry about business."

Part of her bristled at his patronizing attitude, since business had been such an integral factor of her life. But another part wanted to stay in the darkness, where there was a sweet security, and where she could let someone else be in charge.

But as she tried to relax in Zane's reassurances, a gnawing sense of unease began to grow like a malignancy inside her.

THE SHRILL RING of the phone woke them at eight the next morning, and Laura sat up and looked at Zane, who seemed to be undisturbed. "Zane, the phone."

"Answer it!"

She had to look around for it, since she hadn't been here long enough to know where it was. Reaching over to Zane's side of the bed, she picked it up. "Hello?"

"I need to speak to Dad! Put him on now!" Laura didn't know if it was Blue, Ford or Rally, but feeling as if she'd been slapped in the face again, she shook her husband. "Zane, wake up."

"Tell 'em I'll call back," he muttered.

Swallowing, she put the phone back to her ear. "Uh... he's sleeping. Can he call you back?"

"No, he can't call back! Tell him I'm at the office and the place is swarmin' with IRS agents goin' through his desk, his files, everything!"

"What?" Clutching the phone, she tried to grasp what he was telling her. "What do you mean, they're going through his files?"

"Put him on the phone now!" he shouted.

Tears came to her eyes, and she shook Zane more insistently. "Wake up, Zane! He says IRS agents are swarming over your office."

Zane sat up quickly and snatched the phone. "Ford? What's going on?"

"You'd better get over here, Daddy. This looks real bad."

Shaking, Laura got up and began dressing as fast as she could, and when Zane slammed the phone down, she turned on him. "Zane, what is going on?"

"What does it look like?" he shouted. "I've got to get down there."

"I'm going with you!"

"Oh, no you're not! I told you I can handle this!"

"You told me a lot of things, Zane! Now I'm going to see for myself!"

They reached the offices of Berringer Publishing, where much of Zane's income was made buying, selling and licensing songs, within fifteen minutes of the phone call.

Already, the IRS had confiscated half of his files, and Zane bolted into his office and grabbed the man who looked to be in charge. "Do you have a warrant to do this?"

"The IRS doesn't need warrants. We have the right to examine your files if we think you've falsified your tax returns."

"You slimy muckrakers, you've already audited my label. You don't have the right to come onto my private property and start rifling through my things without my permission!"

"Yes, we do, Mr. Berringer." The man calmly turned back to the box of files he was identifying, and Zane grabbed his shoulder, swung him around and planted a fist on the side of his jaw.

Laura screamed as the agent fell back against the wall, and three other agents descended on Zane, complete with guns and handcuffs, before he could make another move.

Within minutes, the building was swarming with more agents and police officers, Zane was being read his rights, and Laura was left in tears with nothing to do but follow the squad car to the station.

ZANE'S ATTORNEY, Leon Ritchter, and his accountant, Bill Walters, met them at the station, having been called by Ford in a fit of panic. Both sternly reprimanded Zane for antagonizing the very people who could do him in, but he wasn't in the mood to listen. He went before the judge when it came time for his hearing and was astounded when his bond was set at a hundred thousand dollars.

"That's no problem, is it?" Laura asked Bill after an officer had taken Zane out through another door to incarcerate him for his sins. "I can just get the money out, and they'll release him today, won't they?"

"He doesn't have it," he told her.

"What do you mean, he doesn't have it? Zane's got plenty of money."

"He's not very liquid. Apparently, he hasn't shown you his bank account. We'll have to get a bail bondsman to loan it to us."

Laura was shocked by the state of their finances. She had assumed that Zane was as successful as his opulent life-style seemed to boast.

He was in a sour mood as she drove away from the jail, having borrowed the money for his release, and when he realized that she wasn't heading home, he asked her where she was taking him.

"To Bill's office. He told us to come by and form some kind of game plan." Her lips were tight and her words clipped. "He seems to think that if we don't find some way to appease the IRS, your bank account will be frozen by morning, along with all of your other assets, they'll auction everything you own, and we won't have anything to live on."

"Now, don't start acting like a godforsaken wife."

She glared at him. "I can't believe you said that! You lied to me about the IRS, and now when I insist that we face up to this mess and take care of it, you have the nerve to say that? I *am* your wife, Zane!''

"I won't have you tellin' me what to do. This is my problem."

"Well, somebody has to figure out how to solve it. Otherwise, our marriage is going to break down to nothing but conjugal visits in prison." They reached the accountant's parking lot and she screeched to a stop. "Now, come on."

Sulking like a child, Zane got out and followed her.

"I'm not in the mood for lectures," Zane thundered as they reached the office and he dropped into a chair.

"No, I wouldn't think so," Bill said. "But, Zane, when you deck an IRS agent who holds your future in his hands, you're asking for trouble. And you've got it. They've frozen all of your accounts, taken all of your files, slapped a huge fine on you to add to your ten million dollar debt, and now they're giving you a week to come up with everything you owe or they're taking the house, the cars, your land and everything that goes in them, on them or with them. Do you understand what I'm saying?"

Zane laid his head back on his chair and didn't answer.

"I understand," Laura said. "So, what do we have to do?"

"Well, I've been negotiating with them until I'm blue in the face, trying to hold them off. But in one swing today, Zane set us back months. The truth is, unless we can come up with a substantial amount, and somehow convince them to give you a pretty big extension, you're sunk. And, Zane, I don't think I have to remind you that if you go down, so do all of your kids. The houses they're living in are still in your name, and they're working in *your* company and managing *your* career...."

Again, Zane only stared at the ceiling. "What do you want me to do, Bill? I'm not made of money. I guess they'll have to send me to jail."

"No!" Laura sprang out of her chair, and faced the accountant squarely. "What's the least amount they'd accept to extend his deadline?"

"I don't know," Bill said. "If we could come up with a hundred thousand dollars and convince them that everything possible is being done to get the rest, we might be able to buy a few more months."

"A hundred thousand dollars," Laura said as tears burst to her eyes. "The magic figure. Throw a hundred thousand at the judge and they'll let him out of jail. Throw a hundred thousand at the IRS and they won't take your house." She looked at Zane, disbelieving. "Don't you have it somewhere, Zane? In stock or bonds? In a retirement fund? There must be something...."

"Zane doesn't believe in estate planning," his accountant interjected helplessly.

"No, I don't," Zane said belligerently, then shot her a what-do-you-want-to-make-of-it look, just like the boys she remembered from the fifth grade.

"You've spent everything you've ever made?" she asked, sinking back into her seat.

"I don't need lectures," he said again, closing down that line of questioning.

Her mind reeling, she turned back to Bill. "What do you suggest?"

He turned his hands palm up. "I don't have a clue. I hope you kept your apartment. At least you and Zane will have a place to live."

Her mouth fell open and she shook her head. This must be a nightmare from which she'd wake soon. And the worst part of the nightmare was the growing evidence of Zane's duplicity in his reasons for marrying her. Evidence that indicated Sly might have been right. Her mother might have been right....

"Unless..."

Slowly she met Zane's eyes, and she knew before he spoke just what he was going to suggest.

"Unless what?"

"Unless *you* had it somewhere. You have bank accounts, don't you? Stocks and bonds. A trust fund. You could probably get your hands on a hundred thousand real easy."

As if it were tangible, she felt the fist of her mistake walloping her right below her ribs, knocking the breath from her. "I told you, I don't have anything, Zane."

"What do you mean? You're a Rockford. Your signature alone would be worth a fortune."

"I'm not a Rockford anymore, Zane. I'm a Berringer. And when I became a Berringer, my mother took away all my Rockford privileges. I have no bank account, no stocks or bonds, no trust fund, no credit cards, not even my own car. And I hope to God you didn't marry me so I could bail you out of this, because if you did, you made as big a mistake as I did."

The silence in the room was so thick it almost smothered her, and finally, Zane's face reddened. "Do you mean to tell me that you're not worth a blasted thing?"

She rose to her feet again then, fighting the tears in her eyes. "I'm worth a lot more than you'll ever know. But I don't have a penny to my name."

With that, she stormed out of the office and headed for the car. She had started it and was pulling out of the lot when Zane came running after her. When he ran in front of her to stop her, she put her foot on the brake.

She braced herself as he got in, but the rage she expected didn't follow. "I'm sorry, darlin'," he said softly. "I was panicked. I didn't mean any of that the way it sounded."

"You lied to me," she cried. "And I have no reason to think you married me for anything other than money." Her voice cracked, and she dropped her head against the steering wheel and let the pain wash over her.

"Oh, honey, that's not true." He pulled her into his arms, rocked her gently and crooned into her ear, "I married you because you make me feel young again, because you brought me sunshine after I'd been living in the dark for so long. I married you because you make me laugh, and because you make me warm, and because you have a body that makes me feel like a teenager dealing with my hormones for the first time. And I married you because you made me fall in love when I thought all that was behind me. I married you because I want to spend the rest of my life with you."

Through her tears, she looked up at him, gauging his face for sincerity and the honesty she needed so desperately to see. And she saw it. At least, she thought she did. "Are you sure?" she asked.

"Positive," he whispered. "Now, let's go home. We don't have to think about any of this tonight."

BUT LAURA COULDN'T HELP thinking about it. Zane's way seemed to be to ignore it and it would go away. Laura knew it wasn't going away.

She waited until he was asleep, then went into his study and found the few meager records he kept in a file drawer in his desk. She found the checkbook and the record of his other accounts, with balances that made her wonder how he'd kept the lights on this long.

He was a man who barely made ends meet, yet he owned a fleet of antique cars, enough acreage to build an air force base, a mansion and several homes in which his children lived....

And she didn't know what she was going to do.

She was sitting in the easy chair beside his study window, staring out into darkness, when Zane came to find her.

He looked so innocent, so handsome, standing in the doorway in nothing but his boxer shorts, apprehension in his eyes. "What's wrong, darlin'? I missed you. The bed was cold."

She looked up at him. "I can't ask my mother, Zane. I just can't."

He knew what she referred to, and slowly, he sat down across from her.

"You know how upset she was about the marriage, and she honestly believes that things are going to fall apart for us and that I'll run to her for money. I just can't do it."

Zane rested his elbows on his knees and stared down at his feet.

"But I've been thinking. If they did take everything, we could just start over, couldn't we? We could move into my apartment and book you a tour. You could earn some money that way, for us to live on, and slowly, we could build back up. It might even be kind of nice, starting from scratch together."

Zane was quiet for a moment, and finally, he rubbed the back of his neck and looked up at her. "That's easy for you to say. These aren't your things."

"But they are just things, Zane."

He got up and went to stand over her, gazing out the window, his silver eyes pensive. "I should have given the deeds to the kids' houses over to them. They asked me to a time or two, but I never got around to it. I sure hate for them to lose everything because of me. At least Haven's tuition has been paid for this semester."

She sighed and tried to imagine all his children without homes. "What do you think they'll do?"

"I don't know," he said quietly. "Most of 'em work for me. They'll have to get other jobs."

She closed her eyes and tried to think. "Isn't there somebody you could borrow from? Friends?"

"You start telling your friends you need ten million dollars, and they're not your friends anymore. I learned that the hard way. It's funny how quick friends can disappear when they know you're in trouble."

"I don't mean ten million. If you could just borrow a hundred thousand."

"I've tried," he said. "And the truth is, I *have* borrowed from a few. That's how I've held the feds off this long. But I'm tapped out."

"What if you sold a couple of your cars? They'd raise at least a hundred thousand."

"There's no way I could get them sold within a week for what they're worth. No way."

The moonlight illuminated one side of his face, and the other was cast in total darkness. She got up and put her arms around him. "I feel like I've jinxed you. Your family's mad at you, and now you're losing everything."

"Not because of you, honey."

"I know, but... I wish there was something I could do. I've always taken money for granted. It's always been there. And now when I need it most of all..."

"I understand why you're too proud to ask your mother," he whispered.

Something about his choice of words disturbed her. "It's not just pride, Zane. She wouldn't give it to me, anyway. Not without some terrible price."

"Well, then, I guess that's that."

THE NEXT MORNING, Zane didn't go into the studio as he was supposed to, and when she searched the house to find him, he was sitting on the staircase, looking up at the pictures of himself with the people he'd called friends in his lifetime. One with Dolly Parton, another with Hank Williams, a third with Porter Wagner. They covered the wall, pictures of Zane with Willie Nelson, with President Jimmy Carter, with Oliver North.

When she got closer to him, she saw him wipe his face, and she knew that he'd been crying. "Are you okay?" she asked.

"Yeah," he said. "I was just thinking that the IRS will probably take those, too. They're just my little mementos, with nothing but sentimental value, but they might fetch a good price in an auction. I sure wish I could hold on to them."

She knelt on the step below him and put her arms around him. "What about your platinum albums?"

He smiled through his tears. "They date me. Notice I don't have any platinum CDs."

"You will," she said.

He sighed. "Well, I guess they'll take them, too."

Not knowing what else to do, she kissed him, but in her heart, she knew it wasn't enough.

LAURA DIDN'T SLEEP at all that night. Images kept flying through her mind—of government agents moving the furniture out of Zane's home, taking his treasured pictures off the walls, selling his cars, bolting his doors, evicting his children. And as irrational as the thought seemed, she felt responsible.

She got up in the night and stole down to the living room, where she sat for hours sorting out her future. The one in which she and Zane started over from scratch, in the apartment Sly had got for her, seemed unacceptable. Zane would turn into a bitter, broken man, and he would blame her. She knew he would.

As dawn intruded through the windows, an answer came to her. Michael.

He had told her he'd always be there if she ever needed him, but she'd never asked him for anything. Surely, he could help her now.

She waited until she was certain he was awake, then called him. The sound of his voice made her feel instantly better.

"Michael?"

"Laura, is that you?"

"Yeah. I hope I'm not calling too early."

"Too early? I'd say it's a few days too late. I heard you got married!"

She tried to laugh. "Yeah. I was going to call you, but we decided to elope at the last minute, so I didn't call anyone."

"You could have called when you got back."

"Things have been a little hectic."

He was quiet for a moment. "Well, I hope you're happy, Laura. I really do. I've said a few special prayers for you."

"Thanks. It looks like I need them."

"Uh-oh." His voice was flat, and when he spoke again, it had more inflection. "Laura, is everything all right?"

"Yes...no... Oh, Michael, it's complicated. I love Zane so much. He's what I've been wanting all my life. But—"

"But what?"

"But he's in trouble. *We're* in trouble."

"What kind of trouble?"

She sighed again. This was harder for her than she'd expected. "Michael, do you remember when you and Mother divorced, and you told me that if I ever needed you, you'd be there?"

"I do."

"Well, if I ever needed you, this is the time. Only this is a biggie, Michael."

"What is it?"

"This has got to be kept quiet. I have to tell you to ask the favor, but I'm telling you in confidence."

"I understand. What is it?"

"Zane's in trouble with the IRS. He owes ten million dollars, and he has a week to come up with it or work out some other solution."

There was silence at the other end of the line. "Did you know this before you married him?"

She felt the sting of his question, the sting that targeted Zane Berringer. If she told the truth, he would think she'd been had. But if she didn't, he would think she was stupid. She chose not to answer either way.

"I married Zane because we were in love," she said. "And now I want to help him. I have to help him, because I'm his wife."

"I can't give you ten million dollars, Laura."

She laughed then. "I know that. I wasn't asking for that much."

"What then?"

"His accountant thinks that if he offered a hundred thousand, and a plan for coming up with the rest in the next few months, that maybe they'd wait. I was hoping...that we could borrow a hundred thousand from you, to be paid back within a year."

Again, he was quiet. When he finally spoke, his voice was low. "What did your mother say about all this?"

She let out a frustrated sigh. "You know Mother. She's cut me off completely, disowned me, threatened me, pulled every rug she had to pull out from under me. She took my car, my credit cards, my bank accounts, my trust fund...I can't go to her."

"As much as I hate to say this, honey, I think I have to agree with her. I'm not real interested in saving Zane Berringer's butt."

"Are you interested in saving mine?"

After a slight pause, he said, "If I thought it would, yes."

"It will, Michael. If Zane goes down, I'll go down with him. I'm his wife. He's my husband. That *means* something to me. I'm committed to him for life, Michael. That's not something Mother can begin to understand. But I thought you could."

She heard the struggle in his sigh. "I do understand that, Laura. I just hope Zane's as committed as you are."

"He is. I know he is."

"All right, then. I'll loan the money to you."

She felt a heavy burden flying off her chest and sucked in a deep breath. "Oh, thank you, Michael! I knew I could count on you!"

"I have one condition," he added.

"What?"

"That you be happy. No matter what that means."

"I will be happy, if Zane is," she said, and from the bottom of her heart, she meant it.

LAURA MET WITH TWO representatives from the IRS, with Zane and his CPA present, to offer them the payment and convince them to give her more time. By the time she left the office, she had done most of the talking, this twenty-one year old, almost-college graduate, who knew less about the world than she did about what she wanted from it. Because of her name, they listened attentively as she told them her plans for Zane. She would get his album released much sooner than the lead time usually required by the record companies, and Zane would go on tour to promote it. He would beef up his publishing company and utilize more of the songs he had in his inventory by selling them to big artists. His new album would have a novelty song with a line dance that would be released on video, and Zane would start selling off some of the luxuries he could do without.

Zane watched her, astounded, as she wheeled and dealed on his behalf, using weapons she hadn't even discussed with him. Still, the government agents remained unconvinced. They had given him ample time already to make good on his debt.

Finally, when she felt she had no choice, she said, "If even these things don't get us the money we need, I'll come up with it on my own. You must realize that I have my own resources."

"We assumed you did, Mrs. Berringer. What we don't understand is why you haven't already tapped into them."

"None of them are available to me right now," she lied. "But within a few months, they will be."

The clock seemed to tick too loudly as the two agents stared at her, thinking it over. When they finally left the room to discuss it between themselves and check back with their own superiors, Zane laughed out loud. "Blazes, darlin'. I sure didn't know I'd married a wheeler-dealer. I'm gonna have to put you to work."

She didn't find the remark funny. Whatever she gained from all this, it had cost her a lot more. She was exhausted and felt sick, but still, she sat stoically in her chair, waiting for the verdict.

After a few minutes, the two men came back in. "We've been authorized to accept a $100,000 payment now and postpone your deadline until six months from now. But if we haven't been paid in full by July 15, we will have to seize your property and all your assets, Mr. Berringer."

It was a victory that Zane celebrated all the way home, laughing and waxing poetic about Laura's powers of persuasion. But she was too deep in thought to celebrate, for she had a lot of work to do, and not much time to do it.

CHAPTER TWELVE

"WILL YOU HELP ME learn the business?" Laura's soft plea came as a surprise to Sly, and frowning, he gazed across the control board at her.

"Why?"

"Because I have to save Zane's career. He won't...or can't...do it for himself."

Sly smiled and shook his head. "Zane doesn't like taking advice, Laura. He doesn't listen, and he has an ego the size of Montana. He's not going to let you get involved."

"He doesn't have a choice," she said. "I've bailed him out twice now, and I have to make sure that what I told the IRS is true. It's my reputation on the line here now."

"No one will blame you if he fails, Laura," Sly said softly. "Zane was heading downhill before you ever came into his life."

"Well, I intend to change all that."

Sly sat back in his chair, surprised at the determination he saw in her. He wouldn't have expected it. "What have you got in mind?"

Laura pulled out a chair and sat down next to him. "I have several things in mind. First, I want to make sure that this album is his best in years. I want to pull out all the stops. I want to use every trick you know to punch it up and make it appeal to younger audiences. Then I want to get it out in record time and book a dynamite promotional tour that will get people's attention. The album's almost ready, isn't it, Sly?"

144 CATCH A FALLING STAR

Sly hesitated. "Almost won't get you very far, babe.
We've got a long way to go. And Zane's a stubborn man,
Laura. He can't admit that the younger audiences aren't
buying him, so he won't do anything different. I've tried
offering suggestions, slipping studio magic into the mixing,
hiring different kinds of backup singers.... He's rejected
every idea I've had."

"Then do it behind his back," she said. "Sly, we don't
have a choice here. I've been through the royalty state-
ments of all his records in the last five years, and they've
been falling drastically. I say we go for broke on this one,
whether he likes it or not."

Sly grinned and lifted his brows. "You know, there's only
so much I can do. Even if I produced his best album, he
doesn't have the kind of appeal anymore that he used to. It
still might not sell."

"I have other ideas," she said. "I want to hire a chore-
ographer to create a line dance for one of his most upbeat
tracks on the album, and then do a video with the dance in
it. It worked for Billy Ray Cyrus."

"Billy Ray has his own appeal, and he had a good song."

"You don't think Zane has any good songs?"

Sly hesitated. "We recorded forty songs and can only put
twelve on the album. The ones I think will be hits are the
ones Zane wants to leave out."

"We'll put the ones you want on the album," she said.
"I'll convince him somehow. And I want to be involved in
the mixing."

"You what?"

"I want to be involved," she insisted. "I know I don't
know a thing about it, but I know what I like in music. I
want to work with you on it, Sly, because Zane won't. From
what I can see, he only wants to hear the finished product
and accept or reject it. I want to help make the decisions. I
want to learn every aspect of the business, and I'm a quick
learner."

If it had been anyone else telling him that he had to teach them the business in "ten days or less," and allow them to make major decisions on his turf, he would have told them what they could do with their determination. But this was Laura, the woman who had been so deceived by Zane's charm, the woman who was waking up from the illusions he'd painted for her about their marriage. It was Laura, who he had hoped would have more backbone than he'd seen in her so far.

Laura, whom he liked so much to be around.

"All right," he said finally. "I think I can teach you a few things, and maybe you can teach me a few things. Together, maybe we can come up with a hit album for Zane."

"Do you think so?"

He couldn't say that he was optimistic, but the idea of having new blood working on Zane's material was promising. "I think if anybody can bring Zane Berringer good luck, you can, babe."

She smiled. "Okay. Then I can come to you when I run into a glitch in his business that I don't understand? You'll talk me through it and not get impatient?"

"I'll try."

"Good enough," she said. When she beamed up into his eyes, he felt something stir in his heart, something he had no business feeling. But he couldn't look away.

"So, where are we with this album?" she asked.

"Still mixing. Trying to find some compromise for Zane that'll still sell a few albums."

"Forget the compromises," she said. "Show me what you would do if you had your way."

THEY CHOSE THREE SONGS that Zane believed could never be hits, dropped three that he thought would, added some saxophones and more backup singers, with some extra reverb here and overdubs there. And they did it all without consulting Zane once.

Meanwhile, Sly urged Laura to meet with Zane's agent, Philly Johnson, the massive, four-hundred pound enigma who wheeled and dealed for many of the most popular acts in Nashville, about booking a tour to coincide with the release of Zane's new album.

Philly chewed on the smelly cigar in his mouth and regarded Laura cautiously. "Where's Zane? Does he know you're here?"

Laura refused to be intimidated. "I'm taking care of some of Zane's business so he can concentrate on finishing his album."

Philly took the cigar out of his mouth and tapped it, letting the ashes miss the ashtray. "What about Blue? He's Zane's manager. He's the one I usually do business with."

During the summers that she'd spent working for Rockford Enterprises, there had been many times when she hadn't been taken seriously. Her mother had taught her that any meeting entered without confidence was a waste of time, and that if one had confidence, it could be used to demand respect. This, she decided, was one instance when her mother's wisdom would serve her.

Leaning forward, she fixed Philly with her piercing eyes. "From now on, you talk to me. Whatever Blue has done for Zane hasn't worked, and I'm going to find some things that will."

He gave a phlegmy cough, shifted in his seat and shuffled some papers until he found a pen. "We're not gonna be able to get him the biggest bookings unless he fronts for somebody bigger."

"No way. I may be new in this business, Philly, but I know that Zane can't be billed as a warm-up act for anyone else. He has to be the headliner. He's a legend."

"He was, once. But we have the little problem of losing money on his tours. The last one we did for him almost didn't break even."

"This is different," she assured him. "It's his best album, and when the video comes out on the first release, with the new dance and his new image, I think you'll see a lot more interest. We're also thinking of getting him a new band to tour with. I've been watching tapes of his last tour, and the band lacks charisma. It needs a new spark, and I think if we got some younger, hotter musicians, maybe some sexy backup singers who could dance, it would breathe new life into his image."

Philly nodded, his double and triple chins wobbling in agreement. "You may be right. Tell you what. Let me make a few phone calls, pull a few favors and see what I can come up with. There might be a little something we can do."

As Zane recorded the last few cuts on his new album, Laura got to know some of the other artists recording for the label and sat in on their sessions, soaking up every ounce of savvy she could get about the business of music and image-making. She saw the way they got together, one artist from studio A with the artist down the hall in studio D, the way they collaborated on unfinished songs, jammed together and sometimes even jumped in as cameo backup singers on each other's albums.

Zane set himself apart, as if he were in a league different from the others and didn't have time to hobnob with the up-and-coming stars. He virtually ignored them, like a team starter ignored the freshman rookies.

But Laura didn't, and when Jerry Joe Wagner was signed to the label and showed up for the first day of his recording session, things took a turn for the worse.

Jerry Joe Wagner would have been nothing more than a skinny mechanic who wrote poetry if it hadn't been for the awesome voice that reverberated from his lungs and his God-given talent on the guitar, which mesmerized even the most seasoned musician. That he was known to be a creative genius so gifted that he almost couldn't function in the real world was common knowledge, so common in fact that some people treated him like a complete idiot.

But he was no idiot, and while others stored up conceptions and misconceptions about him, Jerry Joe filed those slights away for future reference. He had little time for petty jealousies and competitions, yet he was so young that he was sometimes easily influenced, until his creative intuition kicked in and set him straight.

And his choir-boy looks didn't help matters any when it came to being led down the wrong path. He'd been propositioned and seduced by some of the reigning stars of Nashville, the wives of the reigning stars of Nashville, the daughters, the sisters and the fans of the reigning stars of Nashville. And after five years in the business, he was just beginning to see and understand how Samson had been duped by Delilah, and how Adam had been enticed by Eve.

In fact, it was a woman who had seduced him into switching labels, even though it had been against his better judgment. Now he was stuck here, hoping beyond hope that the new label would give him the freedom to cut his tracks the way he wanted and market them in a way that made sense.

But the first day that he walked into the studio and saw Zane Berringer recording down the hall, he knew he'd made a mistake. The man hated his guts, and he couldn't say the feeling wasn't mutual. They had a hate-hate relationship, he and Zane. He knew that Zane believed it stemmed from Jerry Joe's little rendezvous with Rosy years ago, but Jerry Joe's feelings had begun long before that. Rosy was just his way of seeking revenge. And it had worked. Zane had blown a fuse.

But those days, he hoped, were over, and Jerry Joe took his career too seriously to sabotage it with wayward wives of stars. He was more spiritual now, given more to the creative experience and the divine gift he'd been blessed with than to satisfying his human lusts.

So when Zane's new little wife walked into his studio one afternoon to introduce herself, he didn't have the urge to jump her bones that he might have had in his younger days. Instead, he told himself that enough was enough, and Rosy had been more than payback to Zane. He had no intentions of drowning in the water under his bridge. Given the choice, he'd rather swim in it.

"How would you feel about doing a duet with Zane on his new album?" she asked boldly after knowing him only twenty minutes.

He couldn't help erupting in laughter. "You've got to be kidding."

"No. It would be a great career move."

"For who?"

"Well, for both of you."

Jerry Joe laughed again. "I'll tell you what, Laura-love. If you can get Zane to do a duet with me, you've got a deal."

She left his studio so hopeful and starry-eyed that he almost felt sorry for her. It had been a darn sight easier to give her that answer than to tell her there was no way in Hades he'd ever grace the same microphone as Zane Berringer. But it didn't matter, because it would come out the same either way.

"WHEN I WANT your advice I'll ask for it!" Zane slammed his fist against a beam in the wall, cursed, then turned back to Laura and Sly. "But frankly, I'd rather starve than take such asinine ideas from some ignorant socialite who doesn't know a recording studio from a telephone booth!"

Sly saw the look on Laura's crestfallen face and thought that if a man ever deserved hell's wrath for one transgression, this was it, and Zane was the guy. "I think it's a terrific idea."

"You would!" Knocking over a chair, he faced them with rabid rage. "Blast you people. You have no sense of reality. No sense of creative integrity. Neither one of you knows what in blazes you're doing."

When he stormed out, Laura stood stunned, staring after him, her eyes big and fragile with unshed tears. After a moment of tightly wound silence, she cleared her throat. "I'm such an idiot," she whispered. "I should have known. He's so jealous of Jerry Joe. I just thought it would be so great if they could make peace and help each other...."

"This isn't your fault, Laura. It could have worked. Of course, Jerry Joe never would have gone for it in a million years."

"He said he would if Zane would. But it was all a joke, wasn't it?"

"Looks like it."

She half smiled, but he knew she didn't mean it. "And the joke was on me. Again."

Something about that hopeless statement made his heart swell, and he got up and went to lean against the wall next to her, gazing at her misty eyes until she looked up at him. "Don't let Zane's attitude get you down. You have more business instinct than he does. I've seen a lot of people come and go, people like Zane who got to the top and thought they could never lose their throne. They lost it when they stopped listening to people with instinct, like you."

"And you," she whispered.

"Yeah, well, I'm often ignored and cursed at and undermined, too. I figure if somebody's smart enough to listen, they deserve what I can do for them. If they're not—"

Suddenly, a tear slipped over her lashes, and she looked down, but Sly hooked a gentle finger under her chin and lifted until her eyes met his again.

"You're too good for him, Laura. You know that, don't you?"

She didn't answer.

"And you know that he doesn't deserve to have you save his career, just like he didn't deserve to have you save his butt with the IRS."

"He's my husband" was all she could say in response. "I'm committed to him."

"But do you love him?"

More tears fell. "I wouldn't have married him if I didn't."

"But things aren't the way you thought they were when you married him, Laura. Do you still love him, knowing what you know?"

She sighed. "I was raised in a house where love was as disposable as paper plates. But I don't want to be like that. I want to believe that a commitment is a commitment."

Sly knew what she was saying. In her soft way she was telling him to back off, that she wasn't going to stray, that if he harbored feelings that there were any possibilities for the two of them, he should dispense with them right now. But she was also evading. She was having trouble admitting that she loved Zane anymore, and the thought frightened her to death. He hated the fact that it provided him a measure of the hope she seemed to warn him against.

"You don't have to worry about me," he whispered, drying her tears with the pad of his thumb. "I don't mess around with married women."

Her fingers closed around his wrist and she removed his hand from her face. "Then you shouldn't touch me," she whispered.

"Why not?"

"Because it's dangerous."

He tipped his head. "I was just wiping your tears."

Their eyes locked and held for a moment, and if she had not been married, if it would not have hurt her, he would have leaned over and kissed her, and lived out the fantasy that had plagued him like a fatal disease. He saw the awareness in her eyes and suddenly abhorred himself for compromising her.

"Go after your husband," he whispered finally. "You have some ruffled feathers to smooth out."

As if she'd been released from a prison she wasn't ready to leave, she started slowly to the door. "Laura," he said, before she reached it. "If anybody ever accuses you of being shallow or weak or superficial, just because you're a Rockford, you send them to me, all right? I can tell them differently."

Something about that approval satisfied her more than all the love Zane had given her, and feeling even more confused, Laura went to find her husband.

CHAPTER THIRTEEN

SLY PERFORMED EVERY studio miracle he knew to give Zane's work a more commercial appeal, then hired the best mixers in Nashville, specialists who were masters at covering vocal flaws and clarifying murky tracks. But Zane, who believed his work was best in its simplest form, fought them every inch of the way. By the time the album was released, it was a study in futility. Zane got his way, and the fans *went* their way.

The tour Laura had convinced Philly to book was canceled as soon as the album was released. Zane wasn't a big enough draw, according to the miracle-working agent. Everyone would lose money on him. "There is something we could do, though," he said.

"What?" Laura asked hopefully.

"We could book him in clubs. Let him get back in touch with his roots. But it's been a long time since Zane's done one-night stands in bars, and I don't know if he'll do it."

Laura knew. And because of his volatile mood swings, she chose not to approach him with the idea. The money wouldn't be enough to save them from the IRS, and the crowds would be too small to impact the sales of his album. So if it wasn't going to make a difference, why risk enduring his wrath?

She racked her brain for more ideas, consulted with Sly on possibilities, but ran into brick walls at every turn. When they tried to get the label to pay for the video of the song they thought would be a hit single, the company passed, claiming that they hadn't heard anything on his album that would warrant airplay on the major stations.

"Let's face it," Laura was told. "Zane's not the talent he used to be. We're not putting any more money into him, and we're gonna pass on renewing his contract."

Zane hid his dismay in the bottles of his choice and went on a three-day drunk that cost him a brawl in every watering hole in Nashville.

And the moment he was dried out, he got the news that the Grand Ole Opry had dropped him from their roster, and Jerry Joe Wagner would be taking his spot.

Laura sat outside the door to his study, with Blue and Ford standing sentinel, and listened to the sound of breaking glass, crashing chairs and objects being flung against the walls. "He's going to hurt himself!" she cried. "We have to stop him!"

"Just let him get it all out," Blue said.

She wilted back in her chair and looked up at his sons. "What do you suggest I do? I'm at my rope's end. I'm fresh out of ideas."

"Do what you should have done six months ago," Ford said. "Pay off the IRS and get 'em off his back. Then he at least wouldn't have this tickin' bomb followin' him around."

She gaped at them. "Where would I get ten million dollars?"

"Give me a break," Blue jeered. "You come from one of the richest families in the country. Ten million dollars is tipping money to a Rockford."

"I'm a *Berringer* now," she said. "My mother won't give me a dime as long as I'm married to Zane. Don't you understand that if I could get the money, I would?"

"We understand that you're too proud to go crawling to your mother. That you'd rather suffer with your dignity than save your husband."

Laura suddenly felt exhausted, and she glared at the two men. "It's not my husband you're worried about, is it, guys? It's yourselves. What will happen to you if Zane goes under? You'll lose your homes, your land and even your jobs. But other than bullying me about getting the money, I haven't noticed one constructive idea!"

Something crashed against the wall, making them jump. "We're doin' the best we can!" Blue said. "We do have a lot to lose. This is our life, Laura. Our families."

"Then why didn't somebody make him pay his income taxes?"

The words came out of thin air and landed with a thud, and both men reddened.

Laura stood, tears coming to her eyes. "Answer me! You all lived real high and got great jobs and great houses at your father's expense. But when it came to keeping this little kingdom afloat financially, what did you ever really do to help? I've spent the last six months trying with every ounce of energy I have to dig him out of this hole he's in, despite his every effort to stop me, and still it's sinking!"

They stared at her for a long moment as she broke into tears, and for a second she thought she saw compassion in their eyes. Maybe this was the moment, she thought, when they would connect. When they would accept her with respect and see her as something more than some bimbo her father had brought home to share his bed. When they would include her in their family.

But that didn't happen. Another crash sounded on the opposite side of the wall, breaking the spell, and Ford shook his head. "It doesn't have to sink, Laura. You're the only one who can help us now. For God's sake, call your mother."

LAURA DIDN'T KNOW where to go, so she just drove. And as she drove, she struggled to think of someone she could turn to. But there was no one. She was as alone now, married into this huge family, as she had been when she was a child.

She drove until she found herself at the condominiums where Sly lived—and where she'd given up her apartment after she'd got the extension with the IRS—and asked herself why she would turn to him in her despair. Could it be because the gentleness and patience he had shown her seemed more like love than anything Zane had given her?

She sat behind the wheel, staring toward Sly's condo, and wondered what it would mean if she knocked on his door and fell, weeping, into his arms.

The door opened, and she saw him step out with a woman...a pretty brunette who made him smile. He leaned down and kissed her on the cheek, and something painful twisted in Laura's heart. What was it? Envy? Disappointment? Jealousy?

She watched as the woman said something that made him laugh, then headed for her car on the other side of the parking lot.

Only then did Laura recognize her. The woman was his sister, Sharon.

Closing her eyes, she let out her heavy breath, cursing herself for entertaining such foolish emotions. She was married, after all, and had no business reacting to any woman Sly saw.

Still, she was glad it was only his sister.

She watched as the car drove away, then glanced back at Sly's door. He still stood there, only he had caught sight of Laura by now. Slowly, he started toward her.

She rolled down her window as he reached the car and grabbed a tissue to blot her eyes. "Hi," she whispered.

"Hi." He leaned in her window and gave her a grim look. "Hey, are you okay?"

She shook her head. "No. I don't know what to do. I wouldn't have come here, but it just occurred to me that I don't have that many true friends...."

He smiled softly and opened the car door. "Move over," he said.

She scooted over a little, and Sly got in. Instantly, he put his arm around her and drew her closer. "I'm glad you counted me as a true friend."

"I wasn't going to come in." She buried her face in his shirt and felt his steady, capable hand stroking the back of her hair.

"Why not?"

"It just... seemed inappropriate."

"So you'd rather sit out here all by yourself and cry?"

"It's better than sitting in Zane's house with his sons condemning me."

"Zane's house is supposed to be your home."

"It's not, though. It never has been. I was just fooling myself when I envisioned how this marriage was going to be. I pictured people around who hugged me when I came home, and laughed and talked in the kitchen, and gave me pep talks when I was down. I pictured companions, best friends, camaraderie, like you have with your sisters."

Sly tipped her chin up. "Did you marry Zane or his family?"

"Both, I guess. I needed him, too. He filled something in me, Sly. Something I was hungry for."

"A father figure?"

"Maybe," she admitted. "And all the psychology aside, what's so wrong with having what you need? Maybe that's why I let him push me around in the beginning, and let him make my decisions. It felt good knowing that there was a man who cared what I did. A man who had a stake in who I was."

"And now?"

She sobbed softly, then tried to catch her breath. "Now I don't think he does care. But, Sly, he's been under so much pressure, and his career is falling apart no matter what we do. He's about to wind up with nothing. Absolutely nothing. You can't blame him for acting this way."

"He'll still have you, Laura. That'll make him the richest man in the world. He just can't see that."

It began to rain, soft, whispery raindrops on her windshield, then fat, heavy ones that streamed down the contour of the glass. There was peace in the sound of those raindrops, just like the peace in Sly's big arms, and slowly, her sobbing ceased. "Thank you, Sly."

"For what?"

"For seeing something in me that no one else sees."

"Lots of people see it, babe. You'd be surprised."

She leaned her head against him and tried to think about the future. Tonight she would go back to her husband, and he would still be in a foul mood. She would walk on egg shells with him and hope he could lose himself enough to hold her for a while. And she would hold him. That's what marriage was all about. Giving comfort to each other when all the world seemed bleak.

"They said it was my fault."

"Who did?"

"Blue and Ford. They told me that I could stop this whole thing if I'd just pay off his debt. But I don't have it, Sly. And I can't get it."

"They have to blame somebody, babe. You know they do."

"But don't they see that I've done everything I can?"

"You've done more than they have, and more than Zane's done for himself. You should *feel* proud."

"I don't, though." She took a deep breath and whispered, "Maybe I'm just giving up too easily. Maybe there is something else I can do."

THE HOUSE WAS DARK when Laura got home, and she walked quietly through it, wondering from where the next glass might fly. She stepped into the door of the study and saw the overturned furniture, the broken glass, the torn pictures and mementos lying on the floor. Was she supposed to clean it up?

And then the extent of Zane's despair hit her, making her slide down the wall to the floor and collapse in tears again. She saw the phone lying on the carpet next to an overturned plant. Feeling as if she were taking five steps backward, she picked it up.

Her hands trembled as she dialed, and her stomach tied itself into knots. Her mother answered on the third ring.

"Mother?"

Her mother was quiet for a moment. "It's been months, Laura. I had almost given up on you."

Something about that didn't ring true, for her mother never gave up.

"How are you?"

"I'm...fine." She cleared her throat, wishing her mother had the grace to make this easier. But grace had never been one of her assets.

"I read about your husband's tax problems in the paper," Catrina said coldly. "I can't say it surprised me. He married you in such a rush for a reason. I guess that was it."

"We got married because we love each other," she said weakly. "I told you that."

"Yes, you did. And I told you that you can't trust a man's profession of love. There's always a catch."

Laura closed her eyes and fought the urge to hang up. Zane needed her. Blue and Ford and Haven, they all needed her. "I called to ask you a favor, Mother. I think you know what it is."

She could almost hear Catrina smile. "You want me to pay off his debts."

"No, Mother. I want you to give me a loan, so I can. A simple business transaction that will be paid back."

"For how much?"

Her mother was playing with her, and Laura knew that the questions weren't out of cooperation but spite. She was laughing at her, playing along, just so her next wallop would have greater effect. Still, Laura had no choice but to continue.

"Ten million dollars," she said. "It's a lot of money to Zane, Mother, and a lot of money to me. But it isn't to you. It's not much at all to you."

"Why should I give a bloody dime to the man who tricked my daughter into marrying him?"

"He didn't trick me, Mother. And you should do it because *he* is my family now. And if you care about my future, about my happiness, you'll see how much this money could help me. Have I ever asked you for anything before? Ever?"

There was silence on the other end as Catrina obviously realized that she hadn't. This was Laura's first real request, the most important thing she would ever ask her mother. But Laura wasn't sure that her mother knew the cost of this phone call, and what she was sacrificing of herself to make it.

"No, you haven't." Her mother's voice seemed to soften, and a tiny thrill of hope rose in Laura's heart. "And I don't think you'd do it now, if he didn't encourage you to."

"Who can I turn to, if not my own mother?"

Catrina sighed then, and her voice grew decisive. Laura had always given that decisiveness a grudging admiration. She wished she could be as sure as her mother about the things she wanted.

"I'll give you the loan," Catrina said, and Laura let out the breath she'd been holding.

"Thank you, Mother."

"Don't thank me yet. I have two conditions."

Laura's stomach tightened again. Leave it to her mother to make a split-second decision and still come up with terms as excruciating as possible. "What are they?"

"One, you must repay the debt in three years, unless you agree to finish your degree, continue with graduate school and come to work for Rockford Enterprises. In that case, your debt will be forgiven."

It was tough, but it left Laura some hope, and she felt herself relaxing again.

"And the other condition?"

"Simple," her mother said. "You have to divorce Zane Berringer."

She felt the blood pumping into her face, the rage burning in her cheeks, the tears stinging her eyes, and she stood up, her mouth tight.

"Did you hear me?" her mother asked after a moment.

"I heard," Laura replied tersely.

"And what do you say?"

She struggled to find the right words as tears streamed down her face.

"I can only think of three words," she said. "Go to hell."

CHAPTER FOURTEEN

MOST OF THE BERRINGERS attributed Haven's graduation from Princeton to the grace of her guardian angels, lots of prayer and the mistakes of professors who, they were certain, had meant to fail her. Since Haven picked up her degree in the registrar's office and begged off the graduation ceremony, claiming that she wouldn't be caught dead in one of those hats, no one in the family bothered to attend.

She stayed in Princeton a month after graduation because she'd gotten into a band there and had a four-week gig. Then, when she was unable to convince any of her musicians to move to Nashville, she parted ways with them and headed home.

The day Haven was to come home from Princeton, Laura found reason to work out in the front yard, to the chagrin of the gardener. She wanted to greet Haven as she had been greeted the first time she'd come to the Berringer home.

Haven's sisters and brothers had all agreed to come over, and Rosy was already in the kitchen cooking Haven's favorite meal—hot dogs and baked beans from a can. The buzz in the house seemed to ignore the fact that in just a few weeks the IRS would empty the house, auction off everything the Berringers owned and leave them out on the street. No one but Laura seemed to take it seriously, and she had the feeling that they all expected her to save the day at the last minute.

Not that they treated her like their potential savior. For the most part, they ignored her, as if she were a fixture in the house that had to be stepped over. Their usual family banter did not include her, and Zane, who had sunk deeper and deeper into his depression, did nothing to draw her in.

She was more alone than she'd ever been, living in this big house with a husband and so much family. She had done a lot of praying lately, praying about Zane's plight in the music industry, praying about his financial situation improving, praying about restoring her marriage to what she had thought it was going to be, praying about restoring her relationship with Haven.

She watched the driveway from the big gate now, anxious for the moment when Haven would arrive, and wishing—hoping—that there would be a hint of forgiveness in her friend's eyes, that the mellowness that was such a part of Haven would win out, and that her sweetness would help her to see that Laura hadn't meant to hurt her.

But she had learned over the past six months that people rarely behaved the way they were expected to, and so she felt fragile that day, breakable, not certain whether to hold her breath or jump with excitement that Haven was coming home.

She saw the old VW bug put-putting up the driveway, loaded with the few possessions Haven had kept at school. Pasting a smile on her face, Laura walked to the edge of the semicircular driveway to meet her as the car seemed to breathe its last breath.

Haven opened the door, reached for her guitar and got out.

Laura couldn't help the tears rushing to her eyes. "Haven, I'm so glad to see you. I've missed you."

She reached out to hug her, but Haven didn't respond, and finally, Laura dropped her arms. "Did your car give you any trouble?"

"Just the usual," Haven said in a monotone. She opened the trunk and got out her duffel bag and started toward the house.

"Haven, please."

Haven stopped walking, then finally turned around to face the woman who had married her father. "What do you want from me?"

Laura hadn't meant to cry, but she couldn't seem to stop herself. "Nothing. I just want to be friends again. I valued our friendship, Haven."

"Shouldn't that have occurred to you before?"

"Why is it just me you're mad at? Why aren't you mad at Zane, too?"

"Because I understand his weakness for good-lookin' young women," she said. "Any normal middle-aged male who's seduced by a twenty-one-year-old debutante would do the same thing."

"Seduced!" She caught her breath. "Haven, you know me. You know better than that."

Haven started walking back to the house again. "I'm just surprised you're still here."

"Why wouldn't I be?" she shouted. "He's my husband. I love him."

"Yeah, well, he's not gonna be the same person when he winds up on the street. See if you love him then."

"I'll be there with him, Haven," she cried. "We're going down together!"

THEY COEXISTED like strangers after that, she and Haven, while Zane sank deeper into the abyss of despair. He did nothing to pull himself out of it, so Laura set about trying to organize an outdoor concert for the Fourth of July, hoping they'd make at least part of the money he owed and boost sales of his album at the same time.

She spent hours and hours each day at the studio, contacting other artists and trying to get them to commit to performing, arranging for the site, finding financial backing, enticing the two major television networks into covering it live. Her enthusiasm was contagious, and many of the artists she would not have been able to convince otherwise agreed grudgingly to participate. The rest were undecided, but it was difficult to say no to Laura Berringer.

Zane seemed to rise out of his depression a little as the plans began to come together for what she was calling the "Zane Berringer and Friends Fourth of July Picnic."

One night, as Laura was on her way into the house, she passed Haven leaving. Haven barely spoke, but Laura stopped her, anyway. "Haven, do you think you could spare some time on the Fourth to do a set at the picnic?"

It was the opportunity of a lifetime for Haven, one that her father never would have offered her, but she hesitated. "Of my own songs?"

"Absolutely," Laura said. "Sung by you. It could be kind of a debut."

"I don't have a band."

Laura had thought of that. "I was thinking that it would be nice if it was just you and your guitar."

Haven stared at her for a moment, then seemed to soften. "Yeah, okay. I'll do it."

It wasn't much, but it was progress, and as Laura headed into the house, she felt a little more hopeful that things were looking up for Haven and her.

THE CANCELLATIONS STARTED coming at four a.m. on the day of the picnic. One by one, the artists and bands who had committed to be there backed out, until only half of the original number was still slated to come.

A helicopter provided by the landowner who had rented them the site was to fly all of the Berringers, as well as the other stars, to the location in shuttles that day. Laura and Sly had been there since before dawn, Sly supervising the technical crews, while Laura took care of a million other details.

She heard the helicopter bringing the first load—Zane and his family—before she saw it cresting the trees. A feeling of deep dread rose inside her, for she wasn't ready to face him yet.

"What's wrong, babe?"

Laura looked up at Sly, who wore nothing but a tank top and jogging shorts. The tops of his shoulders were reddening over the tan he'd started to develop yesterday when they'd been here, and she wondered why in the world he would put himself through this.

"I'm just bracing myself for what Zane's going to say when he sees how thin the crowd is. Somehow I've got to convince him that the bulk of the fans will come in the next two hours, or he might just get back on that helicopter."

"What if they don't?" Sly wiped his brow with the back of his arm and nodded toward the highway, where a line of traffic was weaving in. People were coming, but not nearly in the numbers they'd expected.

"They have to," she said. "It's our last hope."

She turned back to watch the helicopter as it hovered above the ground, then slowly descended until it touched down.

Sly watched her walk to the edge of the stage, shading her eyes from the sun. Already she was sunburnt, a tender pink highlighting her nose and cheeks. She should have worn long sleeves, he thought, instead of that little T-shirt, and maybe long pants instead of cutoffs. Her hair was twisted up in a loose chignon, and perspiration curled the wisps at her nape.

The urge to lean over and kiss the back of her neck made him angry, and he forced himself to look away.

She turned back to him as the Berringers spilled out of the helicopter, lifting her wrist to wipe her forehead. The movement outlined the generous curves of her breasts beneath the fabric and he forced himself not to stare....

"I don't believe it."

He stepped closer to her, trying to keep his gaze from straying. "What is it?"

"What Zane's wearing." She sounded disgusted. "I told him to dress more casually. I thought it would help his image to quit wearing those rhinestone shirts. And if he didn't agree with me, that was fine, but this beats everything."

Sly shaded his eyes in the direction of the helicopter and saw the two rhinestone shirts, exactly alike, milling through the crowd of Berringers. "Oh, no. Rosy dressed like him again."

He knew it wasn't funny to Laura, but he started to laugh, under his breath at first, then harder. She turned around and shot him a scathing look, but when he couldn't stop, a smile began breaking out over her own face.

"It's not funny."

"Then why are *you* laughing?"

Her shoulders began to shake. "I'm not laughing. You are."

"You've got to admit, it really is a little bit funny."

She turned back to the helicopter and her laughter died. "Sometimes I can't help wondering which one of us is really Zane's wife."

"Imagine the dilemma for him." Sly cleared his throat, trying to stop the laughter, and touched her shoulder. "Don't let it get to you, babe. It's not worth it."

"I know," she said quietly.

Still grinning, he walked back across the stage, and Laura watched his long, easy stride. He looked good, the tank top wet from his own perspiration and clinging to him like a second skin. He was getting nothing out of helping with the concert, yet he'd been here as long as she had and had worked with her all day yesterday. When she'd asked him why, he'd said simply, "I keep hoping we can boost the sales on Zane's album. I get a percentage, too, you know."

But she suspected that it was more than that. He stepped off the stage, and three young blondes rushed to his side. He attracted women the way Zane attracted trouble, and there was no mystery in the fact. He had enough charisma with women to be a star in his own right, with or without talent. One look at him on stage and the ladies would go wilder than they had with Elvis. The thought was enough to keep her awake at night.

But he wasn't Elvis, and he didn't want the limelight. He was just Sly, and he was here to help, and somehow, glancing back at her husband, Laura wished he wasn't so good at making her feel the things that Zane should be making her feel.

Zane climbed onto the stage, his expression dour, and she reached up to kiss him. "Hi, honey. Are you ready?"

He scanned the sparse crowd. "Where is everybody?"

"Uh . . . they'll be here. There's still two hours yet."

He swallowed and looked at the string of traffic outside the fence. "When Willie used to do his picnics, people would camp out the night before, and traffic would get so backed up on the highways that it took hours to get in."

"Things are different now," she said weakly. "People . . . they wait until the last minute." It was a lame explanation, and the moment she said it, she wished she hadn't.

"So have any of the bands gotten here yet?" he asked, looking at the clipboard she held.

"Uh . . . not yet." She didn't want to tell him that half of the acts had canceled, and that the rest were iffy at best. "You're opening and closing, so the others don't have to be here for a while." She glanced down his outfit. "By the way, did she have to dress like you?"

"I have no idea how she knows what I'm wearing every time," he said. "I guess she bribes Eugenia or something. Can't be helped now."

"I thought you were going to dress more casually. Jeans and a T-shirt. Something the crowd could relate to."

"This is what I wear to perform," he said. "Take it or leave it. Haven can wear the T-shirts. And by the way, who told her she could sing in my show?"

"I did." Laura lifted her chin defiantly. "And she's probably nervous, so leave her alone."

"You're crazy, Laura. She's got no talent, and the crowd's gonna be throwing stuff before she gets through. I hope you're not keeping her out there for long."

"Zane, I like Haven's singing. It's different. I think once her voice catches on, she could go really far."

"I don't want my daughter being the laughingstock of Nashville," he said. "I'm telling you, don't let her sing more than one or two songs. Now, who's playing after my opening?" He pointed at the clipboard. "Why do you have a line through him?"

She swallowed. "Because, I...he..." Taking a deep breath, she decided just to blurt it out. The helicopter was leaving, so there was nowhere he could go for a while. "He had to cancel, Zane. Throat trouble. But I've moved Little Texas up..."

He looked as though he'd been struck, and he jerked the clipboard out of her hand and counted the bands with the lines through them. "All of these have canceled?"

He took her silence as her answer and gaped at her, genuinely amazed. "Why?"

"I don't know," she said helplessly. "Sly said there were rumors around the studio that we were in debt so deep that we might not be able to pay them. But we did a little damage control, and the others haven't canceled, Zane. Philly promised me they were coming."

He looked across the sparse crowd of not more than a thousand people so far and shook his head dolefully. "I should have known."

"It could still work out, Zane. Please...don't give up."

But Zane *had* given up, and when the concert started and he came out to perform, he was already on his way to drunkenness and gave the worst performance Laura had seen him give yet.

The only saving grace was that Haven was well received, but just as she warmed up to the audience and had their rapt attention, Zane came out, asked for "a big hand for the little lady," and rushed her off the stage. Before the sun went down that day, before the fireworks could go off, he closed the show and told everybody to go home.

Defeated, Laura stayed behind, intent on making sure everything was undone as meticulously as it had been done. But when the crowd had gone and all the acts had been helicoptered away, and only she and the crew remained behind, she let the failure sink in. Collapsing on a crate behind the stage, she covered her face with both hands and felt the weight of the disaster she had orchestrated.

"Has anybody told you today what a phenomenal job you did with this?"

Glancing up, she saw Sly, as weary-looking as she. "You didn't have to stay."

"Well, what was I gonna do? Leave you with a bunch of sweaty, drunken roadies?"

"I would have been all right." She looked at the equipment still waiting on the stage, as if some other band would step up at any moment and bring the crowd to its feet.

"You did, you know. You did a phenomenal job."

"I couldn't have done it without you." A cool breeze riffled through the wisps of her hair, bringing a little relief from the heat. "I just wish it had worked out better. Maybe made us a little money."

"It worked out great, considering the circumstances, Laura. I'm really proud of you."

She smiled. "Yeah, right."

"No, really." He turned over another crate and sat down, facing her. "You know, the first time I met you, I have to admit I was bowled over by your looks." He grinned. "I do like pretty women. But I'm just starting to be amazed by what's behind those beautiful eyes."

"Tears?" she asked flippantly.

"No," he whispered. "Brains. You could probably pull off anything you set your mind to."

"Anything but earning ten million dollars in the next eleven days."

"It's not your failure, Laura."

She smiled. "Well, you may just be the only one who thinks so."

He touched her bare knees then, making her skin tingle in reaction. "Look at me, babe."

She brought her eyes up to his, hoping beyond hope that he couldn't see the turmoil he incited within her.

"You set up a concert here that would have rivaled Woodstock if it hadn't been for Zane's reputation. With all you had going against you, you still worked a miracle. I want you to feel good about that."

When she didn't answer, his hands squeezed her knees slightly, and her eyes gravitated to them. They were great hands—hands accustomed to being used, hands that conveyed strength and confidence. She tried to remember the last time Zane's hands had touched her, and suddenly, she realized how lonely and isolated she had been.

His face was inches from hers, and she imagined how easy it would be to erase that distance between them, to pull him into the kind of kiss her mind had played out so many times. It would be so easy to forget that ring on her finger when it meant so little to Zane.

"Do you know what I wish, Laura?"

She swallowed. "What?"

"I wish I had the power to give you the kind of happiness you deserve." She sighed, and he reached up and swept a wisp of hair out of her eyes. "I wish I could do something to put joy in those sad eyes."

"You do all the time," she said softly. "Sometimes I wonder if you're the only one who can."

Their eyes locked for an eternity, as they were overwhelmed by the reality of feelings they had no right to feel. So many words lay on the tips of their tongues, so many truths that couldn't be told. They gazed at each other, not saying those things, not touching, not acting at all on the heart-pounding emotions gripping them, until finally, Sly broke the tension. Clasping his hands, he said, "I guess we'd better get back to it."

"Yeah." She got up and stared at the sky in the direction the helicopter had last disappeared. "We need to finish before the helicopter comes back for us. It *will* come back, won't it?"

He grinned.

"I guess it depends on which Berringer is in charge," she said. "Truth is, any one of them would be happy to leave me out here tonight. Although I did get a smile out of Haven after her performance today. First one in seven months. I'll take what I can get."

"The helicopter will be back, Laura."

Not so sure, Laura went back to work.

CHAPTER FIFTEEN

THE HELICOPTER CAME BACK just before midnight and loaded Laura and Sly and the remaining workers who hadn't left in the trucks. As she flew back to Nashville, Laura couldn't escape the dismal feeling that what awaited her at home might not be pleasant.

The helicopter dropped her right on the Berringer estate, where Sly and the others had parked. As the roadies headed for their cars, Laura hesitated at the edge of the lawn.

"What's wrong?" Sly asked.

She shrugged and tried to look less forlorn. "I'm just hoping I can get in and shower before I have to face the music. Maybe everybody's asleep."

"You can't be serious about this. Nobody in their right mind would blame you for what happened today."

"They will, though. Just wait."

The helicopter ascended, stirring the wind as it went, and as it disappeared beyond the trees, Laura felt Sly's hands on her shoulders. "You need to relax," he said, starting to massage the tension out of her. "You need to get in a hot bath and soak until the water cools. And you need to do something about your sunburn."

"It's not bad," she said, allowing his voice to work as much magic as his fingers. "It'll be gone by tomorrow."

His fingers moved to her neck, and he held her head with one hand as he massaged her neck with the other. "And so will your regrets. You'll realize that things weren't as bad as you think."

She shook her head. "I don't know, Sly. Zane's not happy right now."

She felt his chest behind her, emanating heat as if it were the strength she needed to go through that door. But the fact that she would rather turn around and melt into him confused her. It just made things worse.

As though he sensed that, he let her go. "Now," he said, glancing toward the house. "You go in there with your head held high, and don't take any flak from anybody."

She tried to smile, but tears came to her eyes instead. "Thank you, Sly," she whispered. "You've been a lifesaver for the last two days. I won't forget it."

She was glad she couldn't see his face clearly in the darkness, for that meant he couldn't see hers.

"I'll wait for you to get in," he said softly.

Taking his strength and holding it close, she headed into her husband's home.

THE HOUSE WAS DARK when she went in, and praying that Zane was sleeping off his drunken binge, she climbed the stairs quietly. She heard voices at the top and saw the light spilling from her bedroom door.

Haven stood in the doorway and turned when she heard her.

"Hi," Laura said carefully.

"Hey." It was a grudging greeting, but they'd gone so long without speaking that it was easily forgivable.

"Is he..."

Haven nodded and stepped aside. Laura saw Zane sitting on the edge of his bed, head dipped between his knees. He looked up at her, and she realized he had aged a decade in the last few months—ironically, in the same few months he'd been married to her.

Laura stayed in the doorway and said, "It's all broken down and put away."

"Just like my career."

"I tried, Zane. I did the best I could."

"Well, it wasn't good enough."

As if she'd been struck by a blow she'd fully expected, she started toward the bathroom. "Could we just deal with this tomorrow? I'm exhausted."

"No, we're gonna deal with it right now." He grabbed her arm as she pushed past him and swung her around. "You're ruining me, you know that?"

"How?"

"Ever since I met you, my career's gone downhill, my finances have gone downhill, and in no time at all, I'm gonna lose everything I own!"

"That's not my fault!" she shouted. "This was all happening before I ever met you! All I've done is try to save you!"

"By digging my grave deeper?" He knocked a lamp off the dresser, and she jumped as it crashed to the ground. "That concert was a joke, Laura. Why you talked me into it, I don't know. You lied about the acts you had booked, you lied about—"

"Wait a minute!" she screamed. "I did not lie! I told you the truth! But word got around the studio that we might not be able to pay the acts—just like we can't pay our taxes— and one by one they started canceling. I didn't create that problem, Zane. I just tried to work around it! How can you blame me?"

"You want to know how? Because you're a Rockford, darlin'. One of the richest little heiresses on the whole continent! Only you won't give one cent to me. Not one cent!"

"I don't *have* it, Zane. I told you!"

"Your daddy left you a trust fund! If your mama won't give it to you, then get a lawyer and make her! But stop interfering in my business and coming up with all of these cockamamy plans that don't work!"

"My mother is not legally bound to give me the money, Zane. My father's will said that she doesn't have to until I'm thirty. I have nine years to go!"

"Well, now is when we need it, Laura!"

"What do you want me to do? I tried to borrow on it, but she wouldn't let me use it as collateral, and the bank wouldn't loan it. Zane, I've done the very best I can."

"Well, like I said, it's not good enough!"

She closed her eyes and wished from the bottom of her heart that she could wait until tomorrow to have this out. She was so tired, all she wanted was a shower and a soft bed. "Okay, Zane," she said, capitulating. "We've established that I'm single-handedly responsible for everything that's gone wrong with your life in the last seven months. So I guess the question is, do you want me to leave?"

He stared at her for a long moment, then finally smiled bitterly and said, "Yeah, I think that would be a good idea."

Tears sprang to her reddened eyes, but she blinked them back. "Fine." She went to the closet and pulled out her suitcase and started emptying drawers into it. When she'd finished, she closed the suitcase and snapped it shut. "I'll be back tomorrow," she said. "Maybe after we've both had some sleep, we can talk rationally about this."

"Don't bother coming back," Zane told her. "Not until you have ten million dollars."

She stared at him in disbelief. "So I have to buy into this marriage—into this family—if I want to stay? Tell me something, Zane. What's *your* investment?"

He turned his back to her, refusing to answer. Grabbing the suitcase, Laura headed for the hall.

She had scarcely gotten out the door before he slammed it behind her. Tears assaulted her—just one more blow after the avalanche she had experienced today—and she bolted down the stairs. Haven was waiting at the top of the stairs, and she knew she'd heard everything.

"Where are you goin'?"

"Far enough to satisfy him." She bit the words out. "Guess you're all going to get your wishes."

Haven took the suitcase out of her hand. "Who're you callin'?"

"A cab," Laura said through trembling lips. "I don't own a car, remember?"

Haven pulled out the drawer in the telephone table and retrieved a set of keys. "Take the Volvo. It's mine. He can't say anything."

Laura looked up, and their eyes met, darted away, then met again. "Look..." Haven took in a deep breath, then ran a hand through her short hair. "No matter what he says, I thought you did a great job today. It couldn't have been easy."

The tiny acknowledgement moved Laura in a way that she would never have foreseen, and she wiped her eyes and tried to find a smile. "Thanks. You were really good. The crowd loved you. Don't let anybody tell you you can't sing."

Haven looked uncomfortable with the compliment. "Daddy's had a lot to drink today. He's not himself."

Laura stared out into the night. "Oh, I don't know. This is pretty much the Zane I've been living with lately."

"Don't give up on him, Laura."

She laughed harshly. "It's not about me giving up, Haven. He's the one who gave up." She went through the door and stopped on the veranda as more tears overcame her. "The thing is, I really, really wanted it to work. Even if we lost everything...it didn't matter. I just miss the Zane that I thought I married."

Defeated, she went down the steps and out to the car. When she pulled out of the driveway, she saw that Haven still stood in the doorway, watching until she drove out of sight.

As exhausted as she was, Laura didn't sleep much in the musky-smelling motel room. Instead, she played memories over and over in her mind. Memories of those stolen moments with Zane in the early days of their relationship. Memories of how precious he'd made her feel.

But those memories were mixed with the more recent ones of Zane blaming her for all the ills of his life and throwing her out into the night.

Someone knocked on the door, and for a moment she only stared at it. Could it be Zane coming for her, full of the regrets that came with the sobriety of morning? She doubted it. And even if it was Zane, she wasn't sure she was ready to face him.

The knock sounded again, and through the door she heard a man's voice. "Laura? It's me. Sly."

Hope sprang up in her, and along with it, a tremendous sense of relief. Quickly, she opened the door.

Sly leaned against the casing, all clean shaven and rested, looking like the answer to a prayer she hadn't had the energy to utter.

"How did you know where I was?"

"Guessed," Sly said, walking in. "Haven came by this morning and told me what happened last night. This was the closest motel, and I saw your car in the parking lot."

"Haven told you? Really?"

He pulled out his wallet and took a hundred dollar bill from it. "Yeah. And she was afraid you didn't have any money, so she asked me to give you this. She said it was all she had."

"Haven?"

"Yes, Haven." Leaning over to the lamp, he turned it on, banishing the darkness and lighting Laura's face. "Why didn't you call me last night?"

Laura knew how it must look to him. Here she was in this dingy room with the drapes closed tight and all the lights off in the middle of the morning. Slowly, she went to the window and pulled back the curtains. "You were as tired as I was, and besides, what could you have done?"

"Offered you a place to stay, for starters."

She shook her head. "No, Sly. I have to learn to stand on my own."

"Well, that'll be fine, once you get your legs. But right now, I think you need some time to think without the burdens of where you're going to live and how you're going to support yourself hanging over your head."

She sat down on the bed and stared at the hundred dollar bill. "I'll make it."

"You will now," he said. Leaning down, he tipped her face up to his. When she met his eyes, he said, "I want you to check out of here right now, get your things and come back to my house. I have an extra bedroom, and there's nothing more I'd like right now than you as a roommate."

Her eyes widened. "You've got to be kidding."

"Why?"

"I'm a married woman, Sly. I can't move in with you."

"Who said you were moving in? I'm just offering you a temporary place to stay, until some of your problems get resolved."

"Zane would have a fit. And the rest of the family—"

"Actually, Haven suggested it."

"She *what?*"

He shrugged. "From what I can tell, she was really impressed with how hard you worked on the concert yesterday, and then last night, she heard some of what happened with you and Zane. Apparently, she thinks you're the victim here."

"Did she *say* that?"

"Oh, you know Haven. She doesn't come right out and say anything. But she said enough. She still feels a keen loyalty toward Zane, but I think she's giving you a little slack now. She even mentioned that she'd let you borrow her tent, but she didn't think you'd want it."

Laura laughed then, and Sly smiled. "There, that's better. I like to see you laugh."

Her laughter faded slowly, and when he put his arm across her shoulders and pulled her against him, she relaxed against his chest. "I could only stay with you if I knew that nothing would ever happen between us. I still believe in my wedding vows."

He fought the urge to ask her why. "All right," he conceded. "You have my word that I won't jump your bones when you're asleep at night. And I won't flirt, and I won't cajole...."

"You can't help flirting and cajoling," she said. "That's who you are."

"Well, I'll change, then. I won't flirt with you."

She didn't like that prospect much. "And what about all your lady friends? It might discourage them, knowing you have a female houseguest."

The laugh lines around his eyes crinkled. "I can live with that."

"And what about Zane? He'll hate you for helping me. He might even accuse us of having an affair."

"I can live with that, too."

She smirked and gazed at him for a moment. "Then I guess I can, too."

SLY DID THE BEST he could for the next few days. Since Serendipity Chance had fired the engineers on her latest album, she'd hired Sly to cut the last few tracks and mix what had already been done. It kept him busy and away from home, a blessing in disguise since he had so much trouble keeping his thoughts where they should be when he was there.

Laura's spirits seemed to sink deeper and deeper, however, and one night, when Sly came home late and heard the muffled sound of her crying in her room, he couldn't help reacting. He knocked on her closed door and heard her raspy voice call, "Come in."

She was lying on top of the bedspread, fully dressed, crying into the pillow. Her eyes were swollen and red, and the tears had soaked one side of her hair so that it stuck to her face when she sat up. "I didn't hear you come home," she said, reaching for a tissue.

He sat down on the bed next to her. "Are you all right, babe?"

"Just a little panicked, I guess."

"Panicked over what?"

"Zane." She almost seemed to wince. "I guess I thought he'd have second thoughts by now and come after me. I thought he'd miss me."

It defeated him, this undying loyalty to her husband. "Tell me something," he said, pushing her hair back from her face. "Why do you want him to come after you?"

"Because, he's my husband. And I wanted to believe that there was one person in this world who cared more about me than himself."

"That's a tall order, babe, considering how much Zane cares about himself. Truth is, he did you a great favor. When the IRS comes and takes everything he has in a few days, you won't have to be there."

"I *wanted* to be there," she cried. "I married him for richer, for poorer. I meant it, Sly."

"I know you did, babe." He drew her into his arms, and she wept against his shoulder.

"But I've had a lot of time to think since I've been here," she said, "and I realize that I have some decisions to make. Like whether to stay in Nashville or go back home, or go back to Princeton."

Sly's chest tightened. "I sure wish you'd stay here, Laura."

She looked up at him and realized she already had more here, even as a loser and a failure, than she'd ever had in Philadelphia. "I'd like to," she whispered. "But then I have to decide what to do to make a living."

"That's pretty obvious to me," Sly said. "You belong in the music business. You should be a promoter or a manager. You could make stars."

She almost laughed. "Give me a break. I couldn't even get a crowd to my own husband's concert."

"Zane dug his own grave, Laura. What I've seen over the last few months is a herculean effort, and a lot of miracles being worked on a man who resisted every step along the way. If he had just taken some of your advice, things might have turned out differently."

"You think so?"

"I'm sure of it, babe. You have a future in Nashville, if you want it."

She lay back down on the bed and looked up at him, drawing in a deep, cleansing breath. "I've turned into such a weepy little wimp. All I do is sleep and cry."

"You've earned the right to do both," Sly said. "And you'll come out of it soon enough."

THE DAY BEFORE the IRS was to lower the boom on Zane, Laura seemed to fall into a deeper state of mourning than Sly had seen in her yet. When Haven brought Blizzard to the studio for him to give to Laura, he hoped that it would boost her spirits.

He wasn't sure if it was the cat itself or Haven's gesture that made Laura the happiest. "Haven's coming around, isn't she?"

"Looks like it," Sly said. "But she's still supporting her father. She said he was going nuts waiting for tomorrow."

Laura got that haunted look again, and petted the purring cat she had missed so much. "So am I."

He brandished the video he had brought home with him and said, "That's why I got these movies, babe. Tonight we're going to watch *Raising Arizona* and *Monty Python and the Holy Grail*. And if they don't get your mind off Zane Berringer, I don't know what will."

It was just what she needed. Laughter. But it was Sly's companionship that gave her the most comfort.

As *Raising Arizona* came to an end, she looked over at Sly. He sat beside her with his feet on the coffee table, absently stroking Blizzard, who lay curled in her lap. "You're a lifesaver, you know that?"

"Yeah?"

"Yeah," she said. "And when I grow up, I want to be just like you."

He smiled then, but the smile quickly faded as a moment of awareness sparked between them. Their eyes held longer than they should have, and she knew she should look away.

"Do you know that I've never felt more comfortable with anyone in my life?" he whispered.

Her voice was raspy. "I was just thinking the same thing."

He wanted to hold her, wanted to reach over and kiss her, wanted to consummate this desire that had been building within him for too long. But he feared there was nothing that would drive her away faster.

Instead, he settled for touching her face with the back of his fingers, and when her own hand came up to hold his, his heart skipped a beat.

She swallowed. He swallowed. They both wet their lips.

"I sure wish you weren't so beautiful," he said.

Her lips parted as she gazed up at him, and he saw the expectation there, the anticipation, the mirror of his own desire. Slowly, he lowered his face to hers and felt her coming toward him, meeting him halfway, her breath making her chest move with the same unsteady rhythm as his.

The doorbell rang, startling both of them, and before their lips touched, they pulled away. They sat still for a moment, each caught in the spell, until finally, Sly got up and went to the door.

Zane strode in the moment the door was opened. "Laura?" he called out without speaking to Sly.

Laura stood up, still holding the cat. "Zane?"

Zane gave Sly a bitter look. "I don't suppose you'd get lost for a minute while I have a few words with my wife."

"It's his house, Zane!"

"Don't I know it. And he didn't waste any time moving you in."

"I haven't moved in," Laura said. "You threw me out."

His face softened, and he lowered his voice. "I didn't come here to accuse you of anything, Laura. I just want to talk."

Sly shrugged and started toward the back of the apartment. "I'll be in my bedroom, Laura."

Laura stared at her husband for a long moment, searching for the remorse she had wished for. He hadn't been sleeping well, and the lines around his eyes were deep. That he didn't smell of alcohol surprised her, and when he came toward her, tears filled her eyes. "Darlin', I'm so sorry."

She stayed back, not allowing him to touch her that easily.

"I want you to come home," he said. "Tomorrow, I'm gonna lose everything I have. I don't want to lose you, too."

She blinked back the tears, realizing that this was what she'd been longing to hear. "Then why did you throw me out?" she asked.

"I was drunk and humiliated," he said softly. "And then when I dried up, I was so filled with pride that I couldn't admit I was wrong. But I am wrong, Laura. Please forgive me."

She dropped the cat to the floor and ran into his arms, weeping with the relief that he really did care, that he really had come after her, and that money wasn't the driving force in his life. Maybe, if she allowed herself to dream really hard, *she* was.

"Come home with me now," he pleaded in a shaky voice. "I need you at home. None of this is your fault."

He covered his mouth then and broke down in front of her, and the sight of emotions in Zane that she had never seen before filled her with compassion. Holding him closer, she tried to comfort him. "I'll come home," she whispered. "Don't you worry. Just let me get my things."

FROM THE BEDROOM, Sly waited for the yelling to begin, but there wasn't any. And then he realized what was happening. Zane was telling her what she needed to hear, and she was going to go back to him.

The unfairness of that reality clutched at his heart and told him that there was no justice, no logic in life. The first woman he'd ever been absolutely mesmerized with, the first one he'd begun to fall in love with, was married to someone else. And she was bound and determined to make that marriage work, no matter what it cost her.

She knocked on his bedroom door, and he opened it, leaning an arm against the frame and waiting for her decision. "I'm going with him, Sly," she whispered. "I have to."

"Okay" was all he could manage to say.

"It's going to be all right," she assured him. "He's had a change of heart. He really does love me, Sly."

He didn't have the heart to question Zane's motives, not in front of her. "Of course he does."

She wiped her eyes and said, "I want to thank you, Sly. For everything. I don't know what I would have done without you."

Rising on her toes, she touched the back of his head and drew him down to her. Her lips passed across his, soft, sweet, wet, and then she pulled away. "Goodbye."

He couldn't manage to answer her as he watched her disappear down the hall and back into Zane's grasp.

CHAPTER SIXTEEN

THE TRUCKS ARRIVED at 7 a.m. the next morning, before Zane or Laura had had time to get dressed. The agents gave them fifteen minutes to do so, then the movers they'd brought with them began methodically carrying out furniture. Teams of agents nailed auction signs in the yard, on the front door of the house, outside the gates. Laura watched, helpless, as their cars were driven away, one by one, leaving only the oldest and least valuable for them to use.

Upstairs, she heard Zane yelling, and she ran up to see what was going on. One of the agents had insisted that Zane hand over his gold watch, along with all the cash he had in his possession. "Take it," Zane shouted, throwing the watch at them. "Take it all. I should have burned it down while I had the chance."

"If you had, Mr. Berringer, you would have wound up in jail."

"You're the ones who ought to be in jail," he retorted. "You're nothing but a bunch of thieves."

"We think a man who doesn't pay his taxes is the thief," the agent returned. "Just because you have your face on CD covers doesn't mean you're above the law."

She saw how close Zane was to breaking, and when the agent logged his watch and cash, then turned to the platinum albums on the wall and the celebrity photos of Zane with the famous people he'd known over the years, she watched him sink to the floor and cover his face with his hands.

It was more heartbreaking than anything she'd ever witnessed. And it got worse. Choral came running in, carrying a screaming baby on her hip. "Daddy, they took the crib!" she shouted. "The antique one that Granddaddy built. And all the furniture, and Bobby's tools, and now they're takin' the horses! Daddy, our prize stallion is in that barn. *Do* somethin'!"

"There's nothing he can do, Choral," Laura cried. "It's out of his hands."

"Then *you* do somethin'!" Choral screeched. "How can you say you love him, then just sit there and watch everything that means anything to him *or* to us bein' taken away like this!"

"I've done everything I can think of! What do you want me to do?"

"If you loved him, you'd think of somethin'," she said.

The agents pushed past them on the stairs, the pictures and plaques stacked precariously in their arms, and one slid off and tumbled down the steps.

"Be careful with that!" Zane bellowed. "I worked years to earn that, and I don't intend to stand here and watch you treat it like a piece of trash."

The agent got to the bottom of the stairs and picked it up. Tossing Zane a belligerent look over his shoulder, he headed out to the truck.

"Why do they want those, anyway?" Zane asked helplessly, turning back to the empty wall. "They only mean something to me. They can't sell them for half of what they're worth to me." His voice broke, and he slumped on the stair rail, then sat down on the steps again and let the sobs overtake him.

Laura watched as Choral sat next to him, crying herself, along with her baby, and put one arm around her father's neck. Looking up at Laura, she whimpered, "Please, Laura. You're the only one who can stop this!"

MOMENTS LATER, Laura locked herself in the empty bedroom that she and Zane had shared since he'd brought her home from their impromptu honeymoon. It looked different without furniture, and glumly, she realized that nothing in it had been hers. She was just one more fixture that he'd added to his collection of things.

The phone lay next to her on the carpet, almost a reminder that, as Choral had accused, she still did have a little power to stop this. She could call her mother. She could swallow her pride.

As she stared at the telephone, she didn't think about their rushed marriage, the deceptions or the indifference Zane had shown her through most of their relationship. All that mattered were the good times. The beginning, when she'd met him and he'd wooed her and courted her despite the disapproval of his family. And last night, when he'd said all the things she'd longed to hear and begged her to come home.

But now he was out there, slumped on the staircase and crying like a baby, and later on today, he wouldn't know where he was going to sleep tonight or what he'd do to support himself. And everything he loved, all the things that surrounded him and made him happy, would be trucked out of here like the valuables of someone who had died.

Choral was right, she realized suddenly. There was really only one thing to do if she loved him. If she truly loved him—the real love that she'd always believed existed somewhere—then she would do what had to be done.

She picked up the phone and dialed her mother's office. She went through several levels of secretaries and assistants before Catrina actually came to the phone. "Hello, Laura."

Laura might have been any acquaintance her mother had ever had, for all the warmth in Catrina's greeting. "Mother, I won't waste your time with small talk," she said. "I've called to ask you a favor."

"Oh?" her mother asked, amused. "I thought I might hear from you today. It doesn't surprise me at all."

"I need ten million dollars," Laura said.

"I trust you're willing to accept my terms?"

Laura hesitated a moment as the words stuck in her throat. "Yes, Mother," she whispered finally. "I'll file for divorce as soon as I have the money."

THE IRS CALLED the dogs off as soon as they had corroborated Laura's claim that her mother had wired the money to her account. It would take days to get the house back in order, but they had brought everything back in, dropped it where they felt it belonged, then disappeared.

But Zane didn't notice the mess. Nor did he notice the fact that Laura was packing again.

"See, honey?" he said as he bounced down on the bed he had just put back together. "I told you your mother would come through. All you had to do was play along with her a little. Talk about saving the day!"

Laura wasn't going to cry. She was going to do this with dignity if it killed her. "I played along, all right, Zane."

"So, what do you have to do? Go home this Christmas? Make a few public appearances with her? Or does she want me and my band to play at one of her parties? I don't usually play parties, but I'll do it for her."

The more he rambled, the angrier Laura got, and finally, she slammed her suitcase shut. "She doesn't want you to play for her, Zane! She doesn't want anything to do with you or your music!"

"Then what does she want?"

Laura's face reddened further as she struggled with the words. "She wants me to divorce you! And I agreed to do it."

For a moment, Zane gaped at her, a redeeming moment in which Laura thought she sensed a flash of despair, of panic, a moment in which she actually believed it mattered to him. She imagined him picking up the phone, telling the IRS that there had been a mistake, that they could have everything he owned as long as he had Laura. But slowly, a smile crept across his face. "Okay," he said, nodding. "We can work with this."

The tiny hope she'd inflated crashed like a water balloon. "How did I know you'd react that way?"

"No, listen," he said, sitting up. "It's a small price to pay to get the IRS off my back. But it doesn't have to mean—"

"A small price?" she repeated. "How can you say that? This is our marriage! Doesn't it mean anything to you?"

"Of course it does, honey. But don't go off the deep end. As soon as you pay the money back, we'll remarry. No big deal."

"When *I* pay the money back?" she repeated. "And how do you propose I do that, Zane? You're the one with the big career. You're the one who spent the money you should have used for taxes."

"Blazes, Laura, if I had it, I would've paid it by now. Where am I gonna get ten million dollars?"

Laura smeared the tears across her face. "Well, my mother has a terrific idea for my paying back the money. In fact, she'll forgive the debt completely. All I have to do is go back to Philadelphia, give her total control of my life, never remarry without her approval and work for her for the rest of my life."

"Blazes," Zane said. "What have you got to lose?"

The words struck her like a crowbar across the forehead, and she dropped the clothes she'd stacked for her suitcase and stared at him helplessly. Slowly, she sank onto a chair that was placed haphazardly in the middle of the floor. "It was all true, what everyone said, wasn't it, Zane?"

"What's that, honey?"

"That you just married me for my mother's money. And last night, when you said all those things, it was just to push me over the edge, wasn't it? One last-ditch effort to make me sell my soul."

"Of course not, honey," he said, reaching for her. "You know I love you."

She jerked away. "You don't have a clue what love is. I guess my mother really did me a favor, after all."

SLY HEARD THE NEWS the first thing the next morning, that Laura had convinced her mother to give Zane ten million dollars, with the stipulation that she divorce him. The fact that Zane would accept such an offer made him livid. So livid, in fact, that he found himself driving up the long driveway to Zane's mansion, ready to say some things to the man that he'd been wanting to say for years, and rescue Laura while he was at it.

The maid answered the door, as though, just yesterday, the whole family hadn't been ready to hock their socks for a loaf of bread.

"Mr. Sly," she said, inviting him in. "What brings you here?"

"I wanted to speak to Zane." He struggled to keep his voice level. "Is he here?"

"Yes, sir," she said. "I'll get him."

He watched her start up the stairs. "What about Laura? Is she here?"

Eugenia turned around and shook her head dolefully. "No, sir. Miss Laura took all her things and left last night."

Letting that news sink in, he went into the living room and stood in front of the mantel, where photos of Berringers sat in various shapes and sizes. There were none of Laura, and he wondered if Zane had ever bothered to get a picture of her. Idiot, he thought. He didn't even realize how precious she was, or how beautiful, or how lucky he'd ever been to make her fall in love with him.

"I didn't expect to see you," Zane said from the doorway.

Sly turned around, and as Zane approached him with his hand extended, Sly slid his into his pockets. "I came to say a few things to you, Zane."

"What things?" Zane asked with contempt.

"Oh, things like how reprehensible I think it is that you would use Laura that way. How disgusting it is that you'd manipulate her, exploit her, allow her to bail you out, then send her on her way."

"You can leave right now," Zane said, and he started toward the door.

Sly grabbed his arm and jerked him back around. Zane stared up at him, disbelieving. "I'm not finished, Zane. I came here to tell you that I've watched you trample all over people, including myself, to get things like you wanted them, but when I saw you doing it with an innocent young woman who wanted nothing more from you than a little bit of love, something snapped inside of me. And I wanted to tell you that not only has your studio dropped you, but I'm not interested in working with you anymore, either. So when it comes time to do your next album, you can look somewhere else."

Zane's temper was raging and he clamped his teeth together. "I was gonna fire you, anyway. Everybody in the industry knows that you're the reason for the poor sales on my last album."

Sly laughed, surprising both of them. "Right, Zane. You keep believing that. And while you're at it, you can keep telling yourself that you and Laura just had a business arrangement, and that you *didn't* use her until you got what you needed." He shook his head, helpless to get to the heart of his fury. "You stupid fool. Any other man in the world would have seen what a treasure she is, but not you. You're too self-absorbed to see anything but the toys around you, and you treat the people in your life like toys, too. But there's more to life than that, Zane, and it doesn't all revolve around you."

"I told you to get out of my house."

"Just tell me one thing first," Sly demanded. "When is she meeting with her lawyer to draw up the papers?"

"Why?" Zane asked. "Are you interested in patchin' up her broken heart?"

Sly laughed then. He knew that Zane didn't have a clue about how protective he felt of Laura. "I might be," he said.

Zane laughed, too, a grating and bitter sound. "And you say I'm self-absorbed. Your motives are just as clear as mine, Sly. And they're not a bit prettier."

Sly grabbed Zane by the collar and threw him against the wall. Holding him there with his fist at his throat, he muttered through his teeth, "You're nothing but a has-been whose only claim to fame in the last year was the fact that you married the Rockford heiress. Now that she's out of your life, let's see how far you get."

He pushed Zane, then released him, sending the man stumbling forward. And before Zane could get to his feet, Sly was out the door.

CHAPTER SEVENTEEN

LAURA STUDIED THE CHECK she had just made out—a check for the ten million dollars that her mother had wired to her account yesterday. Despite her misery, there was some degree of relief in knowing she had nothing left to lose.

Lane West regarded his client carefully, his eyes soft with concern.

"Laura, are you sure this is what you want?"

"What I want has nothing to do with it." Getting up, she tried to hold back her tears and started for the door. "I never should have come to Nashville," she said, "but the truth is, it's harder than I thought to leave."

Lane got to his feet and looked down at her, his big, imposing frame hovering over her protectively. "Will you go back to Philadelphia?"

Looking down at her hand, she rubbed her bare ring finger. "No, I don't think so. I have things here I still have to do."

"What things?"

Unexpectedly, she laughed. "Who knows? I might try to make somebody a star."

Not checking Lane's reaction, Laura opened the door and confronted the mob of reporters waiting for her outside. They pressed in on her the moment she was out the door, a situation that would be repeated over and over until there was a bigger story to follow. She thought she was going to cry, but with all her might, she struggled not to. She wouldn't give them that kind of satisfaction, she told herself. If she had the strength, she would keep those tears back and let them wonder. Lifting her chin and plastering a tremulous smile on her face, she pushed through the crowd.

"Laura, what does Zane say about the divorce?"

"How is the IRS involved in your breakup?"

"Will you be taking back the name of Rockford?"

"When will the divorce be final?"

"What are your plans, Laura?"

She didn't answer as she tried to make her way to the elevator across the foyer, but she felt those tears gaining on her, threatening to shatter her in front of them all. That was all she needed, she thought. For her mother to see her break down on the national news.

Looking ahead, she strained to see if the elevator was open, or if she'd have to stand there and wait, badgered until she broke. It was closed, but she pushed on, nonetheless.

And then she saw Sly, standing beside the elevator, his brooding blue eyes reminding her that there was one person left in the world who cared. Her plastered smile faded and tears obscured her vision.

Some of the reporters turned to snap pictures of the record producer, but most concentrated, instead, on the honest emotion on Laura's face.

As if by his summons, the doors to the elevator opened, and he grabbed her and pulled her on, blocking the way so none of the reporters could pile in with them. The moment the doors closed, she wilted against the wall. "Thank you," she whispered.

"Baby, are you all right?"

The tears broke free and scurried down her face, and she covered her eyes with her trembling hand. "I'm fine. Just fine."

"Why didn't you call me?"

"It doesn't matter," she said. "It's all over now." Wiping her tears away, she smiled up at him. "Aren't you going to say 'I told you so?'"

Sly punched the Stop button, and as the elevator came to a quiet halt, he pulled her against him. She melted into him, letting her tears fall unhindered, until she was strong enough to stand on her own again. "You should have married me, you know."

Drawing back, she tried to smile. "I know, but you never asked."

He grinned and wiped her tears, and pressing his forehead against hers, asked, "So, what are you going to do?"

Laura straightened and looked up at the ceiling, trying to make her tears stop. "I'm going to try to forget the last few months."

"Don't forget them," Sly said. "Use them. I'll help you."

She drew strength from those intense eyes of his—strength she so desperately needed—and wished so many memories hadn't washed under their bridge. Taking a deep breath, she squared her shoulders, and he saw the determination slowly replacing the tears in her eyes. "Maybe you can at that, Sly," she said quietly. "And maybe I can help you."

He lifted an eyebrow and grinned down at her. "Sounds like you already have something in mind."

"I do," she said. "But you might want to be sitting down when I tell you."

He smiled and punched the button that would allow the elevator to move again. "My place," he said before the doors came open.

"It's as good as any," she said, "since I don't have one."

He ushered her through the mob of reporters, who had beaten them to the first floor, then out to his own car waiting in the parking lot.

When they were both safely inside, he leaned back in the seat and took a deep breath. "Vultures."

"They'll say we're having an affair."

He shrugged. "Whatever." He started backing out of the parking space, threatening to run over several reporters snapping pictures behind him.

"Won't the rumors mess you up with all your other women?"

He grinned. "What other women?"

"The Serendipity Chances of this world who flock to you like little lost sheep."

He laughed. "Oh, those."

She couldn't believe she felt better, not when she'd spent all night crying, but it was comforting, somehow, to hear Sly's laughter. "I'm serious," she said. "Herculean charm or not, it might discourage some of them if they think you're involved."

"You overestimate my appeal, Laura."

Smiling, she shook her head. "Oh, no I don't."

He looked surprised. "Well, you sure haven't had any trouble resisting it."

"I was married," she said. "I *am* married." Her smile faded, and she leaned her head back and closed her eyes. "I guess I will be until the waiting period is over and the papers are signed." Her eyes took on that haunted look again, a look that spoke of suffering greater than any she'd prepared herself for. "It's like a death, you know."

"That's what I've heard."

"But the marriage was all wrong. From the beginning, I guess, it was doomed."

"Then why are you having so much trouble letting it go?"

Those tears came to her eyes again, and she covered her face. "I guess it was just the way it ended. So callously. I never thought Zane could be quite so mercenary. It was just fine with him to trade me for ten million dollars."

Sly was quiet for a while, and when they pulled into the parking lot, she was relieved to see that no reporters had beaten them there. Without wasting a moment, they hurried inside to the sanctuary of Sly's condo.

She saw Blizzard lying on the couch, and quickly she rushed over and scooped her into her lap. "Hi, girl," she whispered. "How has Sly been treating you?"

"She's fine," Sly said, going into the kitchen to start some coffee. "She slept with me last night. Down at my feet under the covers."

Laura smiled, and wondered why that thought seemed so pleasant to her.

He came back in a few minutes with two cups of coffee, sat down across from her and said, "Okay, I'm sitting."

Slipping her shoes off, she pulled her feet beneath her. "You won't laugh, will you?"

"I don't think so."

She smiled at the noncommittal answer. "First I want to remind you that you're the one who put this idea into my head in the first place."

He rolled his eyes. "Are you gonna tell me or not?"

"My mother gave me a choice, Sly. I can go back to school and then work for her, and the debt will be forgiven. Or I have three years to pay back the ten million dollars on my own." Her voice was firm. "I can't go back, Sly."

He nodded and waited for her to go on.

"Well, this may sound farfetched, and I don't expect to start out running, but my mother didn't teach me to think small. What I really want to do is be a promoter."

There was no laughter in his eyes, but the smile that crept across his face revealed absolute approval. "You're a natural. If anybody could have gotten Zane back on track, you could have. Are you planning to get a job with one of the studios or be an independent promoter?"

"Independent," she said. "And I want to start with Haven."

"Haven?" he asked. "Are you sure?"

"I believe in her," she said. "Some people don't like her voice, but I think it has a uniqueness that is going to require special promotion. And her songs are fantastic. With the right push, I think she could be a major star."

"There's just one problem," he said. "Money."

"I know that's a problem right now," Laura said. "But if I can get her bookings in places that really make money, we can probably scrape together enough to finance an album. Or maybe we can get her a contract with somebody, and a budget that could be spent on her promotion. I haven't thought it all the way through yet, Sly. The idea just came to me this morning, and I haven't approached her yet. She may not even go for the idea.''

Sly was quiet for the longest moment, and Laura began to think he was struggling to find the right way to tell her that it couldn't be done. It was unfeasible, unpractical, unrealistic.

''You've got a lot of nerve, babe, for a twenty-one-year-old, but I think you can do it. Alone, probably. But if you had a partner, your chances of success would be a lot greater.''

''Well, sure, but who?''

Again, he only stared at her, then finally, he said, ''How about me?''

She sat up slowly and frowned. ''You? You're not a promoter.''

''No,'' he said, ''I'm a producer. A talented one who has a lot of vision, if I do say so myself.''

She grinned. ''I won't argue with that.''

''Well, the studios do. All of them. They argue that any innovative things I try, or any risky efforts, or anything even a little different from the mainstream, will fall flat in the marketplace. They're all so much more concerned with commercialism than art. But I've always felt that good art will sell no matter what.''

''I think you're right.''

''So I've been giving a lot of thought to opening my own studio, with my own label. Fully digital, thirty-two tracks, the works. And I believe in signs, Laura. I think your decision is a sign that this may be the time.'' He leaned forward. ''I think with you as the promoter and me as the executive producer, we could shoot Haven Berringer to the top. And she would just be the tip of the iceberg.''

Laura's eyes widened. ''You mean we'd work together?''

"Why not?" he asked. "Between the two of us, I know we could get investors. We could build a state-of-the-art studio...and sign some new talent, maybe even get some stars that are already established. Maybe even rejuvenate some careers, like we tried to do with Zane. Catch a few falling stars."

She sank back against the couch. "I think it sounds too good to be true."

"It's not, Laura. It's not."

Their eyes held for a long moment, and she saw in him all the appreciation and admiration that she had never seen in Zane's eyes when he regarded her. Her heart responded to that, but then her head reminded her how vulnerable she was, how hungry for that kind of attention. It was just the kind of vulnerability that could ruin her again. She looked away.

"I have so many scars, Sly," she said in a voice barely above a whisper. "It would be so easy to cling to you, but it wouldn't be fair."

"We would be two adults starting a business together," he assured her. "What's wrong with that?"

Her eyes were sad as she looked up at him. "Sly, even after the divorce is final—"

"Strictly business," Sly cut in. "That's all I'm interested in, and the only thing I'm suggesting."

She didn't know why that reassurance only disappointed her, but she took it as the answer she needed. "Then I guess it looks like we've got a deal."

HAVEN COULDN'T HELP the disappointment she felt that her family's possessions would be saved. She had almost looked forward to losing everything. That way, for the first time in her life, she could balance on that tightrope without a net. It was the stuff of which wonderful songs were written.

But now everything had been restored, and she still had that cushy bedroom in that big house. But it did her no good, for her father's influence had done little to get her the recording contract she'd been striving for.

She had enough songs ready for three albums, but each time she convinced a record executive to come to hear her sing them with her band, something happened to keep them from showing up. She'd gotten a few nibbles after the Fourth of July picnic, but so far, nothing had panned out.

And she wasn't absolutely sure that her father wasn't going behind her, slamming shut the doors that she had pried open.

Hoping that wasn't true, but unable to stand another minute of the fake feel of the air conditioner or the softness of her muslin sheets, she grabbed her sleeping bag and decided to head out tonight and sleep under the stars, find some private communion with her maker and her guitar.

But just before she had left her room, the phone rang. She almost didn't answer it, but something told her it was important. "Hello?"

"Haven? Sly. How's it going?"

She smiled and lifted her eyebrows. "You've got a lot of nerve callin' here, after what you did today."

"What, exactly, did Zane tell you I did?"

"He said you barged in and started accusin' him of all sorts of things."

Sly laughed. "Well, he would. What I did, Haven, was tell him that I'm not going to be working with him anymore. And I told him how I felt about the events of the last few days. And I may have grabbed him or something, but—"

His voice trailed off, and Haven smiled. "Well, I figured it wasn't as bad as he told it. But I didn't expect you to be callin' here again soon."

"I'm not calling for him," Sly said. "I'm calling for you. I need to talk to you. It's business. Could we meet somewhere tonight?"

She shrugged. "I had plans, Sly."

"We can do it late or early, or first thing in the morning. Just give me a few minutes, Haven. I don't think you'll regret it."

She frowned. "Business, huh?"

"Yeah, business."

She took a deep breath. "All right. I'm gonna be on the ridge overlookin' the old furniture store on Picadilly Road, by the lake. In my tent. If you really want to talk to me, you can come there."

"You're kidding."

"Nope."

"Haven, that's dangerous. A woman shouldn't be sleeping out by herself at night. You could get killed."

"Who's gonna kill me?" she asked. "There's not another soul around there."

"Well, anybody. Or a snake could come along..."

"If you're scared, Sly, we can wait 'til tomorrow."

He hesitated. "I'm not scared for me, Haven. But no. We'll...I mean, I'll be there. Eight o'clock all right?"

She shrugged. "I don't own a watch. Just come when you're ready. I'm not goin' anywhere."

LAURA SAW THE PUP TENT perched on the ridge exactly where Haven had told Sly it would be, and she laughed softly."

She's crazy," Sly muttered. "You do know that, don't you?"

"No, she's not," she said. "She's just Haven. She marches to her own drummer. I think it's wonderful." She opened the car door and looked back at Sly. "Well, if I don't come back in thirty seconds, it means she's talking to me."

He peered up at the pup tent again. "Well, I'm going to sit here just in case. You sure you don't want me to come with you?"

"I'm sure," she said. "Haven and I have to talk alone."

Getting out, Laura walked through the brush and half climbed, half ran up the hill to the ridge. As she approached, she heard a guitar playing and Haven's soft voice, clear and simple, singing along. She rounded the tent and saw Haven leaning back against a tree, strumming.

Haven looked up at her, and immediately her hand stopped. "Hey," she said, without getting up.

"Hi."

Haven eyed her for a moment, then glanced back at the trees. "Where's Sly?"

"He didn't come. The phone call was just a ruse to get you to talk to me."

Looking down at the strings of her guitar, Haven started strumming again.

Cautiously, Laura sat down on the ground, facing her. "Haven, I'm really so sorry about everything that happened with Zane. Believe me, if I had it to do over again, I'd have gone back to Princeton with you and never given him a second thought. But I can't undo what I did."

Haven leaned her head back and gazed over the ridge to the trees below. "Nobody's keepin' score."

It was a tiny concession, and Laura felt a little of her burden lifted. But it wasn't enough. "I'm especially sorry for what it did to us. I never meant to ruin our friendship."

"Ruin's a strong word," Haven said.

There, Laura thought. It was forgiveness in Haven's own special way. Laura smiled.

"I've been thinking a lot about where to go from here, what to do with my life, and I've decided to stay in Nashville."

Haven kept strumming. "Yeah?"

"Yeah. And Sly and I are starting our own label—him producing, me promoting."

Haven's hand stopped strumming, and she stared at Laura for a moment. She nodded infinitesimally, a tiny acknowledgement that it made sense. "I can see it."

"Good." Laura smiled. "That's the main reason I wanted to talk to you tonight."

Haven's eyebrows came together, but she didn't say anything.

"We want you to be the first artist we sign, Haven. We want to give you a contract and try to promote you into the star that we think you have the potential to be."

Haven's expression didn't change. "Sly . . . he's heard me sing, right?"

Laura smiled. "Yes, Haven. We've talked about getting you a vocal coach to work with you to enhance your strengths, but we both believe you have the makings of a star. The crowd at the picnic loved you. We can do this, Haven."

Haven swallowed and looked away, and slowly she began to strum again. "And you'd let me do my original songs, and record them myself?"

"We would," Laura said. "And you'd be able to have more input into how they're mixed and how we promote you than you could at a major label. We'd protect your integrity, Haven. I can promise you that."

For a moment, Haven kept playing, her eyes fixed on the top of a tree below the ridge. Finally, she glanced at Laura. "So, where do we start?"

It was as close as Haven would ever come to agreeing to anything, so Laura accepted it as that. "Well, we need to talk contract. We can't offer you an advance since we don't have any cash flow yet, but you'll get points. The reward will come after the work's done."

Haven shrugged. "You bailed my family out. We'll consider that the advance."

"Then come by Sly's tomorrow afternoon, and we'll discuss the contract."

Haven nodded. "I'll be there."

"Good." Laura sat still for a moment longer, listening to Haven play. After a moment, she got to her feet and dusted the dirt off her jeans. "I'm gonna make you a bigger star than your father, Haven."

The strumming stopped again, and Haven looked up at her. "Is that what this is? Revenge?"

Laura tried to glance away before Haven saw the tears pushing into her eyes, but Haven held her in her firm gaze for a moment. "No," she said softly. "The hurt's still too fresh for me to get even. Besides, that's not my style." Laura knew that if there had been any deception in her, Haven would have seen it.

"I'll bring some of my newer songs," she said finally.

"Yeah, do that," Laura said. "Sly can start working with you on the arrangements."

The strumming resumed and Laura started to walk away. Just before she rounded the tent again, she looked back at Haven, and saw that she was smiling.

"So what did she say?" Sly asked when Laura got back into the car.

"She's in."

Sly laughed. "Really?"

"Really. We're all meeting tomorrow to nail down the details."

"Fantastic!" Sly held up a hand and Laura gave him a high five. Turning the car around, he said, "I just hope she isn't maimed up there tonight."

"She'll be fine," Laura reassured him. "I think God's assigned special angels to watch over Haven."

CHAPTER EIGHTEEN

THE DOOR WAS UNLOCKED. Though she'd only had the apartment for a week, Laura knew that she hadn't made the mistake of leaving it that way when she'd gone to meet Sly at the bank to talk about a loan for their studio. An instinctual fear rose inside her, but as she turned the knob, she realized that it wasn't a fear of danger but one of confrontation. Slowly, she opened the door.

Her mother sat in the center of her couch, her legs crossed pristinely at the knee, the lavender pump on one foot swinging impatiently as she looked up at her.

"Mother." Laura stopped cold at the door. "How did you get in here?"

Catrina stopped swinging her foot and rose to greet her daughter with a half embrace and a pseudo kiss. "Aren't you glad to see me, darling?"

"Yes, of course, but..." She glanced back at the door, growing more annoyed by the moment. "I know I locked the door this morning."

"You did, darling. But I persuaded the superintendent to let me in to wait for you."

"Oh." Of course, Laura thought. She had probably waved a hundred dollar bill under his nose, and he was putty in her hands. Dropping her briefcase and keys on the table, she tried to look pleasant. "So, what brings you here?"

"You, of course," her mother said, fixing her perfect gaze on her. Laura regarded her mother, and the beauty she had spent a lifetime cultivating, and recalled how many times in her life she had envied that beauty. But it was an expensive beauty, she knew now, and for the price Catrina had had to pay, Laura had decided she would rather do without it.

Catrina watched with cool eyes as Laura went into the open kitchen and found two glasses. "Would you like a drink, Mother?" she asked over the counter that divided the two rooms. "I don't have anything alcoholic."

"Nothing then," her mother said. "Let's go out."

Laura set the glasses down and turned around, crossing her arms. "No, Mother. I'm not interested in having you get me in a crowded restaurant where neither of us will make a scene. Say what you came to say."

Catrina looked as if she'd been slapped, and wearily, she dropped back onto the sofa. "I came to tell you that I miss you, Laura. That I was truly expecting you to come home after all that happened."

"I never told you I was coming home."

"But why on earth would you want to stay here?"

"I have plans, Mother. A goal. I've found something I'm good at, and I have to see how far it can take me."

"And would you care to share it with me? Unless, of course, it's a secret."

Laura came back out of the kitchen and sat down across from Catrina. It occurred to her as she faced her mother that they'd had very few talks like this in her life. Most of their serious conversations had taken place in public settings. When she'd tried to corner her mother at home, Catrina had been in control and had refused to sit still long enough for any type of confrontation. It was a major step, she thought, that her mother was sitting still now.

"I'm going into business with a record producer I know. We're starting our own label, and we'll be recording new artists. My job will be promoting them."

"Promoting them? What could you possibly know about that?"

"Come on, Mother. I was bred to be a businesswoman, and I've spent the last ten summers of my life working in PR for Rockford Enterprises, not to mention the training I got at Princeton. Besides that, I've learned a lot in the past few months. My marriage to Zane was an education, if nothing else.''

Catrina looked astounded. Speechless, perhaps for the first time in her life, she gaped at her daughter. ''You don't have any money,'' she pointed out. ''How can you start a business without money?''

''We're getting investors,'' Laura said. ''Sly and I have already been able to borrow some money, and before long, I'm sure we'll have a few investors to complete the picture.''

Her mother's face hardened. ''You realize, don't you, that I'm not waivering on my agreement with you. You pay me back in three years or you have no choice but to leave Nashville.''

Laura didn't flinch. ''I know that, Mother. I never for a moment thought that you would let me off the hook. I intend to pay my debt to you.''

Catrina glanced away, apparently at a loss for another threat. When she focused on Laura again, there were tears illuminating her eyes. ''Why are you doing this to me, Laura?''

Laura almost laughed. ''Why am I doing it to *you*? You've got to be kidding.''

''I don't understand it,'' Catrina said, her voice raspy, though she kept her expression in tight control. ''I've always been very generous with you. You've had the best possible childhood, wanting for nothing.... Why do you keep defying me so?''

''It's semantics, Mother. You see my growing up as defiance. None of this is about you.''

''Yes, it is,'' Catrina said. ''You wouldn't have jumped into that marriage with that hick if you hadn't been trying to shock me. And now this. My daughter working in the country music business. It's disgraceful. Your father would roll over in his grave.''

"I doubt it," Laura said. "And it's not defiance, Mother, to want to follow my own dreams instead of yours. I have my own life and my own ideas."

"I only want what's best for you. Wasn't I absolutely right about Zane?"

Laura couldn't admit that yet. "Mother, I may not always make the right decisions, but you don't have any better idea what's best for me than I do."

"Yes, I do," she said. "It's best for you to come home and work with me. I'll train you to take over the company someday. You'll be the richest woman in the country, if you just do what I say."

"I just want to be happy, Mother. And all the money in the world hasn't given that to you."

Catrina's perfect countenance registered insult. "I've been very happy, Laura. I have everything I could want, except you at home."

"You never wanted me home when I was growing up."

The faint beginnings of a flush mottled Catrina's skin. "I didn't send you away to get rid of you, Laura. I sent you because I wanted you to have the best education possible. And now you've thrown it away with just one semester left, made unspeakable choices that have cost me millions, and you still aren't any closer to getting your life on track than you were before!" She got up and paced across the room, trying to calm herself. "You want happiness, Laura? Well, let me tell you something. It's difficult to achieve, and not just anyone can have it. It comes with power. Power over other people, power over your destiny, power over your future."

"I think you're wrong, Mother. I don't think power has one thing in the world to do with happiness. And I'm willing to stake my life on it."

"Then you'll wind up with neither."

"We'll see," Laura said. "I want to find out."

Catrina snatched her purse up then, and looking forlornly at her daughter, headed for the door. "When you've hit bottom, when you have no place else to turn, when you realize that I was right all along and that you've done nothing but waste time trying to prove me wrong, you call me. And then we can talk about how happy you are.''

She slammed out of the apartment then, leaving Laura to stare at the door as numbness washed through her.

"I'VE FOUND YOU an investor who's willing to put up a third of the money you need to build the studio and get started in business.''

Chase Jackson, Sly's lawyer, told Laura and Sly the news a few days later as they sat in his office.

"Who is he?'' Sly asked.

Chase shook his head. "I can't tell you, because I don't know myself. I was contacted by the investor's attorney. The terms would be that this partner would share in the profits of the company, but would have no say in how you choose to run it. It looks to me like the best of both worlds, actually. He gives you the money you need, and you never have to take one word of advice or instruction about running your company.''

"But what's in it for him?'' Laura asked.

"I guess he thinks you stand to make a lot of money. He wants a cut.''

"Why the secrecy?''

Chase shrugged. "Who knows? Maybe he's someone you know who just wants to give you a hand without changing your relationship. Or maybe he's just modest and likes to keep a low profile. Whatever the motive, I haven't found any reason to suspect that it isn't above board. His attorney is highly reputable. I've known him for years, and I trust him.''

Sly shot Laura a disbelieving look, but Laura seemed troubled. "What do you think?''

"I don't know,'' she said. "This would keep us from having to have several investors, people we might have to answer to. But I don't like going into something with a blindfold on."

"Well, whoever it is, he's obviously wealthy. He believes in our venture, and he wants to be a part of it without calling attention to himself. I don't really have a problem with that."

"But problems could come up," Laura said. "What if this investor decided that we weren't earning him enough money and wanted to sell his shares? What if he sold them to someone we couldn't work with?"

"I would recommend a clause that the partners have first option to buy another partner's shares in the event that one of you wanted to sell," Chase said. "I'd also stipulate that each partner has the right to reject a new partner by buying the share that's for sale."

"So, if this investor wanted to sell his share," Laura repeated, "Sly and I would have the right to buy it. But if we didn't, and he found a buyer, we could decide whether or not we approve the new buyer."

"And if you didn't," Chase said, "you'd have one further chance to buy the share yourselves."

"That sounds fair," Sly said. "Don't you think?"

Laura hesitated. "I guess so."

"There are other safeguards I can put into the partnership agreement," Chase said. "But it looks like a relatively clear-cut deal to me. I don't think you'll have a problem."

Sly sat back, grinning like a man who'd just won the lottery. "Well then, I guess we've got a deal."

Laura nodded slowly. "I guess so."

CHAPTER NINETEEN

LAURA STOOD OUTSIDE the almost-finished facilities of Renegade Records, and clutching her coat around her to battle the January cold, she peered up at the sign that had been hung yesterday. Renegade Records, Your Refuge From the Norm. She laughed quietly. She'd almost been kidding when she'd come up with the slogan, but Sly had latched onto it immediately.

His urgency in getting her here today made her a little anxious, for he'd indicated on the phone this afternoon that there had been a glitch in the electronics and some of the work might have to be torn out and started over. That would delay their opening, and Haven was already chomping at the bit to get into the studio.

Pushing through the glass doors into the empty front office, she peered up the hall. "Sly!" she called. "Where are you?"

"In here, Laura," he called back.

She shrugged out of her coat, tossed it over a folding chair and started up the hall. The light was on in Studio B, where he'd said the trouble originated, so she headed there.

She wondered why she didn't hear the noise of the myriad workers who'd been wiring and welding and splicing all week. It was too quiet. Something was terribly wrong.

But the moment she stepped into Studio B, a horrendously loud noise assaulted her, making her jump, and a horde of people leapt out at her screaming "Surprise!"

Dumbfounded, she looked from one face to another, recognizing Haven and Sly, some of the staff they'd already hired, friends she'd made over the last few months, artists who'd been vying for contracts with them, songwriters who never missed the opportunity to rub elbows with someone who might buy their songs. A banner was hung at the back of the studio, and she read, Happy Birthday, Laura!

Sly stepped out of the boisterous crowd and slipped his arm around her shoulder as she covered her face and began to laugh. "How did you know it was my birthday?"

"I got it off the loan applications," he said.

She punched him playfully and scanned the room. "And you had me scared to death that there was a problem with the equipment."

"Problem?" he teased, looking around at the electronic engineers who'd been designing the studio. "Do you guys know of any problems?"

"No problem here, Sly," someone said. "In fact, we're just about finished up with A and B."

Laura gave them a disbelieving look. "Really? We're almost ready to start working?"

"By next Monday," Sly said, glancing at Haven. "What do you say, Haven? Are you ready?"

"Just try to hold me back," Haven said, hugging Laura. "Happy birthday, Laura. Wait till you hear the sound. It's unbelievable. Are you hungry? There's cake and nuts and all kinds of junk."

Dazed, Laura let them lead her to the birthday cake, which had a caricature of her on it, and when she had blown out the twenty-two candles, she turned back to Sly. "How about some music? I'm dying to hear how it sounds in here."

"You got it, birthday girl." He went into the control room, pushed a few buttons and started a Jerry Joe Wagner CD. Coming back out, he took her hand and pulled her against him. "I paid everybody off to make sure I got the first dance. So, what do you think? Is this a phenomenal sound or what?"

Her eyes closed as she laid her head against his chest. "It's beautiful, Sly. You did a fantastic job."

"And so did you."

Others coupled off and began to dance around them, but for all Laura cared, they could have been the only two people here. "I never celebrate my birthday," she said softly. "Not in years. I had practically forgotten."

"Why wouldn't you celebrate the day when every angel in heaven rejoiced because such a beautiful little life came into the world?"

If anyone else had said it, she would have laughed, but there was something very moving about the emotion in Sly's words. "I guess others didn't rejoice much," she said. "After I went away to school, I celebrated most of my birthdays there. They were pretty uneventful. I learned not to put much stock in them."

"Well, it's time that changed. I think a lot of things are about to change."

The song switched to a soft, romantic ballad, and the crowd grew quiet as the perfect, crisp sounds filled the room.

Sly dipped his head and buried his face in her hair. "Remember the first time we danced?"

"At the Guitar Pit," she said, looking up at him, startled at how close their lips were. "I remember."

"Was it my imagination, or did we have sparks?"

She smiled. "It wasn't your imagination."

The humor faded from his eyes, and a sweet, gentle longing replaced it. "I wonder what happened."

She sighed. "I was at a fork in my road," she said. "And I went the wrong way."

"Thank God for second chances."

His voice was seductive against her ear, arousing shivers down her back. She rested her head against his chest and breathed him in. He smelled like clean clothes, with a hint of wind and sun mixed in. His was a scent that couldn't be bottled, but if it could, she knew women everywhere would be spraying it on their pillowcases and sleeping with it at night.

But it was his eyes that made her heart skip a beat as she looked up at him again. They were so blue...such clear, honest eyes, the kind of eyes that every woman dreamed of waking up to in her old age.

And that was precisely why she was so relieved when the song came to an end and she was able to step out of his embrace and put some distance between them. This was all too confusing, and she desperately feared jeopardizing the relationship this business was built on and the friendship that had come to be so vital to her.

Sly recognized her withdrawal and tried to lighten the moment. "Are you ready to open your presents?"

"Presents?" she asked. "You're kidding."

"Nope," he said, escorting her to the table. "Over here. And be careful. Some of them are gag gifts, and I heard one ticking."

HAVEN PUT AS MUCH ENERGY into her recording sessions as she did into her vow of poverty. Her specific ideas for her own sound actually gave Sly the opportunity to be more creative. And as the album came together, Laura became more optimistic that Haven could be the star that she had envisioned.

When she was able to convince the band Kentucky Blues to hire Haven to go on tour with them as their warm-up act, she felt they were on their way. Haven, however, wasn't sure.

"Kentucky Blues?" she asked. "You mean, they've heard me and they still want me to front for 'em?"

Haven's humility never ceased to amaze Laura. "Haven, they heard some of the finished tracks on your album, and they think it'll fly out of the stores. They wanted someone different."

For the first time, she saw a blush creeping up Haven's cheeks. "But they're so big...."

"It's the opportunity of a lifetime. Anybody would kill for it."

The smile dawning across Haven's lips made all the wheeling and dealing worthwhile. "So what did *you* do to get this?"

Laura threw up her hands. "What can I say? I'm good at what I do. And I only promote the best."

Haven stared at her for a moment, and finally, her hands came up to cover her face as she considered the possibilities. "The money. It'll be a lot, won't it?"

Laura handed her the contract and pointed to the figure she'd negotiated.

Haven let out a long breath. "That'll change so many things."

"You can't reject an offer for being too high, Haven! That's un-American!"

Haven leaned back against the wall, her eyes glazing over at the thought. "People will start to recognize me."

"Is that a bad thing?"

She shrugged. "Well, there goes my hitchhiking across the country." She eyed Laura suspiciously. "Hey, you're not gonna start making me wear those frilly little costumes, are you?"

"Nope. You are what you are. That's how I'm selling you."

Haven's smile came back. "Kentucky Blues, huh?"

"The one and only."

"Have you told Daddy?"

Laura's smile faded. "I don't talk to Zane anymore, Haven. You know that."

"He's not gonna believe it."

"He will when he sees you performing before a club full of fans. They're planning a preview concert at a club here in town—to work out the kinks—so he can see you there."

Again, that pink blush colored Haven's cheeks. "Finally, he'll have to admit that I've got somethin'."

"You've got something, all right," Laura told her. "Something that I'm willing to stake everything on."

SLY LIKED TO MIX in the dark, completely alone, with nothing but the music and the glow from the meters and the board. There were times when he had to work with others in the room, and Sly had to sacrifice the solitude and almost hypnotic concentration that was what made the process so special to him. But on the occasions when a cut was recorded clean—as Haven's had been—he could bury himself in the art of mixing and get lost in the sounds and colors of perfection. There was nothing like going on pure instinct and watching those greens and reds shimmy across the meters. The joy in that creative play was what enabled him to stay here all night after recording all day. And until he'd met Laura, there had been no one in the world he would allow to intrude on that time.

Now, however, he found himself wondering when she would look in on him, wishing she was here to offer an opinion about whether to use reverb on one of Haven's best numbers and whether to cut the drum track out entirely.

When the door finally opened, spilling light into the dark room, Laura hesitated at the threshold. "Sitting in the dark again?"

"I can hear better in the dark," Sly teased. "You're not going home now, are you?"

"I thought I would," Laura said. "Some of us need more than two hours' sleep a night."

"Come here a minute," he said. "Listen to this."

She closed the door, locking out the light, and went toward Sly, whose face was barely outlined by the reflection of the reds and greens. The room was full of Haven's voice, and smiling, Laura sat down next to him. "Haven has a wonderful rainy day style, doesn't she?"

"Funny that you'd describe it that way. I used to think of rain when I heard Joni Mitchell."

"Rain is a compliment," Laura said. "It's peaceful, introspective, almost lonely. You've done a great job with her, Sly."

"It's been the easiest album I've ever recorded. Her arrangements have been so near perfection that all I've had to work on is her voice."

"So your opinion about Haven has changed?"

"No," he said with a chuckle. "I still think she's crazy."

She punched him. "I mean her talent."

He listened for a moment to the words Haven sang, words that painted such vivid pictures he sometimes dreamed of them. "If I ever had any doubts about Haven's talent, I don't now. Her voice gets under your skin after a while. If we play our cards right, we may be able to make a zillion bucks with her."

"I've been thinking about strategies for doing that," Laura said, "and I want to take a trip to Philadelphia."

"Philadelphia?"

"Yeah. I need to visit Michael."

"Michael? The guy who was your stepfather?"

The fact that he'd gleaned that information from her months ago and remembered it—when Zane had never cared—pleased her immensely. "Yeah, that Michael. He owns a string of radio stations and some magazines, you know. I want to coerce him into helping me with Haven's publicity. See if he'll finagle a little more airtime than their play lists call for, set up some interviews, get his DJs to spread some excitement...."

"Do you think he'll do it?"

"He might," she said. "And if he doesn't, it'll be nice to see him anyway."

"And your mother?"

Laura hoped her face was less visible in the darkness than Sly's was to her. "I'll probably stop by to say hi to her, too." When an uncomfortable silence passed, she added, "You know, I'm not staying away from her out of choice. I wish

I had the relationship with her that you and your family have. But it just isn't that way."

"It has to start somewhere, babe."

She sighed. "You don't know her, Sly. You couldn't understand."

"I can't imagine being all alone in the world without some form of family."

"You can be alone whether you have family or not, and I've really never known it to be any other way."

There was something abysmally sad about her words, and Sly reached through the darkness and took her hand.

"I don't like knowing you feel that way," he whispered.

Her face was painted in a pale red glow, and she smiled at him.

"Truth is, I've felt less alone in the last few months. I've never been happier, Sly. I feel like I'm in the middle of the good ole days, and I don't want them to end."

"I'm not going anywhere," he said.

For a moment they sat in the darkness, gazing at each other with eloquent looks that revealed so many things that neither of them could say.

He leaned over and took her hand in his, feathering his fingertips across her palm, stroking the length of her fingers, massaging her wrists. "You know, this friendship stuff is fine and all, but does it ever cross your mind that you and I might be really good together as more than friends?"

She swallowed and watched his fingers playing across her hand. "You know it does."

He nodded quietly, then looked up at her and slowly stroked one fingertip up her neck, across her throat, to the tip of her chin. "Sometimes I think if I could just kiss you one time...."

Her eyes sparkled in the light from the meters, and she found it significant that her heart didn't race with alarm but with anticipation. "What?" she asked on a whisper.

"I don't know," he said, moving infinitesimally closer with each word. "Maybe I could concentrate better, sleep longer, dream less...."

His lips touched hers before he'd finished the last word, and she closed her eyes and surrendered to the euphoria, the sweet relief, the bittersweet ecstasy warmly washing through her. She opened her mouth to deepen the kiss and felt her heart racing, her hormones raging, her soul yearning...

He weaved his big hands through her hair, moving her head along with his, and she gripped his collar with one hand and slid the other behind his neck.

The kiss grew hotter, wetter, more urgent, and she felt the floodgates of her feelings for him being gently pried open. If they were allowed to open, if those feelings were exposed to the light before she'd had time to deal with them, she might lose control and ruin the delicate bond that she and Sly had forged between them.

Haven's song ended, and Sly broke the kiss, his breath coming unsteadily as he rubbed his forehead across hers. "I was wrong," he whispered.

"About what?"

"About my kissing you solving my concentration...I have a terrible feeling that it's all about to get worse. I could see myself becoming addicted."

She tried to steady her breathing, and closing her eyes, she touched his face, feeling the stubble that felt so good against her face.

He drew back, and when she opened her eyes, he was studying her closely. "I wish you could see the terror on your face."

She shook her head, denying it. "There's no terror, Sly."

"Yes, there is," he said, stroking her cheek with the back of his knuckles. "You're not ready for this, are you?"

Tears sprang to her eyes. "I've lost everyone I've ever loved," she whispered. "I don't want to lose you."

He swallowed and wiped the first tear as it fell. "I think your head knows that won't happen, Laura," he said. "But until your heart knows it, I'll wait. When you're ready, you'll let me know."

She couldn't say for sure whether it was disappointment or relief that passed over her heart, but she knew that kiss wouldn't be easy to forget. Was he putting the ball in her court now? Was she going to have to make the next move? For the life of her, she didn't know if she'd ever be able to. And she realized that it might not be possible for him to wait. Others would come along...

"So... when are you going to Philadelphia?" he asked softly.

For a second she didn't answer, and he knew she struggled to hold back those tears. Part of him hated himself for being so vulnerable to her, but another part chastised himself for heaping more pressure on her. Maybe they were only supposed to be friends. There were worse things.

"I thought I'd leave tomorrow," she said. Slowly, she got up and went back to the door. When she opened it, he was struck by how lonely she looked, silhouetted against the light in the hall. "Laura? Make sure you see your mother while you're there, okay?"

"I'll try," she promised weakly, then closed him back in the darkness.

THE STREETS of Philadelphia had changed little since she'd last seen them, but that very constancy of her home city made her realize how much *she* had changed.

Michael had aged only slightly. His temples had grayed and there were a few more lines on his face than when she'd last seen him, but that only seemed to add character to the man she had so often wished was her father.

Laughing at the sight of her, he welcomed her with a hug. "Look at you. You're all grown up."

"Yeah, well, marriage and divorce have a way of doing that to you."

"Tell me about it." He seated her in a chair and leaned back against his desk, grinning as if she'd gone from eight to twenty-two in a matter of seconds.

"How's your marriage?" she asked him.

"Fantastic," he said, and she knew he meant it. "I've finally found my soul mate."

Laura smiled. "I'm so glad. I hope I get to meet her someday."

"Well, how about tonight?"

She hesitated. "I don't know. I really came here on business, but I thought I'd at least try to make contact with Mother tonight. Maybe even stay at the house, if she could tolerate such a thing. And then I'm leaving tomorrow."

"Rain check?"

"Sure," she said. "I'd love to meet her the next time I'm here."

"So, what's the business part of your trip?"

She smiled slyly, then cocked her head, the way she always had when he was her stepfather and she wanted to hit him up for ice cream. "Actually, my business is with you."

"Me?" he asked with a laugh.

"Yes," she said. "I need your help. I'm promoting Zane's daughter, Haven, and her new album is going to be released soon. Right after it's released, she'll be touring with Kentucky Blues. But I want to introduce her with a splash. We need some radio attention."

He went to the chair beside her, turned it to face her and sat down. "Well, I'm sure if she's any good, all my country stations will be giving her air play. If she gets on the *Billboard* list, it's guaranteed."

"I want more. I want you to play her even more often than that." The audacity of her request brought a smile to his lips, and Laura mirrored it. "I was hoping I could persuade you to start getting your DJs to talk about her, build excitement. I could release tidbits of information about her a little at a time so they'd have material coming in a steady stream. And I thought maybe you could incorporate clips about her on the news and have some of your magazines feature her. She's a real interesting person. There's a lot to tell."

"Like what?" he asked with a smile.

"Like the fact that she only wears jeans and green or brown T-shirts, and she prefers to sleep outside in a sleeping bag rather than in her bed, and she's an avid environmentalist, and she cuts her own hair, and she's a genius when it comes to writing, and all of Nashville is vying to record her songs, but she's determined to record them all herself...."

He laughed, cutting her off. "All right. I get the picture. But you think Haven Berringer is more important than wars brewing across the world?"

"Not *more* important," she teased. "Just *as* important."

He leaned his head back and grinned. "Don't you think this is a little underhanded?"

"What?" she asked innocently. "Asking a close friend for a favor? Absolutely not. It's no different than our hiring a big PR firm to do exactly the same thing."

He stared at her for a moment, genuine affection in his eyes. "I don't usually do favors like this, Laura. You know that. It compromises my integrity."

"I'm asking you to tell the truth about an up-and-coming new star," she said. "If you think about it, *I'm* doing *you* the favor."

He chuckled and rubbed his forehead. "I've heard her, Laura. The coverage you got for Zane's picnic a few months back. She's not that good."

"Good is relative," she said. "She's unique. Different. She writes the kind of songs that could probably make even my mother cry—if she'd ever actually listen to them—and she has the kind of voice that you never forget. Since she's been working with a vocal coach, she's learned how to enhance her style and her delivery. She's star quality now."

"I always knew you had the kind of determination to pull something like this off. If anyone could work that kind of miracle, I guess you would be the one."

"So... are you going to help me or not?"

"I'll think about it," he said.

"Good." She got out a pen and jotted a note, then handed him an envelope full of tickets. "Haven will be performing at Rudy's on West Ridge Street in Nashville every weekend until the album comes out. And before she goes on the Kentucky Blues tour, they'll be previewing in Nashville. There are enough tickets there for as many of your DJs and reporters who want to go. You could play on her being Zane's daughter. Rising offspring of the falling star."

Michael was becoming more and more amused. "I'll keep that in mind. But the truth is, our listeners would probably be more interested in what *you're* doing than what she is."

"Then use that," she said. "Haven is my business now. Take any angle you can find, as long as it's positive and makes Haven the star I've decided she's going to be."

"I think she will be, too, sweetheart. How can she go wrong with you in her corner?" Sighing, he shook his head. "I can't believe you've grown into such a woman. You've got the best parts of your mother, but in a package that is a lot more pleasant to be around." He leaned forward, his expression serious. "I'm sorry your marriage didn't work out, sweetheart."

"Yeah, well." It was still painful, humiliating, talking about it, so she tried to change gears. "Listen, about that loan you gave me. As soon as the album is released, I'll pay you back. I promise. So you see, it's in your best interest to make it a success."

He shook his head. "I'm not worried about the money, Laura. I would just like to see you happy. Look at me."

Laura met his eyes directly. "What?"

"Tell me what's really going on with you, Laura. There's got to be more than work. Are you seeing anyone?"

She forced herself not to look away. "Not really."

"What about Sly Hancock? I read an article about him in *Rolling Stone* last month. It hinted that there might be a little something between the two of you."

She smiled. "People are always trying to find drama where there isn't any."

"Are you sure?"

She thought for a moment and realized she had no reason to hide from him. "There's something really special about him, Michael," she admitted. "If I have the gall to fall in love again, it'll probably be with him."

He chuckled. "What do you mean, gall?"

She fought the mist forming in her eyes. "It takes a lot of gall to keep trying something that obviously isn't in your cards."

"One mistake doesn't mean it's all over, Laura."

She glanced away, struggling to put her feelings into words. "I guess I just need to do a little growing up first," she said softly. "A big part of me is still that little girl praying for a father. If I ever do fall in love again, I want it to be with a person, not a concept."

Michael smiled softly at her, like a father overwhelmed by the wisdom in his child. "I'm really proud of you, Laura. And I think when the right time comes, whether it's Sly or someone else, you'll be so overwhelmed with love that you won't even remember all the sadness."

"I hope you're right, Michael," she said. "I really hope you're right."

LAURA DIDN'T CALL her mother before arriving at her door. Some small, still-childlike part of her hoped to see surprise—and maybe a little joy—betray itself on her mother's face. Instead, Catrina looked annoyed. She had never liked surprises.

"You might have called to let me know you were coming," her mother told her tightly.

"I'm glad to see you, too, Mother," she clipped. "And you didn't exactly send an announcement the last time you showed up in my living room." Glancing into the sitting room, she saw a man she didn't recognize. Was her mother entertaining while her husband was out of the country? "You have company," she said. "I'm sorry. I'll just go and—"

"Might I assume from this that your business isn't working out as well as you hoped?"

Again, Laura glanced at the man. It wasn't like her mother to start a scene in front of a guest . . . not unless she knew him very, very well. "No, Mother. Things are going well. I was just in town on business and wanted to say hello."

"I see." Her mother's disappointment that she hadn't run home with her tail between her legs was apparent. She turned back to the man. "Donald, this is my daughter, Laura. Laura, Donald Morrison. He's our congressman."

"Yes, of course." Laura shook his hand and quelled the urge to ask how his wife was.

"Laura is in the middle of a little adventure," Catrina went on. "She's decided that music is her life, although she couldn't have been less interested in it when she was growing up."

Laura's face burned. "I'm not performing, Mr. Morrison. I'm a promoter. And my mother doesn't know *what* I was interested in while I was growing up."

Catrina flinched slightly at the rejoinder, but it did nothing to satisfy Laura. Instead, she felt ashamed.

"Look, I can see that you have plans, and I'm really tired, so I won't keep you."

She started back to the door, but her mother stopped her. "I called you on your birthday, Laura. You weren't home."

"I have a machine," she said.

"I chose not to leave a message. But I do have a gift for you. If you'd like to stay the night . . ."

She thought of telling her mother that she had other plans, but some part of her, some part she would never in her life be able to explain, needed to know that she was still welcome here. "Thank you, Mother," she said. "If it's not too much trouble, I would like to stay. But I don't want to intrude."

"You're welcome to have dinner with us," Catrina offered stiffly.

"No, thank you. If you'll just tell me which room, I think I'll turn in early."

"Which room?" Her mother gave her a bitter smile. "Your room is just as you left it. And your gift is on the dresser."

"It was nice to meet you," she said to Donald as she started up the stairs.

"Likewise. If you're ever in Washington, don't hesitate to come by the office."

Nodding, Laura hurried up the stairs.

Her mother was right; her room was exactly as she had left it. It was still cold and sterile, still too elegant for comfort, and as she walked in, she realized this had never really been a home. She supposed the dorms had been the closest to a home she'd ever had until the condo she lived in now.

That was what being an adult was about, she decided. Righting childhood wrongs. She wondered if Sly could help her with that.

Quietly, she went to the dresser and saw the small wrapped box lying there. The fact that her mother had remembered her birthday surprised her, and she tore into the silver wrapping paper and opened the box.

An exquisite bracelet lay there, with diamonds and rubies interlaced with gold. She placed it across her wrist, saw how elegant it looked next to her skin and realized it had cost a fortune.

Dropping it back into its box, she went to the bed and stretched out. She lay staring up at the eight-inch molding on the ceiling, with the Elizabethan faces carved like demons in the wood. Those faces used to frighten her when she was very small, but over the years she had learned to live with them.

She closed her eyes and compared the feeling of being here, near her mother, with being near Sly. They were two vastly different feelings, worlds apart. One was ice. The other was fire.

She fell asleep dreaming of Sly holding her, kissing her again, and of their restrained passion breaking loose and sweeping them both away. She dreamed of comfort and joy in the aftermath. And she dreamed that there was still joy in his eyes the morning after.

She didn't wake until the next morning, when she realized that the butler had brought her suitcase up and set it inside her door. She hadn't even undressed or slipped under the covers.

Quickly, she showered and changed, then went down to thank her mother for the gift.

One of the maids met her in the breakfast room. "Your mother had an early meeting," she said. "But Cook will prepare whatever you like for breakfast."

Laura's heart sank. The fragile hope of a real conversation with her mother died, and she started back to the staircase. "No thank you. I'm not hungry."

Gathering her things quickly, she called a cab. And she left the bracelet right where she'd found it.

CHAPTER TWENTY

THE NIGHT OF HAVEN'S opening concert for her tour with Kentucky Blues, Zane threw around the idea of going to hear her. Sitting on the back porch with the radio tuned to his favorite country station, he tossed back his glass of bourbon and reached for the bottle.

He saw Rosy coming from her house across the yard, all dressed up and ready to go, and he wondered what young stud would be escorting her tonight.

"I'm sending Haven flowers tonight," Rosy said. "Do you want me to put your name on 'em, too?"

He shrugged. "I don't need you sending my daughter things in my name. If I want to send her flowers, I'll do it."

"Well, you are at least goin' to hear her, aren't you?"

"I might," he said.

She eyed his denim shirt. "So, are you wearin' that?"

"Whatever I decide to wear, Rosy, you can bet I won't be telling you about it. I'm not in the mood to play twins with you tonight."

"Why are you in such a lousy mood?" she asked. "This is Haven's big break. You ought to be proud of her."

"Haven's gonna fall flat on her face. She doesn't have the talent God gave a gnat, and I don't know if I can stand to watch her do it."

Rosy crossed her arms and shook her head dolefully. "And they wonder why I ever divorced you."

"You didn't," he said. "I divorced you."

"Right," she taunted. "You keep tellin' yourself that."

She started to walk away, when the opening chords of an old Zane Berringer tune played on the radio, and Zane caught his breath and leaned over to turn it up. "Will you listen to that?"

He hadn't heard the song in so long, he'd almost forgotten about it. It was the first song he'd recorded, back when he'd owned two pairs of boxer shorts and one pair of socks, a hand-me-down pair of jeans, one button-down shirt with a hole in the elbow, and a battered truck that was in worse shape than Haven's bug. Some diaper company had offered a five hundred dollar flat fee for the rights to "Long Ago Lullaby," and not knowing that the song would likely make millions, he'd signed his rights away, taken the money and run. It had become the Dry-Baby theme song for the next several years.

But something was different about the intro. Rosy turned back around, listening. "You didn't have a piano in that, did you?"

He frowned. It was true. He hadn't. And yet there it was, different, yet the same . . .

And then he knew why.

Another man began singing the words, a younger man, his voice clear and sweet, but with an upbeat that gave the song a whole new flavor.

"Who *is* that?" Rosy asked.

Zane strained to listen. "Could be any of two or three different people."

"Well, at least you'll start gettin' royalties on it again, won't you?"

"No!" Zane blurted. "I don't own it. I sold the rights, remember?"

Rosy frowned and drew closer to the radio. "Uh-oh," she said, wincing up at Zane. "I think I know who that is."

But just as she uttered the words, the voice came to Zane. With murderous rage, he shot to his feet.

"Jerry Joe Wagner stole my song!"

IN THE DRESSING ROOM backstage, Haven looked up to see one of the roadies bringing her a vase of flowers. "Probably from Daddy," she told Laura. But when she took the flowers and checked the card, her face fell. "Oh. They're from Mama."

"She's here, Haven. She told me to tell you, but she wanted to go ahead and get a good seat."

"And Daddy?" she asked.

Laura wished it didn't matter to Haven. "He hasn't gotten here yet."

Haven glanced in the mirror at the small concession to makeup she'd allowed to keep her from looking pasty. "Do you think he's comin'?"

"Sure he is," Laura said. "I'm sure he wouldn't miss your debut."

But he had still not shown up when it came time for Haven to perform, and when Laura nudged her out onto the stage, she realized that Haven's energy level was significantly lower than it might have been if he'd stopped in just to wish her luck.

But the crowd didn't seem to notice.

After the first song, she was a hit, and she warmed up to the audience in a way that she was never able to warm up to anyone in her personal life. Her rapport with them amazed Laura, and reinforced the wisdom behind all the decisions she had made on Haven's behalf.

Sly came up behind Laura backstage and playfully slid his arms around her waist. In her ear, he whispered, "What do you think?"

"She's wonderful. They love her."

"*You're* wonderful," he said. "That's why they've had the chance to love her. Actually, we're both geniuses."

She laughed aloud, exuberant at the realization that dreams were beginning to come true.

DESPITE THE CALL for an encore, Haven stormed off the stage after her last song with no intention of coming back. "Did Daddy show up?"

Laura had to admit that he hadn't.

"Are you sure? I mean, he isn't out there somewhere... in the audience?"

"Not unless he came in disguise," Laura said gently. "I told everyone at the doors to let us know as soon as he got here. We had special seats for your family. But it doesn't matter, Haven. You were fabulous. Listen to that crowd! They're calling you back for more."

"I'm not doin' more," Haven said, yanking the guitar strap over her head and thrusting her beloved instrument at Laura. "Tell the guys they'll have to find a new front band. I don't wanna go on tour with 'em anymore."

Laura gaped at her. "But, Haven...don't you realize how much they liked you?"

"I wanted *him* to realize it, Laura!"

Laura scrambled to follow her through the crowd of people backstage, and when she caught her, she saw rare tears forming in Haven's eyes. "Haven, you'll feel better tomorrow. You can't quit. We have a contract."

"I'll pay the money back. I didn't need it anyway."

But I do, Laura wanted to say, but somehow she couldn't, for the pain on Haven's face was too real. "You would really give up this tour because your father didn't come to see you?"

"You couldn't understand," Haven said simply, and before Laura could stop her, she was gone.

THE BERRINGER house was dark when Laura showed up at the front door and banged on it. After a moment, the housekeeper, dressed in a robe, opened it. "Miss Laura!"

Laura stepped inside and looked around. "Has Haven come home?"

"No, ma'am," Eugenia said. "She had that concert tonight."

"I know that," Laura snapped. "Where's Zane?"

"Upstairs, I s'pose," the woman said. When Laura bolted up the stairs, she protested, "Miss Laura, I should tell him you're here!"

"I'll tell him myself," she shouted, then stormed down the hall to Zane's bedroom.

She threw the door open, but Zane wasn't there. On a mission, she dashed through the house, looking in every room until she came to his workout room.

There he was, sitting on his rowing machine, covered with sweat and swigging on a half-empty bottle of bourbon as if it were water.

It was the first time she'd seen him in months, and something about the sad picture he made sitting drunk in the midst of all those machines meant to improve him twisted her heart. "I was hoping you were bleeding...that there was a good reason why you missed your daughter's debut concert. Something that would help me to think better of you. Something that wouldn't remind me of the man you were at the end of our marriage."

He stared up at her, bleary-eyed, and mouthed a curse. "I had something else I had to do."

"Funny how three thousand others found the time to see her."

"They came to see Kentucky Blues, not Haven," he blurted. "You know it, and I know it."

"They begged her for an encore," she said, going in and standing over him, "but she wouldn't give them one, because she was so crushed that her father hadn't shown. In fact, she's breaking her contract and refusing to do the rest of the tour."

"Give me a break."

"No, Zane. I'm tired of giving you a break. Everybody's tired of giving you a break. It's time for you to stop thinking of yourself and think of somebody else for a change."

Furious, he got up, steadying himself on the handlebars of a nearby stationary bike. He wore nothing but a pair of jogging shorts, and the toll the alcohol had taken on his body was obvious. His skin was pale and his stomach sagged, and she wished he would put on his shirt. "You want to help Haven?" he demanded. "Then get out of her life."

"My getting out hasn't done you any good, Zane," she said, picking up the bottle. "What's happening to you?"

"You, that's what!" he shouted, jerking the bottle away from her and letting some of the bourbon slosh onto his carpet. "I was doing fine until I married you! Then everything came tumbling down!"

"Everything was tumbling down before you even knew me, Zane. All I did was try to help you."

"All you did was interfere in my career and clear a path for Jerry Joe Wagner to bulldoze right over me." He took a swig of the dark liquid, wiped his mouth with the back of his arm and staggered toward her. "In fact, everything that's gone wrong in my life dates right back to you. And the rest I blame on Jerry Joe Wagner."

Laura couldn't follow where Jerry Joe fit into the picture, but in his drunken state, Zane didn't need to make sense. "Fine," she said, her hands trembling as she clenched them at her sides. "We've been all through this, Zane, and there's really no need to hash it all out again. Blame me. Blame him. But don't blame Haven. She's the only one who's really stuck by you. She needs your approval, God only knows why. Please, Zane. If you have one shred of decency left in you, let her enjoy her moment. Give her what she needs! It won't cost you anything!"

Zane dropped down onto his weight bench and stared between his feet. "Just get out of my house," he rasped. "Nobody wants you here."

Giving up, Laura left him alone with his bottle. As she drove home, she fought the urge to respond to Zane's accusations in the way he'd intended. There was no truth to what he'd said. She hadn't been responsible for the ills of his life any more than Jerry Joe Wagner was responsible for the downturn in his career. He had tricked her into marrying him, had used her for her money, had emotionally blackmailed her into paying off the IRS. And the worst thing he had done, she thought, as her heart remembered its old bruises, was that he hadn't cared at all when she'd had to file for divorce.

By the time she got home, she was outraged all over again, and she was glad to see Sly sitting in a lawn chair beside her front door. "Where've you been?"

"I went to lambaste Zane," she said, jabbing the key into the door and letting him in. "But it didn't do any good." She held up the bag she carried. "This is a bottle of vodka, Sly. I'm going to get drunk tonight. If you care to watch me, you're welcome to."

Slightly amused, Sly sat down on her couch. "You shouldn't let him ruin your success, Laura. We were a hit. Kentucky Blues is still going, and when I left, they were tearing down the house. But before they went on they said to tell Haven that this was gonna work out great. You should be ecstatic."

"Yeah, I should, shouldn't I? Only Haven's refusing to do the tour."

"She didn't mean it," Sly said. "Things will look better in the morning."

"You don't know her like I do."

She opened the bottle and poured herself a drink. "So, why aren't you out partying?"

"I wanted to be here," he said with a grin.

"Yeah, well, you didn't know I'd ruin your mood. And you didn't know I'd get drunk."

"You're not going to get drunk," he said. "You can't even stand the taste of vodka."

"Watch me," she said, and gulped some down. "See?"

"And what is this going to prove? That Zane always brings out the worst in you?"

"Call it a celebration," she said. "I haven't celebrated my divorce yet."

"All right," he conceded. "I'll buy that."

He watched her drink and listened as she raved about all the things that Zane had done, and finally, slipping his arm around her and drawing her close, he said, "Do you want me to beat him up for you?"

She considered that for a moment. "No," she said. "*I* want to beat him up. You can hold him while I do it."

"That could work," he mused. "Only he'd probably heal too fast and forget the whole thing. How about if we humiliate him publicly?"

"Yeah," Laura said, lighting up. "I could write a book about his sexual dysfunction."

Sly's mouth fell open. "*Is* he sexually dysfunctional?"

"He would be after he read the book."

She laid her head on Sly's shoulder as gales of laughter overtook them.

"We could ruin his career," Sly suggested, "but he's doing that all by himself."

Laura recalled Zane's accusations against Jerry Joe and laughed even harder. "The worst thing would be if we signed Jerry Joe Wagner to record with us, and I could promote him into the next Elvis. That would really do Zane in. We wouldn't even have to kill him. He'd just shrivel up and die."

They became hysterical at the thought and Laura drained her glass.

Finally, late into the night, she fell asleep on Sly's shoulder.

Sly took the half-empty bottle from her hand and hoped that the price she would pay in the morning wouldn't be too severe. Quietly, he set it down on the end table, then moved her shoulders slightly forward to make her more comfortable. She slid across him, and he caught her in his arms, cradling her.

She looked like an angel, he thought, with her face in repose and her cherry lips slightly parted. Something in his heart twisted and he felt a surge of sadness that only when she was sound asleep could he finally hold her and look at her the way he'd wanted to since that kiss.

But he blamed Zane for the scars that made her so afraid to love again. In fact, the idea of beating him to a pulp was looking better all the time.

And then he realized Laura had been right. There were better ways to beat Zane.

A soft smile skittered across his lips as he remembered the time about a year ago when he'd run into Jerry Joe Wagner at a club. The singer had bemoaned the lack of good material to put on his latest album, and Sly had conveyed his frustration at trying to get Zane to rerecord his early hit "Long Ago Lullaby," which Zane had insisted was passé and of interest to no one. Before he knew it, Jerry Joe had been writing down the name of the song and the publisher who owned it.

Since that time, Jerry Joe had recorded it, and this week, the first week after its release, it had debuted on the Billboard Country Chart at number one.

If he wasn't mistaken, Jerry Joe owed him one.

He bent down and pressed a kiss on Laura's temple, chuckling softly as he realized that her idea to sign Jerry Joe, though conceived as a joke, was a good one. If they could somehow convince him to record with them . . .

The idea began to have more and more merit as Sly considered how much Jerry Joe could do for them. He knew for a fact that Jerry Joe hadn't been happy with his label the last time they'd spoken. He'd complained about being too constrained, about feeling that the studio was trying to fit him into an image, rather than working around his own. If he could promise the singer autonomy in his recordings, there might be a possibility . . .

A name like Jerry Joe Wagner could push their label over the edge and draw more of the major stars in Nashville.

The ideas reeled through his mind as he lifted Laura in his arms and carried her to her bed. The moment he laid her head on the pillow, she woke and looked up at him. With glazed eyes, she reached for him, and he went willingly, stretching out beside her.

Her brazen kiss took him by surprise, and he felt her body stirring to wakefulness, inciting a maddening desire in his own. Her hands were liberated, moving across him with stark hunger, and he found his breath coming harder as he trapped her hands in his own and held them still.

She was drunk, he told himself. And as much as he'd fantasized about just such a scene, he wasn't going to let his first experience with Laura be tainted by the fact that she didn't know what she was doing. When he made love to her, they would both be fully aware, and there would never be any regrets.

"Go to sleep, baby," he crooned.

"Don't wanna sleep," she rasped. "Want you."

"I'm yours, baby," he whispered. "But not until you have full use of your faculties."

"My facilities are . . . just fine. . . ."

He grinned and pulled her closer. "Just be still," he whispered. "Close your eyes. . . ."

She did as she was told, her face pressed against his neck, and his heart nearly burst at her nearness. He wondered if any other woman would ever feel so good, or fit against him so perfectly.

Before she drifted off to sleep, she whispered, "I love you, Sly."

His eyes misted, and he kissed the top of her head. "I love you, too, baby," he said as raw emotion filled his throat. "I love you, too."

LAURA WOKE AS THE SUN intruded through her window, and for the first time in her life, she cursed it. She started to sit up, but the ache in her head stopped her, and she had to lie back down.

What had she done last night? She looked around, saw the half-empty bottle beside her bed and groaned. What must Sly think of her?

And then she remembered that Sly had been the one to bring her to bed. The rest was blurry, and she didn't know what had happened next. But she was still fully dressed, and he was gone.

Disappointment flooded her, and she wasn't sure why. She turned on her side, trying to ease the pain, but it didn't help. And then she remembered lying like this in Sly's arms, feeling as if all the empty places in her soul had suddenly filled up.

And she remembered telling him she loved him.

She covered her face and groaned out loud, wishing she could rewind time and do things differently. She would erase that stupid confession, would not let it happen....

But it had, and he was gone, and now she felt sure that it was the beginning of the end.

Forcing herself to sit up, she dropped her feet to the floor and told herself that she'd have to find him and tell him she hadn't meant it, that she had been drunk, that she hadn't known what she was saying. She'd have to set things right before he started hardening himself against her, before he started slipping away, as everyone she'd ever cared for had done.

She stumbled to the shower, turned it on and stripped as fast as she could. But the hot water spraying down did little to comfort the ache in her head or the anxiety in her heart.

THE PHONE HAD RUNG unanswered, and when she'd walked across the courtyard to his condo, Sly hadn't been home. Confused and a little worried, Laura went home, chastising herself with both barrels.

She had almost convinced herself that whatever she'd done or not done, or said or not said, had driven Sly away. When the doorbell rang, she dashed to it. Sly greeted her with a huge smile, and Jerry Joe Wagner at his side.

"Sly. Jerry Joe." Frowning, she let them in. "What's going on?"

Sly leaned against the wall and grinned down at her. "I decided I liked your idea last night. So I acted on it today."

"What idea?"

He chuckled and shot Jerry Joe a look. "Laura's probably a little vague about last night. How are you feeling, babe?"

She tried to pretend she was fine, though her head hadn't stopped throbbing. "I'm great, but I still don't know what idea you mean."

"The one about signing Jerry Joe to our label."

Her eyes widened. "I suggested that?"

Jerry Joe laughed and took one of the chairs. "Geez, it must have been real important if you don't even remember it."

She dropped onto the couch and closed her eyes. "No...I think it's a terrific idea. I just wish I remembered it."

Sly sat next to her and turned slightly to face her. "Anyway, I made him an offer this morning that he couldn't refuse."

"Really?" she asked, not yet believing.

Jerry Joe leaned forward and cocked his head, and she noted the boyish charm that had made him so popular. "I sort of owed Sly one anyway for turnin' me on to 'Long Ago Lullaby.' It's gonna make me a mint."

Slowly, the events of the previous day began to come back to her. "Zane's song. Now I remember. He was livid, you know. He blames you for the fall of Rome, the destruction of Atlantis and all of his tax problems."

Jerry Joe laughed. "Yeah, well, that's Zane. But the fact is, there's no love lost there. I've detested that man for years."

Laura frowned. "Does it have anything to do with your little fling with Rosy?"

Jerry Joe's smile faded, and he looked uncomfortable. "Uh...no, actually. That was the result of it." He sat back and took a deep breath. "I used to work on the crew of one of Zane's road tours, and after twelve weeks of backbreaking labor, setting up and breaking down so he'd have the best stage show of anybody in country music, Zane refused to pay us. Claimed he hadn't made enough on the tour, and that he'd run out of money. He even had the gall to tell us that he'd supported our butts for twelve weeks and given us the experience of a lifetime, and we didn't have any right to demand what he'd promised."

Laura shot Sly a look. "Sounds like Zane. But why didn't you sue, Jerry Joe?"

"I didn't have a contract. Just a verbal agreement. It was stupid of me, but I was only seventeen, and I didn't know any better."

"So, where did Rosy fit in?"

"Couple years later, when my band and I were just starting to get noticed, Zane came in one night. He came backstage like the big star, lowering himself to speak to us peon performers, and I guess I got my feathers a little ruffled. I told him I used to work for him, and I swear, he acted like he didn't remember. And then the opportunity just presented itself. Rosy warmed up to me first, and when she made the invitation, I took it."

Sly raised his hand over his mouth to cover his grin.

"It felt good to get even with him, guys," Jerry Joe said. "I know that sounds awful, but it's true. When he found out, I thought he was gonna kill me. But I'm bigger than he is, so I held him off. 'Course, he's done things over the years to sabotage my career. It's usually backfired on him, though."

Laura gauged him seriously for a moment. "And you think working with his second wife as your promoter will pay Zane back for the rest of what he's done?"

Jerry Joe shrugged. "Won't hurt."

Laura's smile faded. "I'm not into revenge, Sly," she said. "It was all just a joke. I love the idea of signing Jerry Joe, but not to get even with Zane."

"I know that, babe," Sly said. "But the more I thought about it, the more sense it made to our studio. Forget Zane. Just think of what Jerry Joe can do for us."

"And don't forget that I've been wanting to work with Sly for years now," Jerry Joe assured her. "I figure Zane's career would have been in the dumper three albums ago if Sly hadn't done his thing on them. I want to stretch and try new things and cultivate the image I want instead of the one the company wants. I really like what you're doing with Haven Berringer, and how you've maintained her integrity while you're promoting her."

A slow smile drifted across Laura's face as she realized Jerry Joe had the potential to give their studio the prestige it needed—and bring in enough money to pay off her debt to her mother, as well as the one to Michael. She held out a hand. "Welcome to Renegade Records, Jerry Joe. We're going to make a fortune together."

CHAPTER TWENTY-ONE

THE MOMENT THE ALBUM that Jerry Joe recorded in their studio hit the stores, and his new video hit the major television stations, his picture was splashed over the front page of every tabloid in the United States, and articles and reviews peppered the mainstream papers. The first release from the album shot to number one and stayed there even longer than "Long Ago Lullaby" had.

"Guess y'all hit it big with him," Haven commented one afternoon as Laura charted the cities included in Jerry Joe's upcoming tour. "Daddy's fit to be tied."

Laura regarded her carefully. "I'm sorry this puts you in a bad position, Haven, but you can't blame us for signing him."

Haven pulled her foot up onto her chair and hugged her knee. "I never blamed you. When I pulled out of the Kentucky Blues tour, I guess you had to find somebody else to set your hopes on."

"We never gave up on you, you know."

"Well," Haven said with a sigh, "I guess the fact that you believed in me in the first place was mind-bogglin'."

Laura leaned across her desk and faced Haven squarely. "Haven, it's not too late, you know. I have all sorts of ideas for picking up where we left off. There are two more songs on your album that might hit the charts if we released them as singles, and your first album has already sold over 100,000 copies. That's not bad for a first-timer. We just need to get your name out."

"And how would you do that?" Haven asked.

Laura's eyebrows came up. "Get you another tour."

Haven was skeptical. "Come on, Laura. Even I know I cut my throat when I cancelled with Kentucky Blues. Who in their right mind would take a chance on me again?"

"Someone who loves you," Laura said. "Someone who understands you better than you think."

Haven's eyes narrowed. "Who?"

"Me." Laura got up and went around the desk, her eyes animated, and she leaned on the edge of her desk to focus on Haven better. "I talked to Jerry Joe about it, Haven, and he really, really likes your music. The word *genius* came up more than once."

Haven wasn't buying. "Come on."

"No, really. And when I suggested letting you front for him on his tour, he loved the idea."

Haven frowned. "Does he know how...unreliable...I am?"

Laura couldn't help laughing. "He knows you're a little...eccentric. But so is he. And, Haven, I believe that if you give us your word not to back out of the tour, for any reason, that you'll go through with it."

Haven dropped her foot to the floor and considered the idea for a moment. "How many cities?"

"Forty." She held her breath, hoping it wouldn't seem too many to Haven.

"It's not easy." Haven got up and went to the window, looked out, then turned back to Laura. "I mean, I have trouble with all the fame and stuff. And the money. It's not me."

"But the music is, Haven. That's the bottom line. Nobody's going to hear your music unless you take it to them."

"Jerry Joe's a big draw," she said pensively. "He'll pack an auditorium as full as Kentucky Blues did."

"One can only hope."

Haven crossed her arms and leaned back against the wall. "I want to talk to Jerry Joe about it first," she said. "Make it clear that I'm not into the drug scene, or the all-night parties, or any of that adulation stuff. I'm in it for the music, and I have to have my quiet times or the spirit will run right out of me."

"Fine," she said. "Come by my apartment at seven tonight, and I'll have Jerry Joe there. The two of you can work this all out."

JERRY JOE arrived at Laura's early, anxious to talk Haven into joining him on the tour. Haven arrived thirty minutes late, making them both sweat for a while. In her best low-key voice, she asked Laura, "Would you mind if I talk to Jerry Joe alone for a minute?"

"Of course not." Laura grabbed her coat and started for the door. "I'll be across the courtyard at Sly's. Call me when you're ready for me to come back."

Haven waited for Laura to leave, then looked at Jerry Joe, the man her father hated so deeply. "Daddy would rather have me be abducted by aliens than go on tour with you."

Jerry Joe nodded. "I can believe that. But I don't really care what your daddy wants. I want somebody different goin' on tour with me. And you're about the most different person I know."

Haven's expression didn't change. "I've never smoked a joint in my life. Did you know that?"

"No, I didn't," Jerry Joe said, although he looked as if he didn't have a clue why she brought it up.

"And I don't drink. Not even beer."

"Why not?" Jerry Joe asked.

Haven shrugged. "I just can't feel very spiritual when I drink. I mean, I know Jesus drank wine and everything, but I guess he could hold it better than I can."

Jerry Joe grinned. "I'll buy that."

She gazed at him for a moment. "Are you one of those performers who has the roadies line the groupies up after the show so you can pick the ones you want to take back to your room?"

His grin faded. "No, but a couple of times, my roadies
have seen girls in wheelchairs who couldn't get very close to
the front, and on my orders they brought them backstage
for a hug and an autograph."

Haven nodded. "I like that. What about the partyin' on
the buses?"

"I don't allow drugs," Jerry Joe said, "but there is usually beer floating around. A lot of card playing, video games
and good music. Probably not a lot different than a weekend at the Berringer house when everybody lived at home."

Haven's eyes remained intense. "You slept with my
mother, didn't you?"

The question obviously surprised him. "Well...just
once."

She stared at him quietly for an uncomfortable time, then
said, "It wasn't really your idea, was it?"

He smiled and looked down at his feet. "No, not really.
But I ain't runnin' from the blame."

"You know if I go on tour with you, it'll be as good as
puttin' a knife to my daddy's heart."

"Well, from what I hear, any reaction at all from him
would be better than nothin'."

She looked offended. "What do you mean by that?"

"I mean, Haven, it's common knowledge that your daddy
has never supported your career. And that just shows how
shortsighted he is. You're one of the most talented artists I
know, and if I were you, I'd go right along with my business and forget about what he has to say about it. He hasn't
been right yet."

There was a lot of truth to what he said, but it was hard
for her to swallow. "I believe in loyalty. And he is my
daddy."

"Bein' true to yourself isn't bein' disloyal to him," Jerry
Joe said.

She had to agree, despite herself. "I'll never change the
way I dress."

He smiled. "Then we can swap clothes in a pinch. I like the way you dress. And I like the way you write. But most of all, I like the way you sing."

Her smile was tentative, but profound. "I like to sleep outside under the stars every chance I get," she said. "It helps me get closer to God when things start gettin' crazy."

"Maybe you'll let me come along sometime."

She studied him for a short eternity. "Maybe I will."

"Then we've got a deal?"

She paused for just a moment before nodding her head slowly. "I guess we do."

THEY TRAVELED IN A CONVOY of five vehicles, one bus for Haven and her band, one for Jerry Joe and his band, one for the roadies and sound engineers, and two eighteen-wheelers that held all their equipment. Laura shared Haven's bus and slept little the nights they drove straight through and bunked on the pull-down beds. She longed for the nights when they actually stayed in hotels and took long showers and slept in real beds.

Haven, on the other hand, seemed to thrive on the vagabond life-style, and more often than not, she and Laura rode on Jerry Joe's bus, where Haven and Jerry Joe collaborated on a number of songs that Laura was certain would be hits. After their third concert together, Jerry Joe suggested that Haven come back onstage during his set and do a duet with him. The crowd went wild, and they made it a permanent part of the show.

As successful as it all was, Laura couldn't escape the fact that none of it seemed complete without Sly. He'd stayed behind to keep the studio running smoothly. Other artists had signed with them now and were deep into recording their new albums. There was more work than Laura had ever anticipated, and she began to wonder if she had the stamina to keep up with all of it.

That worry was evident in her voice the night she called Sly from a motel in Arizona where they'd decided to stop for the night.

"So, what's the matter, babe?" he asked in his gravelly, intimate voice.

"I guess I'm just tired," she said. "I'm ready to come home. I wish we had time to break for Thanksgiving."

"I do, too. But at least you'll be home by Christmas."

She smiled. "No chance of you joining us for at least part of the tour, is there? It would boost morale."

"Whose?" he asked skeptically.

She laughed softly. "Mine, actually."

She could tell that he enjoyed that. "Good," he whispered. "I was beginning to think you were getting along too well without me. Serendipity told me yesterday that she hadn't seen me smile in two weeks. She suggested that I was getting sour."

She let the idea that he hadn't smiled because of her absence slide right past her and focused, instead, on Serendipity. "I thought she wasn't going to start recording until next month."

"Yeah, but she's been hanging around the studio a lot, trying to find the right material. Every time I turn around, she's here."

"Oh." Something twisted in her heart, and she recalled the way she had seen Sly holding her so long ago. Was there something between them?

"Are you sure you're okay?"

She nodded and tried to swallow the lump in her throat. "Yeah."

"You should be happy, you know. You're doing a bang-up job with the tour."

"Somehow it's not as much fun without..." Her voice trailed off, and she stopped herself.

"Without what?" His voice was expectant.

Finally, she forced herself to say it. "Without you. It never seems like work when you're around."

His sigh expressed heartfelt relief. "I miss you, too."

She hadn't said she missed him, and she wouldn't have, not in those words, but the fact that he knew it made her smile. "Well, I guess I'd better go."

"Don't hang up yet. I'm not ready to let you go."

Her heart swelled. "Okay. If you're sure you're not keeping anybody waiting."

His laughter warmed her heart. "What do you mean by that?"

"Well, you're no monk, Sly, and you're certainly not lacking in the virility department. It would be a little naive to think that you're alone every night."

The moment she said the words, she hated herself, for they gave too much away.

"I like to think I'm a man of integrity, baby," he whispered. "And I can wait for what I really want. It isn't always easy, but finding a substitute wouldn't ease the wanting."

Her heartbeat accelerated and her mouth went dry, yet she was afraid to think that he meant what she thought he did. "No," she whispered. "There are no substitutes for the real thing."

Several moments of crackling silence went by, and finally, Sly said, "Do you know what I think, Laura Rockford?"

"What?"

"I think you're healing."

She smiled. "I think maybe you're right."

IT WAS TOO HARD to sleep after she hung up. Sly's voice kept running through her mind, filling Laura's heart and intruding on her dreams. Finally, she decided to go to Haven's room.

Some of Haven's band members were sitting outside their rooms, drinking beer and playing cards, and when Laura knocked on her door, they looked up. "Haven's not there, Laura."

She turned around. "Where is she?"

"Campin' out," one of them said.

Laura's jaw dropped. "Are you kidding me? She doesn't even know what town we're in. What if she gets lost? What if she gets kidnapped or murdered, or worse?"

"Jerry Joe went with her. He can protect her."

Laura groaned and slapped her hands against her thighs. "Terrific. Our two stars out in the middle of the desert together. Did anybody think of consulting me before they left?"

The band members began to snicker. "Haven never consults anyone. You ought to know that by now."

A FEW MILES from the motel, Haven and Jerry Joe lay side by side in separate sleeping bags, looking up at the heavens.

"Do you believe in the stars?" Jerry Joe asked her softly.

"I believe they exist."

He chuckled. "No, I mean, do you believe in astrology? Horoscopes, that sort of thing?"

She thought for a moment. "I don't put much stock in that stuff. All I know is that God put them there. How he wants to use 'em is up to Him."

She watched the red light of an airplane cut a path through the Big Dipper. "Why? Do you believe in that stuff?"

He shrugged. "I don't know what I believe, really. That's why I envy you so much."

She looked over at him. "What do you mean, you envy me? I'm not somebody you should envy."

"Why not? You know what you believe in, and you live by it. That's something to envy."

"Well, that's not so hard," she said, staring up at the stars again. "All you have to do is think about it awhile. You have to believe in something. Just look at those stars and try to tell yourself you don't believe."

He looked at them and saw the absurdity of denying a higher power. "You're right."

"You know, my daddy only believes in himself," Haven said quietly. "But he's one of the most miserable men I know."

Jerry Joe didn't say anything.

"I wish I could get him to look up at the stars now and then, and see what I see. I really worry about him sometimes."

"He's not worth it."

"Oh, yes, he is," Haven said. "He's worth it, because he's my daddy. I can't ever give up on him."

THE NOISE LEVEL had finally died down in Sly's condo when he'd put *Aladdin* on the VCR for his nieces and nephews to watch. In the kitchen, all four of his sisters buzzed around the pies they were making today so that they wouldn't have so much to do tomorrow for Thanksgiving.

His mother, a spritely white-haired lady with bright eyes and a smile to match, brought him a glass of iced tea and bent over to kiss his cheek. "I hope we're not driving you crazy, Sly. We could still have Thanksgiving at Sharon's."

"No, Mom," he insisted. "You're staying here, so that's where most of the cooking's being done. It would be silly to drag everything over to Sharon's."

She sat down across from him with a huge sigh. "Well then, if it's not the company that's getting you down, what is it?"

Sly smiled and propped his jaw on his hand. "What makes you think I'm down?"

"Because you're not in there watching *Aladdin* with the kids!"

He laughed then, and she nodded. "That's better. Now, tell me about her."

"Who?"

"The woman, whoever she is. Is she that pretty little Rockford girl you work with?"

Sly covered his face and shook his head. "I wonder what ever makes me think I can keep secrets from you."

"You never could," she said. "It is her, then, isn't it?"

He threw his palms up and shrugged. "All right, Mom. Yeah, it's her."

"Unrequited love?" she asked cautiously.

His smile faded. "Yes . . . no . . . I don't know. Actually, I think we're starting to get somewhere. It's about time. I've known her for two years now. But . . ."

"But what?"

"But I'm in Tennessee, and she's in Utah, and I haven't seen her in weeks . . ." His voice trailed off, and he rubbed his tired eyes. "And I think I'm just about to go crazy."

"I see." His mother smiled and sat back, proud that she had finally got to the bottom of the problem. "Then tell me one thing. Why are you sitting here with us, when your studio's closed for the holidays and there's nothing stopping you from being with her?"

He looked surprised. "Well, you guys were coming all the way from California . . ."

She waved a hand at him, dismissing that excuse. "We can fend for ourselves, Sly, and we certainly see each other enough that we can skip one holiday together. You go pack your bags right now. Your sisters and I will go on about our business, using and abusing your house as if you were here, so you don't have to give us another thought."

He hesitated. "Are you sure, Mom?"

"Go!" she said, pointing toward his bedroom. "You may be missing a flight as we speak."

THE CONCERT Haven and Jerry Joe did in Salt Lake City on the night before Thanksgiving was a phenomenal success, and after four encores in which Jerry Joe returned to the stage with Haven, they finally ran out of material and had to leave the crowd screaming.

It was only then that Laura realized both artists had reached the goal she had set for them. They were becoming huge stars, and they were loved by everyone who saw them. The fact that the band wasn't going to get a break for Thanksgiving didn't seem to faze any of them. They were glad for one day in which to rest in a hotel, and Laura had rented a banquet room so they could have their Thanksgiving meal together before traveling on to their next destination.

Why she felt on the verge of tears, she wasn't sure. She took care of the details that had to be attended to after the concert, fielded questions by the media, and then went backstage to congratulate Haven, as she always did. It had become routine that she would bask in Haven's excitement and compare notes about the way each song went. She never knocked, and tonight was no different.

She waited until the hallway outside Haven's dressing room was clear, so that no wayward fans would catch a glimpse of her half-dressed. Then quietly, Laura opened the door and slipped inside.

Haven stood in Jerry Joe's arms, embroiled in the sweetest, wettest, longest kiss that Laura had ever walked in on.

They both glanced up when she closed the door behind her.

"I'm sorry," she said quickly. "I didn't mean to interrupt."

Haven looked embarrassed, but she didn't let Jerry Joe go.

"I'll just...go now," Laura said with an awkward smile. "You two just...carry on."

Haven and Jerry Joe laughed as Laura backed out of the room and closed the door.

Laura shoved her fingers through her hair and grinned. Why hadn't she seen it? Haven and Jerry Joe had been spending an inordinate amount of time together, and she had no reason to think that either of them wasn't cut from the same cloth as she. Of course they were falling in love. And in Haven's case, it was probably for the first time.

Then suddenly, as quickly as the joy for Haven filled her, she was stricken with a profound sadness. It was happening for Haven, but it hadn't happened yet for Laura. Sly was hundreds of miles away, and she was here, at Thanksgiving, just as alone as she'd ever been.

She left the building and went back out to the empty bus, got on it and found the cellular phone. Aching, she dialed Sly's number.

Her heart raced as the phone was picked up.

"Hello?"

It was a woman's voice, and Laura froze.

"Hello?" the woman said again.

Laura hung up, kicking herself. Of course he wasn't alone, she thought. It was the night before Thanksgiving, and no one wanted to be alone....

She set the phone down and sat on the bus by herself, and suddenly she realized that all of the things she had been striving for were a waste. All the success and the money and the fame she directed toward her stars...none of it mattered if she was still alone.

And she was. Just as alone as she'd been when she was four years old and praying for a father. Just as alone as she'd been when Michael moved out. Just as alone as she'd been when she was married to Zane. Just as alone as she would ever be, for she didn't have whatever it took to make a relationship work. And now Sly was so far away, with someone else, probably not giving her a thought....

She began to cry, and she dropped her face into her hands and let the sobs overtake her. There was a kind of loneliness that friendships and success couldn't fill. The kind of loneliness that could be soothed only by a soul mate, someone who knew your emotions before you felt them. But if Sly had ever been meant to be her soul mate, she may have made him wait too long.

She heard the bus doors opening and someone stepping on. Quickly, she got up, turning her back to them, and headed to the bathroom so she could wash away the evidence of her tears.

"I've looked all over for you."

The voice sounded so familiar, and yet . . .

She turned slowly around and saw Sly standing there smiling at her, and suddenly she started to cry again. "Sly . . ."

As if they had come together like this a thousand times before, he took her in his arms and crushed her against him. "Why the tears, baby?"

She shook her head. "It doesn't matter now." She laughed and wiped them away. "What are you doing here?"

"I closed the studio for Thanksgiving, and I wanted to see you. . . ."

"To check up on me, huh? Make sure I'm doing my job?"

"No," he said. "To be with you. To hold you. To look at you." He smiled down at her. "Do you have any idea how good you look to me?"

Closing her eyes, she pulled him closer and held him for a long moment. She wouldn't think of how this could impact their friendship, or change their working relationship or effect their lives. All that mattered was that he was here. "I called your house just now," she whispered. "A woman answered."

She looked up at his grinning face as the answer that should have been so obvious finally hit her. "Your sister, right?"

"Right. I left a house full of company. But it couldn't be helped."

He bent down and she buried her face against his neck, kissing the skin there, which smelled so uniquely of him. "Haven and Jerry Joe are an item now," Laura whispered, as if that had anything to do with what was happening between them.

"You don't say." The laugh lines around his eyes creased, and he looked down at her mouth.

She wet her lips.

"And they've been collaborating on some of their songs...."

His face began to descend to hers.

"He took her out on his encores tonight, and they—"

"Be quiet," he whispered, just before his mouth met hers.

She stopped talking as his lips grazed hers, gently, softly, sweetly at first, and then at her own moment of surrender, the kiss moved deeper. It was a rebirth, an awakening, a rekindling of feelings that Laura thought she would never feel again for anyone. It was so joyous that it was sad. It was so wonderful that it was terrible. It was so calming that it was terrifying.

When the kiss broke, Sly pressed his forehead against hers and his breath came hard against her lips. "I missed you so much."

Her own voice was breathy as she whispered, "Me, too."

"I only have two days," he said, "and then I have to get back. And I want to cram as much of you as I can into those two days."

The doors to the bus opened again, and they heard voices as the others started to climb on. She stepped back, out of his arms, and wiped her lipstick from his mouth. "I'm glad you're here," she said with tears in her eyes. "But we're driving straight through tonight. We aren't stopping at a hotel until tomorrow. Do you mind sleeping on the bus?"

"Is there room for me?"

"Sure," she said. "We can find a place for you."

The look in his eyes told her he was disappointed that they wouldn't be alone, but there was always tomorrow. And as the others filed onto the bus, that same look told her that tomorrow would be worth the wait.

THEY TALKED for most of the night, just the way they used to do when their planning sessions took them into the wee hours of the morning. He told her of all the goings on at the studio, and she told him of all the shenanigans she'd experienced on the buses. And the more they talked, the more she remembered how sweet it was to have Sly around.

But the looks that passed between them became more longing and more sensual, and as they settled down in their separate bunks to sleep, Laura realized she had bided her time with Sly too long. It was time to cross the threshold from friendship into love. Time to admit how she really felt about him, time to take another risk, to make herself vulnerable again. She prayed that this time it would be different, that there would be no rejection, no surprise, no heartbreak. But even as she embraced the hope of love with Sly, memories came back of being crushed and used by Zane, of being neglected and tolerated by her mother, of yearning and praying so hard for a father.

But things changed, she told herself, and it wasn't a father she was looking for now. It was a soul mate, and she was pretty sure that was what she'd found in Sly.

Telling him would be more difficult than admitting it to herself. She still bore the scars from her experience with Zane, and they made her afraid.

It was noon before they reached the hotel where they were to have their Thanksgiving dinner, and before they checked in, the host ushered them all into the banquet room, where a feast had been set up. But Laura's mind wasn't on the turkey. Instead, it was on Sly, and the fact that, finally, she would have the chance to be alone with him.

After dinner, Sly offered to help her take her things to her room, rather than getting a bell boy. The moment the door closed, he took her hand and pulled her against him. "It's been a long wait," he whispered.

She rose up on her toes and met him halfway. The second their lips touched, she felt the floodgates of her restraint release, and myriad feelings rushing through, feelings that could drown her completely or float her upstream.

She felt his heart beating with a breakneck pace, and her own responded in kind as the kiss deepened. She touched the dark stubble on his face that he hadn't had a chance to shave off this morning, reveling in the sandpapery feel beneath her fingertips.

And all the while she sank deeper under his spell, but it was a spell that she knew he cast on himself, as well. Joy flooded through her, along with the glorious hope that loneliness was behind her.

He broke the kiss and framed her face, gazing into her onyx eyes. "Do you know...do you have any idea at all...how beautiful you are?"

She swallowed. "As Haven's song says, I'm only beautiful when you look at me."

"Oh, no," he said. "You're beautiful when I'm a thousand miles away, thinking of you, wondering where you are and what you're doing. You're still beautiful when I dream about you at night."

It was almost too wonderful, melting in the essence of those words, seeing in his eyes that he meant them.

He kissed her again, his fingers tangling through her hair, his other hand sliding down her back...

The phone rang, startling them as if they'd been caught in some wrongful act. "Let it ring," he whispered.

She tried, but the caller didn't give up, and finally, she shook her head. "I can't. I'm in charge here. If something goes wrong, I'm the one they call."

"You're right," he said, releasing her. "Go ahead."

With a sense of dread, she picked up the phone. "Hello?"

"Laura? This is Johnny back at the studio. Do you happen to know where I can find Sly?"

"He's right here, Johnny," she said. "Just a minute."

Wondering why their engineer would be calling, she handed Sly the phone. "I thought you closed the studio today."

"I did," he said, frowning. "Yesterday and tomorrow, too." He put the phone to his ear.

Laura turned away, her heart still pounding, and decided that the moment he hung up, she would take the phone off the hook.

"Oh, no." His tone made her turn around, and covering the phone, he told Laura, "Somebody broke into the studio."

"What did they take?"

"The masters of some of our albums. Nothing else." He closed his eyes and into the phone said, "Pirates. It has to be pirates."

Laura's heart sank. Whoever had taken the masters had done so with the intention of making counterfeit albums and selling them underground at a cut price.

"Johnny," Sly asked, "did they get Haven's and Jerry Joe's?"

Laura saw by the despair on his face that they had. "Look, I'll be right home. I'll take the next plane out."

Laura's hopes sank as he hung up the phone and turned back to her, gazing at her with heart-wrenching frustration. "I have to go."

"Yeah," she whispered. "I know you do. The building...was it damaged? Did they hurt any of the equipment?"

"They were just after the masters," he said. "But that damage will be bad enough. They'll be able to make perfect counterfeits, and we won't see a penny of profit for any of the records they sell. It could do serious damage to album sales for Haven and Jerry Joe, especially now when the tour is spurring more sales than ever before."

Laura followed him to the door. "The police must have some idea who did it."

"We'll find out," he said. He touched her face and leaned down to kiss her sweetly, gently. "I'm not through with you," he whispered. "When you get back..."

His mouth lowered to hers again, and he pulled her against him, stroking her hair as his tongue delved deeply into her mouth, evoking a passion that had been buried so deeply that she'd forgotten it existed.

When the kiss broke, he caught his breath. "When you get back to Nashville, we have some serious feelings to confront, Laura."

"I know," she admitted.

"I'm gonna miss you again."

"I am, too."

Then, before the tears in either one's eyes were shed, he was out the door.

CHAPTER TWENTY-TWO

BY THE TIME the tour was over and the buses pulled back into Nashville, it was common knowledge throughout the country music world that Haven and Jerry Joe were in love. And as Haven rode in the taxi out to the Berringer estate and prepared to meet her father, she braced herself, for she knew he wouldn't be happy.

She paid the driver, then picked up her bag and walked up the steps to the front door. It was locked, so she reached into her front pocket, fished out her keys and tried to unlock it.

But something was wrong. Her key didn't fit.

Frowning, she rang the bell and waited a small eternity before it was finally answered.

The maid who came to the door was a small, plump Latino woman who greeted her without recognition. "Yes?"

"Uh ... my key didn't fit." She waited for the maid to move out of the way, then said, "I'm Haven. Zane's daughter?"

"Oh, yes," the woman said, backing away. "I should have known you from your pictures. Come in. I'll tell him you're here."

It was weird, being invited into one's own home and announced like nothing more than a visitor. She'd hoped to come in and dump her bag out on the floor, wash some clothes and take a hot shower. But somehow, she didn't feel that she should. "Where's Eugenia?"

"She left weeks ago, and your father hired me," the woman said, starting up the stairs. "Make yourself comfortable."

Haven let out a frustrated sigh, dropped her bag and started into the kitchen. None of her family had come to welcome her home, and fleetingly, she wondered if her father had passed on the message she'd left him that today was the day.

Reaching into the refrigerator, she pulled out a carton of orange juice, drank from it, and looked out the window to see if she could see her mother's car at the cottage.

"You could at least use a blasted glass." Her father's voice was brusque and unwelcoming, and she swung around.

"Hi, Daddy."

He walked right past her and pulled a glass from the cabinet. "You might as well drink it all," he said. "Nobody's gonna want to drink out of it now."

Slowly, she set the carton back on the rack. "Didn't you get my message that I'd be home today?"

"Yeah, I got it," he said. "What's it to me?"

Tears popped to her eyes, and she shrugged. "Well, I don't know. I thought you'd be glad to see me."

"I told you how it'd be if you went on that tour with him. I told you you wouldn't be welcome back."

"But . . . I didn't really think you'd hold to that, Daddy. You know I didn't do it to hurt you. Aren't you even a little happy about my success?"

"I heard you two were lovers now. What's he trying to do? Work his way through my whole family?"

She wiped the tear seeping through her lashes. "It's not like that at all, Daddy. He's really nice."

Zane reached out and knocked over a chair, sending it crashing onto the cold floor. "Don't tell me what a nice guy he is! He's a thief and a con artist."

"How do you figure that?"

"He stole my song and convinced my child to join forces with me against me."

"He did not!" she returned. "Daddy, everybody knows you wrote that song. You even have credit on the album, whether you get royalties on it or not. And he didn't con me into anything."

"Well, I'll tell you what, Haven," he said. "You like him so much, then maybe he'll take you in. Because you're not welcome to live in my house anymore."

Her face twisted, and she stared at him in disbelief. "But, Daddy..."

"Pack up all your stuff," he said. "I don't want any of it here." He strode to the back door, grabbing his keys off the top of the refrigerator. "When I get back, I want you gone. And by the way, the locks have been changed, so you'd better get everything in one trip."

The door slammed, startling her, and she stared at it helplessly as the tears ran down her face.

The maid came back in. "May I get you anything?"

Covering her face, Haven shook her head and said, "No. No, thank you."

Then she ran up the stairs to try to find what was left of her life to take with her. She looked around the room and realized that she could leave with the bag she'd left downstairs. But there were a few things that meant something to her. The scrapbook of her childhood. The box of mementos she'd saved over the years. Her favorite old records. Her books.

Too many things to carry out to her car. She needed boxes. Something to put them all into.

Wiping the tears so that she could see, she ran down the stairs and opened the door to the basement.

The maid came running through the foyer. "You can't go down there. Mr. Berringer says it's off-limits. He was very clear."

"I just need some boxes," Haven said. "I live here. It's not like I'm gonna steal anything!"

"But he was very clear. Off-limits, he said. To anybody, he told me."

"I'll take responsibility for it," Haven cried. "I just need a stupid box!"

Before the woman could stop her, she flicked on the light and headed down the stairs.

Just as she'd hoped, several boxes were stacked in the corner, and she opened them to see if they could be emptied out.

Several hundred unmarked tapes were stacked there, and she pulled one out, wondering what Zane would have these for. Wiping her eyes, she turned around to see if any empty boxes were lying around.

And that was when she saw it.

One whole wall of the basement was covered with tape recording equipment and tapes were stacked from floor to ceiling behind her.

Was Zane trying to set up a recording studio for himself? But it couldn't be, she told herself as she went closer to the equipment. The basement wasn't acoustically sound, and there were no microphones and no speakers...

But there were at least a dozen tapes turning at one time, recording something she couldn't see.

A sick feeling rose in her stomach, and she eyed the stairs, hoping her father wouldn't burst in and catch her here. Her mind reeling, she turned back to the equipment and found the source disc. With a trembling hand, she stopped the recording and slid it out.

It was the master disc of Jerry Joe's album that had been stolen from Sly's studio.

A wave of dizziness washed over her as reality hit, and she scrambled through the box at the end of the table. Other masters were hidden there—all recorded at Renegade Records—but the one that struck the most painful blow was her own.

It couldn't be, she told herself. Zane couldn't have stolen his own daughter's album to counterfeit it and sell it illegally, could he? Was he honestly capable of that?

Trembling, she went back to the boxes, opened another and saw the counterfeit cassette covers—thousands of them. They looked exactly like the ones on both their albums, complete with liner notes and credits. In another box, she found tapes that had already been reproduced and packaged to look like the real thing.

A sob caught in her throat, and she covered her mouth and tried to muffle it. This was too much. It was unbelievable. He had stolen from Sly and from Laura and from Jerry Joe, but he had also stolen from his own daughter.

Abandoning what she had found, she ran up the stairs and out the door, where the maid still stood waiting. "Look," she said, don't tell him I went down there. It'll just get you into a lot of trouble. I didn't find any boxes, so there's no harm done."

"*Sí*, I can keep it quiet." The maid looked relieved. "He just gets so crazy about that basement. Says it's his refuge. I guess men like to have places that are just their own...."

Haven didn't wait for the rest of the woman's rambling but grabbed her bag and ran out the front door before she had to confront Zane with what she knew.

LAURA WASN'T SURPRISED when Haven showed up, distraught, at her door. She had expected Zane to throw a fit when Haven got back, especially since talk of her relationship with Jerry Joe had already traveled back to Nashville.

But she hadn't expected to see Haven's eyes red and swollen from crying, or her packed bag in her hands.

"Haven, are you all right?"

"He threw me out," she said. "Can I stay with you a few days? Just until I find a place...."

"Of course." Laura took her bag from her and pulled her through the door.

"I thought of goin' to Jerry Joe," Haven went on, "but we're just not ready for that."

"I would love to have a roommate," Laura said. "You don't have to look for another place. I have an extra bedroom."

Haven gave in to her tears, and Laura led her to the couch. "Haven, sit down and tell me what happened."

"He had the locks changed, and he has a new house-keeper who doesn't even know who I am...." She caught her breath. "I don't even think my family knows I'm back. Mama wasn't at the cottage, and I haven't had the chance to call the rest of 'em."

"I'm sure they'll be thrilled to see you. Zane's just bitter, Haven, but I know he'll get over it."

"Did he get over it with you?" Haven shot back.

"Well, no, but I didn't mean as much to him as you do. You're his daughter, Haven. He loves you."

"Not anymore. He's put me in the same category as you, Jerry Joe and Benedict Arnold. Traitors. Enemies. And it's like a little war with him. The things he's doing...."

Laura wasn't following. "What things, Haven?"

She stifled another sob and waved the question away. "I can't... It's just... I never thought he could be this way."

"I've had the same thoughts myself, Haven. And it took a long time to get over him."

Haven covered her face, trembling, and Laura reached over and hugged her. "Why don't you go take a shower, rest awhile, and then call your mother and the rest of your family when you feel better?"

Haven got up, grateful to have a reason to be alone for a while. She needed time to think about what Zane had done, and decide whether she could tell anyone or not. He was her father, but what he'd done was unforgivable. He'd tried to ruin her and Jerry Joe. And Laura and Sly.

She wept in the shower as the hot water streamed over her, and when she got out, she locked herself in the bedroom Laura had given her and tried to sort out what she was going to do.

SLY'S HOPES WERE HIGH when he came to Laura's apartment that afternoon after supervising the unloading of the equipment from the buses. Her eyes had been luminous when she'd climbed off the bus, and there was no question that she was ecstatic to see him. It was as if his long imprisonment had come to an end, and tonight would be his first night of freedom. All he wanted was to hold her without interruptions, to tell her how he felt about her, to ask her to stop the tap dance and decide how she felt about him.

He hadn't been so worked up about a woman since he was fourteen and his first crush, Tammy Simpson, had kept him guessing for six months. But Laura was no teenage crush. It took more than infatuation to keep him preoccupied all the time, make the other women he called friends aware that his attentions had strayed, and make him choose solitude if he couldn't be with her. He'd never ached for a woman before—not in his soul, not in his heart—so that he was just as miserable without her as he was ecstatic when he was with her.

Tonight, he had to tell her that, and he had to show her. Somehow, he had to convince her that he would never use, hurt or abandon her. To do that, he would have to break old patterns, old stereotypes. He would have to be stronger than he'd ever been before.

His hopes, however, were dashed the moment he reached her condo and saw the troubled look on her face.

"Zane threw Haven out," she whispered. "She's here now, and she's been crying for hours. I can hear her in there. I don't know what to do."

Sly closed the front door behind him and tried to push away his disappointment that yet another problem was overriding their time together. "She's just real sensitive, Laura. She'll be okay."

"But something else must have happened. I know she half expected him to throw her out, so that wasn't a surprise. She would be upset, but not like this."

"Have you called Jerry Joe?"

"He's on his way over," she said. "I hope he can cheer her up."

Sly leaned back against the wall and gazed longingly at her. "I guess that means we're not going to be alone tonight."

"Not for a while," she said, her eyes conveying the same disappointment as his.

"And I guess it would be out of the question to leave her when she's this upset."

"Yeah," she said with a remorseful smile. "I think it would."

He pulled her against him anyway and touched her face with his fingertips. "I guess just being here is better than nothing. I've waited a long time."

"So have I," she whispered. Her arms slid around his neck, and she feathered her fingers through his soft hair. Their lips met, hungry, welcoming, urgent.

The doorbell rang, and Sly moaned. "It's not meant to be," he muttered.

Laura went to open the door and Jerry Joe burst in. "Why didn't she come to me?"

"I don't know," Laura said. "But she's really upset."

"Can I go in there?"

"Knock first," she told him.

They listened as Jerry Joe headed for Haven's room, knocked and went in. Then silence followed.

Sly and Laura looked at each other. "Now what?"

"I guess we just sit here and see if we're needed," she said softly. "But I don't blame you if you want to leave. It is frustrating...."

He cupped her face then and raised it to his. "I'm not going anywhere, Laura. I've waited weeks to be with you, and all the evil forces of nature can't keep me away."

Relief seeped into her eyes. "What about the forces of good?"

Sly's smile comforted her more than she could imagine. "Not a problem," he said, "because I happen to know they're on our side."

LESS THAN AN HOUR later, Haven came out of the bedroom, Jerry Joe following behind her. "Guys, we have to talk."

Laura glanced at Sly. "Okay."

Haven sat down on the hearth, rather than the chair, and Jerry Joe sat beside her with his arm around her.

"Tell 'em, honey."

Her eyes were raw from her tears, and she drew in a ragged breath. "You have to promise not to overreact and start callin' lawyers and stuff."

"What?" Sly stood up. "Haven, what's going on?"

"Promise," she said. "What I'm gonna tell you is the hardest thing I've ever done."

"Really," Jerry Joe said. "She's torn up about this. You have to promise to cooperate or she's not gonna tell you."

"All right," Laura agreed. "What is it?"

Haven glanced at Jerry Joe, then took another deep breath. "When I went home, after Daddy threw me out, I went downstairs to get a box out of the basement, and I saw . . . I saw . . ."

"What, Haven?" Sly asked, growing impatient.

"The masters of my albums and Jerry Joe's. The ones that were stolen."

"What?" Sly gaped at her, and Laura rose to her feet.

"He had a bunch of equipment down there that he was using to duplicate the tapes," Jerry Joe went on.

"There were boxes full of the counterfeit tapes," she said. "He even had the covers duplicated. They looked exactly like the real thing."

For a moment, the silence in the room could have smothered them all. Laura was the first to speak. "Are you sure?"

"Would I say this if I wasn't?" Haven asked. "I agonized over whether to protect him or not, but then I realized how much money this could cost all of you, and how he's already cost you so much, Laura. I couldn't decide what the right thing was to do."

"You've done the right thing," Sly said. "And the first thing we've got to do is call the police."

"No!" Haven threw herself between Sly and the phone. "You promised. I don't want to turn him in, Sly! He'll go to prison. Can't we just go to him, tell him we know what he's doin' and talk him into quittin' it and givin' the tapes back? The humiliation will be punishment enough..."

"Are you kidding me?" Sly bellowed. "The guy broke into our studio, stole his own daughter's master disc and is cutting into her sales and putting the money into his own pocket! Don't you see what he's done, Haven? You *can't* protect him!"

"But I have to! He's my father!"

"He doesn't care about you or he couldn't do this! Don't you understand that pirating is a crime? And he committed it against *you!*"

"I know that," she shouted. "I just...I can't hurt him just because he hurt me. We've got to give him another chance."

Sly turned to Jerry Joe. "He stole from you, too, Jerry Joe. Do you want to keep quiet?"

"Whatever Haven has to do is all right with me," he said. "She has to live with it."

Flabbergasted, Sly turned back to Laura, who stared, expressionless, at Haven. "Laura, you must see how ludicrous it would be to keep quiet."

Laura hesitated. "I don't know, Sly. Maybe Haven's right. Maybe we could talk him into giving it up. Threaten him, even."

He gaped at her. "Let me get this straight. The man has emotionally abused you, lied to you, belittled you, tricked you into marrying him, milked your mother of millions of dollars that you have to pay back, stolen from us and cut into the profits of our business together, and you aren't sure whether you want to make him mad?"

Laura clutched her head. "That's not it. I just understand what Haven's saying. He's someone I once cared about. I don't know if I want him to go to prison."

Sly set his hands on her shoulders and looked straight into her eyes. "Baby, if it weren't for you, he'd have been in jail last year for the tax thing. When are you going to let go of him?"

"I'm not hanging on to him!" she cried. "I have no feelings for him anymore. Why would you accuse me of that?"

"Because," he said, his eyes fiery, "I've been biding my time waiting for you to fall in love with me ever since we met, but I don't think it's ever really going to happen until you say goodbye to him, once and for all. Frankly, I was hoping for death, but I guess prison will do."

He stormed to the door. "Think about it for a while. You know where I'll be."

When the door slammed behind him, Laura turned back to the other two. "He's right, you know," she said in a quiet voice.

"No, he's not," Haven protested. "I love my father. I can't send him to prison, no matter what he's done. Can you honestly say you ever really loved him and send him there, either?"

"I don't know," she whispered. "But I do know that he can't get away with this."

THERE WAS ONLY ONE THING for her to do, Haven thought later that night as she sat perched on her sleeping bag on the ridge where she loved to camp. Beside her, she could hear Jerry Joe's rhythmic breathing as he slept.

Leaving him, she quietly slipped away and headed back to the car. When she reached her father's house, the lights upstairs were on. She sat in the driveway for a moment, wondering what he was feeling right now. He was a man with too much pride, she thought. She wondered if he was lonely, and if he regretted, even the slightest bit, what he had done to his daughter.

Wiping the tears from her eyes, she went to the door and rang the bell. In a few moments, the maid opened it. "Miss Haven. I didn't expect you back."

"I have to speak to my father," she said, going in and starting up the stairs. "But I'll find him myself."

"No, miss. You really shouldn't—"

But Haven ignored her, and when she reached the second floor, flew to his bedroom.

The door was closed so Haven knocked, gave him a moment, then opened it. Zane sat in his bed, a bottle of vodka in his hand, and looked up at her through glazed eyes. "I thought I told you to get out."

"You did, and I went. But I had to come back, Daddy." Stepping inside, she stared down at him. "I know what you've been doin' in the basement. You're gonna wind up in prison if you don't stop it. And I don't want you goin' to prison."

Slowly, he set the bottle down and stood up, his ruddy face paling with dread. "What the blazes are you talking about?"

"The pirating, Daddy. The counterfeiting. The break-in at Renegade Records."

His jaw fell, and she saw the guilt on his face where she had hoped to see confusion.

"Laura and Sly know, Daddy, and they're probably gonna turn you in. Jerry Joe says he'll forgive you if I want him to, but they're not that easy. But maybe if you go tonight and give back the masters, and promise that you won't do it anymore...maybe you can come to some kind of agreement and they won't have to get the police involved."

The blood drained completely from his face, and he stepped toward her. "How could you?"

"How could I what, Daddy?"

"How could you do this to me? You spied on me, didn't you? You told them."

"I wasn't lookin' for it! But I did find it, and I had to tell, because you stole from them, Daddy!"

His expression was one of bitter rage, and through clenched teeth, he snarled, "Get out of my sight."

She backed toward the door, starting to cry again, and he grabbed the bottle and flung it against the wall. It crashed into a thousand shards of glass. "Get out!"

Sobbing, she fled back down the stairs and out to her car.

DARKNESS FILLED Laura's condo like a shroud as she sat alone on the couch, replaying the developments of the day in her mind. Was Sly right? Did her unwillingness to turn Zane in to the police indicate that some part of her still hung on to him?

She honestly didn't know. He had lied to her, used her and rejected her in the most destructive of ways, and now she found herself confronted with nothing but pity for the man she had once loved.

Was that pity going to drive Sly away?

The prospect was more dismal than she could confront, and she told herself that she couldn't go to Sly until her thoughts and her feelings had crystallized in her mind. When that happened, it would be her moment of truth—a moment that could free her completely or seal her fate forever.

Across the courtyard, Sly sat in equal darkness, wanting a drink but too miserable to get up to pour one. This was supposed to have been a glorious day—the day when he'd been prepared to profess his feelings to the one woman in his life he'd ever been in love with, the one woman who brought peace and sunshine and every good thing to his world. The one woman he believed God had marked for him.

Could it really be that she still had feelings for Zane?

Something told him that he was overreacting, that he was condemning Laura for the very goodness he found so attractive in her. She gave second chances, and third chances, and it wasn't in her capacity to hate. Not even Zane.

If he loved her, he had to honor her feelings.

This wasn't about his ego or his studio or his bank account. This was about Laura's peace of mind.

He went to the sink and splashed some water on his face, hoping it would clear his mind. It wasn't necessary to have Zane behind bars, he told himself. He didn't need revenge or reparations. He didn't even need the satisfaction.

All he really needed was Laura.

THE URGENT SOUND of the doorbell brought Laura to her feet, and relief flooded through her as she dashed to the door, expecting to see Sly.

But Zane leaned against the doorjamb, his face red and his breath reeking alcohol. Without greeting her, he burst in and closed the door behind him.

"Zane! What do you think you're doing?"

"Haven told me what you and Sly are cooking up," he accused. "I can't believe you'd do it. Not after all we've meant to each other."

Laura stared at him in disbelief. "She warned you, after you threw her out today?"

"Doesn't our marriage mean anything to you, Laura?" he asked, stepping toward her, his bloodshot eyes piercing her. "All the struggling, all the good times...."

"What good times? Our marriage was six months of misery, Zane, and you know it! You never even wanted me to begin with."

He made a helpless sound that suggested he'd been misunderstood.

"I had *always* hoped that once you paid your mama back and got out from under her control, that you and I could get back together...."

Tears sprang to her eyes, and she exhaled a heartless, disbelieving laugh. "You're such a liar! You *never* loved me. All you did was use me."

"That's not true, Laura." His own eyes filled, and he held his palms up helplessly. "I still love you. I may have hidden it, and I may have tried hard to camouflage it, but a man has pride, Laura! It's not easy to know that the person you love most has seen you fail. What else could I do?"

"You could have treated me with respect. You could have treated me like somebody you cared about losing. You could have acted like a man!"

"I have flaws, Laura. You know that more than any-body." His voice cracked, and he covered his face and sank onto her couch. "Paying off the IRS didn't mean anything after I lost you. And then I had to watch you going on with your life, without me, and it hurt, darlin'. It hurt."

She might have expected to feel more, but she found no desire in herself to comfort him. "This won't work, Zane," she said quietly.

"I was so broken up, Laura, that I didn't know what to do with myself. I lashed out, and yeah, it was the wrong way. I shouldn't have done it. But all I knew was that I was broke and my career was in the pits, and there you and Jerry Joe and Sly were..."

"And Haven," she threw in. "Don't forget Haven. You stole from her, too."

"Y'all were making money and going so far," he went on, "and I was jealous. There that Jerry Joe Wagner was mak-ing tons of money off a song that I wrote, and I wasn't get-ting a penny for it. I was just trying to get what was rightfully mine."

He dropped his head in his hands, and when he looked up at her, there was genuine despair on his face. For a mo-ment, she felt a brief surge of pity that Zane had never un-derstood why things didn't work out for him in life. And until he did understand, he would never be happy. His life was his own prison.

"'Long Ago Lullaby' wasn't even on that album," she said, "but even if it had been, it *wasn't* rightfully yours, Zane. None of it was rightfully yours."

"But I see that now!" he cried. "And look, I brought back the masters I stole." He pulled them from his coat pocket and dropped them onto the coffee table. "See? No harm done. It's all over. I realize what I've done, and all I want now is for you to come back. All I want is for you to forgive me, and love me again like you did, and come live with me, secretly so your mother won't know, until we can tie the knot back up again."

She stared at him, dumbstruck. "Why on earth would you want to do that?"

"Because I love you," he said. "And I don't think I can go on living without you for one more day."

It was only at that moment that Laura knew she had grown. Months ago, she would have fallen for the vulnerability, the sweet words, the pseudo commitment that she'd so needed to hear. But it was too late, and the words didn't move her anymore, and neither did his tears or the genuine remorse in his eyes. She saw it all for exactly what it was.

"I don't love you anymore, Zane," she said softly, "and I'm not sure I knew that until exactly this moment. And I'm not going to let you off the hook again. I'm turning you in."

Zane looked stunned as she picked up the phone, and she wondered if he had honestly believed that she would melt under his promises and sell herself again.

Slowly, he got to his feet, and the remorse in his eyes disappeared. In its place came a livid anger, a rage so hot that it almost frightened her. "If you dial that phone, it'll be the last thing you ever do."

Clutching the phone, she stared at him. "So, you're going to go from loving me to threatening me now, Zane?"

"Don't think I won't carry through on it."

"Oh, I know you will," she said. "I've seen how you treat your own flesh and blood. You're out of control, Zane. You need help."

"Put the phone down."

She stared at him, then at the phone, and for a brief moment she considered doing as he said. But something stopped her. A defiance born of abuse and disappointment and humiliation. The ball was in her court now, and she was ready to play it. With no further hesitation she started to dial the police.

SLY WAS CROSSING the courtyard to her condo, anxious to tell her that he would do whatever she wanted about Zane, when he saw Zane's car double-parked behind hers. Something tightened in his stomach and he started to run.

He didn't even knock but burst through the door, just in time to hear a crash and see Laura falling to the floor. Zane was scrambling for the phone, and after hanging it up, he then turned to Sly.

Sly snapped, and without thinking, he hurled himself at Zane, grabbed him by the collar and threw him against the wall. When he let go, Zane almost fell, then steadied himself and came back with a fist across Sly's jaw.

Sly returned the punch, knocking him down this time. Zane didn't get back up. For a moment he lay squirming on the floor, staring up at Sly. "It's a real good thing you've got these fighting skills, Zane, because you're gonna need them in prison."

Twisting Zane's arms behind his back, Sly held him face-down on the floor as Laura groped for the phone.

TWO HOURS LATER the police drove away with their prisoner handcuffed in the back seat of their car. Zane stared dolefully out the window at Laura as if she'd just sold him into slavery. The police had searched his house when she'd told them about the pirating and had found the evidence they needed to indict him. Since Laura had decided not to add assault to his list of charges, she wasn't required to go to the station with them.

Sly stood behind Laura as she watched the police cars drive off into the night, their blue lights flashing. She was tired . . . so tired. He could see it in her posture, in her eyes, in her spirit. When the cars were out of sight, he stepped up behind her and placed his hands on her shoulders. "Let's go in, baby."

"Haven's gonna die," she whispered.

"Haven won't be surprised. We did the right thing. He's out of control."

"Yeah, I know," she said, and for the first time, he knew there was no remorse in her tone.

He put his arm around her, and she leaned her head into his shoulder and let him guide her into her condo.

He sat down first, then pulled her onto his lap, and a slow smile crept back into her eyes. That smile was for him, he knew, and he treasured it as if it were a priceless piece of art. "Are you okay?" he asked.

She slid her arms around his neck and rested her forehead against his. "Tell me something," she whispered.

"What?" His heart was pounding, and he knew she knew it.

"Why did I ever love him?"

"Because you didn't know better."

"You tried to tell me."

He smiled sadly. "It was too late. I should have kidnapped you and married you myself the first second I saw you."

She sighed. "You know what I realized tonight, Sly?"

"What?"

"That I don't love him anymore. I don't even really pity him that much. It's really over."

He closed his eyes as relief washed over him. "Laura, you know how I feel about you."

As if she didn't need to hear the words, she kissed him then, so sweetly and eloquently that he knew everything that was in her heart. She loved him, too; it permeated her fingertips, her cheekbones, her hair. It was in her breath, in the velvety feel of her tongue against his, in her touch as her hands moved to unbutton his shirt.

He felt a tear roll down her cheek, and easing her back, he looked up at her. "Why are you crying?"

"Because I've missed you so much," she whispered, "and being with you now . . . I just can't believe how much I'm in love with you."

It was as if a ten ton boulder had been lifted from his heart, and he felt that familiar choking emotion rise up in his throat, in his eyes, as she kissed him again. Their mouths went from tasting to ravaging in seconds, and that frenzied hunger filled him, making him tremble, making him want her with more urgency than he'd ever felt before.

Her hands were moving over his chest, unbuttoning his shirt. He caught his breath as she wrestled it off his shoulders, down his arms, then, giving up, abandoned the shirt and splayed her fingers over his chest, through the crisp curls of hair there, over his nipples....

He swallowed and broke the kiss again, looking up at her with smoky eyes. It seemed he couldn't get enough of the sight of her face so close to his, dazed with such passion, such smoky longing.

She got up and took his hand, and he rose and tangled his fingers through her hair, stroking her face with his thumb. "I love you, too, Laura. I've loved you for a long time."

"Then show me," she whispered, and another tear trickled down her cheek.

"I will," he promised. "I'll show you what real love looks like."

When he kissed her, she began backing away, pulling him with her down the hall to the bedroom he hadn't seen since she'd had too much to drink. When they reached her room, he felt her hands move between them, felt her unbuttoning her blouse....

His heart threatened to escape from his chest and launch itself across the sky, and he found it harder and harder to breathe. His hands shook as they roamed over her back, feeling her blouse loosen as each button was released.

Inhaling a deep, ragged breath, Sly found the last remnant of control he possessed and stopped her hands. "Don't," he whispered.

She gazed up at him, her eyes still full of tears. "I love you, Sly. I want you."

"I want you," he said, "more than anything in this world. It's all I've thought about, day and night, night and day, for months...years...."

He was still trembling, and when she dropped her hands, he rebuttoned her blouse with an effort that seemed to take more strength than he was sure he possessed.

Slowly, he lowered her to the bed and knelt in front of her. He stroked her hair back from her face, ran his thumb along her lips. "But it's occurred to me that you've never known unconditional love in your life. All you've ever known is a using kind of love, a controlling kind of love. I want to give you more than that. When I undress you, it's going to be more giving than taking. And there won't be regrets or recriminations in the morning. And you'll never have to wonder where you stand with me."

Another tear slipped from her lashes.

"When I make love to you, Laura, it's going to be as my wife and not my lover."

For a moment, she stared at him through her tears, as if unable to believe his words. Her hand came up to cover her mouth. "You want to marry me?"

"More than anything I've ever wanted," he said, still breathless. "And quickly. Real quickly. If we could do it in the next thirty seconds, in fact, it would be perfect."

She caught her breath on a sob, then fell into his arms, clinging to him with all the love and passion and devotion that she had rejected before.

"Say yes, baby, please," he whispered against her ear. "Say you'll be my wife, and we'll build a house together, and a home, and have babies, and I'll be the kind of father to them that you always wanted for yourself, and you can be the kind of mother that you always wanted yours to be. Please, just say yes."

"Yes, yes, yes," she cried. "When?"

He smiled and drew back. "You thought I was kidding about it being tonight, didn't you? But I wasn't."

Unrestrained joy flared in her eyes, then died as suddenly. "I can't."

His heart crashed. "Why not?"

"My agreement with my mother," she said. "I can't get married without her approval...not until my debt is paid off."

"She hasn't turned you down yet," he whispered. "Maybe she'll approve."

Her face drained of color. "I don't think so, Sly."

"Then we'll pay it off," he said. "Together, we'll borrow money on the company's assets. It'll be okay, baby. I swear it will."

And somehow, as her smile was reborn in her eyes, he knew that she believed him.

CHAPTER TWENTY-THREE

"I CAN'T BELIEVE he pleaded guilty." Blue Berringer stood at the mantel, looking down at his siblings as if he had stepped into the role of father to them all. "He knew they'd send him to prison."

Rally, Choral and Ford sat on the couch, Choral wiping her tears and the men shaking their heads as if something terrible had been set into motion and they had been left powerless to stop it.

"They're treatin' him like some kinda criminal," Angel wailed, sitting on the hearth.

From her place on the floor, Haven looked over at her. "What he did was a crime, Angel. It's protocol to treat someone like a criminal when they commit a crime."

"Whose side are you on?" Angel retorted.

"Leave her alone," Ford said quietly. "The crime he committed was against her. She has the right to feel that way."

"So he made a mistake! She didn't have to be so bitter and turn him in!"

"I didn't turn him in!" Haven returned. "I tried to warn him . . . and it might have worked if he hadn't gone off half-cocked and attacked Laura the way he did."

"She probably provoked him," Choral shouted. "She always did."

"That's enough!" Blue bellowed. "We've got to stop pointing fingers. He did it, and he's payin' for it. That's all there is to it. But Daddy wanted me to get you all here for a reason. He's decided to sell the house."

"What?" Choral sprang up from her seat. "He'll need this house when he gets out!"

"This is our home!" Angel cried.

"It's not your home anymore," Blue said. "Since Haven's movin' out, it isn't gonna be home to anybody. And Daddy's worried about the fact that Ford and Rally and me are losin' our jobs, since we worked for him. So he wants us to sell the house and this part of the property—not the parts where we live, but this west end of it—and divvy the proceeds up between us."

"What about Mama?" Angel asked. "Her house is on this part of the property."

"I've already worked it out with her," Blue said. "She'll get a portion, too, and with it she can rebuild on the land where one of us lives."

There was silence for a moment, and finally, Rally said, "I could use the money."

"Me, too," Ford agreed.

"Then it's done," Blue told them. "I'll list the house tomorrow. I don't think it'll take long to sell it."

"There's just one thing you're all forgettin'." Haven took a deep breath and looked from one of her siblings to the other.

"What's that?" one of them asked.

"Laura. The money ought to go to her."

"*What?*" It was Rally and Choral who spoke simultaneously. The others gaped at her as if she'd lost her mind. "You must be crazy to think we'd give a dime of it to her. She got Daddy thrown in prison!"

"She kept him out when she was married to him," Haven reminded them in her soft, thoughtful monotone. "And she saved this house and his cars and all the land by goin' into debt for ten million dollars. If anybody makes any money off of Daddy's property, it should be her."

Blue's face reddened, and he set his hands on his hips. "Tell you what, Haven. If you want to throw money at Laura Rockford, go right ahead and do it with your share.

284 CATCH A FALLING STAR

But I'm not lettin' go of mine so that she can get out of trouble with her mother. They've got more money than anybody in the country. Certainly more than we do."

The others agreed unanimously, and as the conversation revolved around selling the house, Haven didn't say another word.

"YOU'LL MARRY THAT MAN over my dead body." Catrina's voice trembled with rage, and Laura clutched the phone tighter.

"Mother, I really want your blessings. I want to have the kind of wedding you could be proud of. I want a white dress and a veil, and a bouquet, and a big cake, all in a beautiful church. I want to have the kind of wedding I used to dream of as a little girl, and I thought you would want that for me, too. But if I can't get your help with this, or your approval, I don't have to have any of that. The main thing is that I'll be getting Sly."

"Laura, he's not from a good family," her mother snapped. "His father was a postal worker, for heaven's sake, and his mother's a secretary!"

"You had him checked out?" Laura asked. "How dare you!"

"I'm your mother," Catrina said, as though that gave her license to do as she pleased. "I care about you, and I wanted to make sure that you weren't getting involved with someone else who was going to use you to get at my money. I don't trust anyone in the music business."

Laura was livid. "Mother, *I'm* in the music business."

"Not for long," Catrina replied.

Laura let out a heavy breath. "That's a matter of opinion, Mother. And you obviously didn't find anything on him or I would have heard about it by now."

"I learned that his family is not the kind of family that a Rockford should be marrying into. You can do so much better, darling, if you'd just come back home and..."

"I'm *not* coming back home, Mother! Not now, and not ever. I'm marrying Sly."

"Don't be ludicrous," Catrina bit out. "The choice is not yours. Have you forgotten our agreement?"

"No, Mother, I haven't forgotten. Either I pay you back within the allotted amount of time or I come back to Philadelphia and work with you."

"If I recall, there was also a clause about your not getting married without my approval."

"I'm not an indentured servant, Mother. I owe you money. I do not owe you my life."

"Pay back the loan, darling. Then you can do whatever you want."

"And if I don't have it now and I get married, anyway?"

"Then I'll sue you," Catrina said simply. "We have a contract in black and white. No one held a gun to your head to make you sign it."

"You would sue your own daughter?"

"You bet I would. In a second. Don't ever underestimate me, darling."

For a moment, there was silence, and finally, Laura tried again. "I'm going to pay you off very soon, Mother. Even before the deadline. I'm going to borrow money on the assets of our company. Sly has agreed to it. All I have to do is go to the bank."

"Is that so?" Catrina asked, her tone suggesting she had the edge again. "That's very magnanimous of him, but if I recall, there's a third partner in your company."

"Our partner has been very good about letting us be autonomous," Laura told her. "I don't anticipate problems from him."

"Laura, Laura," her mother said, her tone half amused. "You're still so young, and so naive. Don't you realize that there is no 'him?'"

A sense of foreboding tightened Laura's stomach. "What do you mean?"

"I mean that there's only me. I'm the third partner in Renegade Records."

CHAPTER TWENTY-FOUR

"YOU'RE LYING." Laura's voice quivered, and she raked her hand through her hair. "It's not true. You can't be the third partner."

"It's true," Catrina said again. "And now I'm sure you can see how ludicrous it would be to borrow on the assets of a company I own a third of, in order to pay me back."

Reeling, Laura shook her head. "Why? Why would you finance our studio, only to use it against me like this?"

"So that I could see to your best interests, darling," Catrina told her. "Your judgment has proved lacking in the past. You insist on doing things your own way. Sometimes a mother has to do secretive things to look out for her child."

"And looking out for me means putting a noose around my neck and forcing me into doing things I don't want to do?"

"Coming back to Philadelphia would be the best thing that ever happened to you. You'd be the heir to billions, and you could marry well, and you'd be able to do anything, go anywhere, buy everything."

"All I want is what I have here," Laura insisted. "Manipulating me is not going to make me want what you want for me, Mother."

"Then it looks as if we have a problem," Catrina said. "You don't have the money to pay me, and you probably won't before your deadline. If you marry against my will, you'll face a number of consequences aside from a lawsuit. I could start flexing my muscles in your company, now that it's no longer a secret that I'm your partner. Sly might not like it, but he'll be so distracted trying to keep your marriage together under all the stress that maybe he won't notice. Of course, men do take things so personally. It would be rather demeaning when everything he's worked for comes tumbling down. You should know, darling. Zane didn't mind saying goodbye at all when he had fallen."

Tears flooded Laura's eyes, and she caught her breath. "What did I ever do to you? Why do you hate me so much?"

Catrina was quiet for a few moments. "I don't hate you, Laura. It's not possible for a mother to hate her child. But I'll do whatever I have to do, buy whatever I have to buy and destroy whomever I have to destroy to see that you reach your potential."

Slowly, Laura dropped the phone into its cradle and cut her mother off.

She wasn't sure how long she sat in the dark room, staring into space, playing the conversation over and over in her mind like a litany that would soon drive her crazy.

The doorbell rang, and she stared at the door, wondering if Sly's session had been canceled. Slowly, she got up and opened it.

Haven stood there, scruffy and waiflike—the way she'd looked ever since Zane had been sent to prison—clutching her army surplus jacket around her. But according to Haven, Laura was worse. "You look awful," she said. "What's wrong?"

Laura abandoned the door, and Haven came in and closed it behind her. "My mother. I told her Sly asked me to marry him—"

Slowly, Haven smiled. "He did?"

Laura nodded miserably. "Only there's this stupid clause in that agreement I signed with her that I won't get married without her permission until the loan is paid off. Only I don't have enough money yet . . . and we were gonna borrow it on the business, only now she tells me that she's the third partner who invested, and she won't agree to using the business as collateral, and she might destroy it anyway." She broke into a sob, and Haven came to sit next to her on the couch. When Haven put her arms around her, Laura collapsed against her shoulder, crying her heart out.

"Sheesh," she said. "That woman causes you an awful lot of pain."

"I guess I bring it on myself," she said. "I should have learned by now."

"None of us ever learn," Haven said softly. "Not when it comes to our parents, anyway."

Laura let Haven go and slumped back on the couch. "I don't know how to tell Sly."

"Just tell him straight out," Haven said. "He'll understand. He's waited two years for you. He's not gonna give up now."

SLY WAS FAR FROM giving up, and when he told her that he wanted to chance it and get married anyway, despite her mother's threats, she wasn't surprised.

"Sly, she'll ruin the company. And she'll sue us."

"You can't sue somebody for getting married!"

"You can if they signed a contract not to."

"Fine. Then let her sue us. Let her ruin the company. I don't care, Laura. This is our life we're talking about."

She considered the possibility, then sighed in defeat. "I'd be bringing you down, Sly, just like Zane accused me of doing with him. Don't you see? It would be just like my marriage to him. One struggle after another. Failure, defeat..."

"With one difference, Laura. I love you."

It was too complicated, she thought, and she knew firsthand that love wasn't enough to solve so many problems. But problems like these did often have the power to extinguish the love.

The doorbell rang, and wearily, she opened it. Haven was back. "I think I've got the answer," she said.

Laura let her in and slumped back on the couch. "What answer?"

"To at least part of your problem." Haven shrugged out of her jacket, tossed it onto a nearby chair and sat cross-legged on the floor. "See, I've been havin' a problem with all this fame and fortune... I mean, part of me likes knowin' that so many people like my music, but there's somethin' wrong with this. I don't have any peace with gettin' rich off it." She pulled an envelope from her pocket and slipped out the check that was inside.

"That's your first royalty check," Laura said. "What's wrong with it?"

Haven laughed mirthlessly. "Well, the amount, for one thing."

"A million dollars?" Sly was becoming impatient. "It's your first royalty period, Haven. There'll be more."

Haven got up and shook her head, as if she didn't want to hear that. "You don't understand. What am I gonna do with this kind of money? All I need is a couple of T-shirts and a pair of jeans, a roof over my head, *sometimes*, and somethin' to eat now and then. Besides that, Jerry Joe made way more than this. What are two people like us gonna do with millions of dollars?"

"Enjoy it," Laura said. "You earned it. You're worth it."

"But see, that's just it," Haven told her. "I didn't earn it. You did. If it hadn't been for you, none of this would have happened to me."

"So... are you blaming me or thanking me?"

Haven smiled. "I'm payin' you." She handed Laura the check. "I want you to have it as partial repayment of Daddy's debt to you."

Laura couldn't take it, but she sat up straighter. "Haven, I can't take your royalty money."

"You have to," Haven insisted, her face reddening, "or I'll just go crazy. I don't want it, Laura. I *never* wanted it." She dropped the check on the coffee table and pulled another one out of her back pocket. "Oh, and I never wanted this, either. If I'd had my way, you'd have gotten all of it, but I can only give you my part."

"Your part of what?"

"The proceeds from the sale of the house and the land and all of Daddy's cars," Haven said. "I told everybody that we owed it to you, since you had paid to save them in the first place, but they wouldn't listen. But I got a bigger portion than anybody else, since they already had houses and land that Daddy had given them. For some reason, he's gotten real fair-minded since he's in prison."

Stunned, Laura looked down at the cashier's check for four million dollars. "Haven, I can't take this."

"Oh, please, Laura," Haven said. "If you don't take it I'll just give it to some fake organization that claims to feed starvin' children but really finances revolutions in Third World countries. I don't want the responsibility."

"But . . . it's so much."

"It's only half of what you did for my family," Haven said more seriously. "I plan to pay the other half if I ever get that much again."

Laura shook her head. "If I take this, can we call it even? Once and for all? No more payments?"

Haven shrugged. "I don't know if I can make that promise, but we'll see."

Laura hesitated and looked at Sly, her eyes wide and questioning. "What do you think?"

Sly grinned. "I say we go for it, and name our first child after Haven."

Laura laughed and hugged her. "Thank you, Haven. This means so much to me."

But Haven knew, as well as she did, that it wasn't enough. It was only half of what she needed to pay her mother back, and even after she did, she had to contend with Catrina being their third partner. As promising as five million dollars looked in her hand, Laura couldn't help believing that she'd sunk into a mire from which it was impossible to escape.

"WE'LL THINK of something, baby," Sly said later, after Haven had left. "But five million dollars is a darn good start." He pulled her down across his lap and cradled her head with his arm. "And if you think that I'm going to let your mother keep me from marrying you, you're as crazy as Haven Berringer is."

When he kissed her, she felt as if she'd acquired wings and was soaring above the heavens without a single tie to hold her back.

Suddenly, he broke the kiss and grinned down at her. "I've got it!"

She frowned. "Got what?"

"I know what to do!" Sly said. "I don't know why I didn't think of it right away." His eyes were full of fire. "We're going to beat your mother at her own game."

"WE'VE DECIDED TO SELL our shares of Renegade Records to Haven Berringer and Jerry Joe Wagner." Laura smiled and clutched the phone, waiting for Catrina's reaction.

Her mother laughed bitterly. "Oh, no you don't. Our agreement says that I have the option to refuse a sell to anyone. And, darling, I'm refusing."

Laura made a great show of sighing. "You have the option to buy us out yourself, Mother, as long as you match the offer by the other parties."

Catrina was silent for a moment. "I'm not stupid, Laura. This is a scheme, and I'm not falling for it."

"It's all legal, Mother. You're such a stickler for legalities that we had our lawyer review the fine points of this sale. And Jerry Joe and Haven have offered us a total of five million for our part in the company."

"That still won't get you out of my debt."

"Not yet," Laura said, looking down at the two checks totaling five million that Haven had already given her. She wasn't ready to tell her mother about them yet. Not until it was time. "But it will get me out of your control, at least where the company is concerned."

Catrina was dead silent for the next several moments, and finally, Laura said, "What'll it be, Mother? Do you acquire two new partners, or do you buy us out for five million?"

Catrina finally cleared her throat. "You win this battle, Laura," she said through clenched teeth. "But the war isn't over. As long as you owe me five more million, you can't marry Sly or anybody else. Because if you do, I'll drag you through the court system so fast that you won't know what hit you."

"And you'll really get the jury's sympathy," Laura said. "The mother who's suing to control her twenty-three-year-old daughter."

"Everyone will understand that I've done nothing but bail you out since you quit Princeton," she said. "When I drag the details of your marriage to Zane and the way he used you and abused you in front of a jury, and the fact that I even tried to help you get started in a new business by financing it completely as a silent partner, I don't think anyone would see me as anything but a caring mother who's determined to keep her child from making more mistakes."

"It doesn't matter what *I* see, does it, Mother?" Laura asked quietly. "As long as you can convince the public."

"You're a child," her mother said, "and you'll never see things as they truly are."

"I saw things as they really were when I was eight years old," Laura whispered. "None of this surprises me. But I still have a few surprises for you."

When she hung up, she looked down at the checks in her hand, and suddenly it didn't matter anymore if her mother loved her or approved of her or made peace with her. All that mattered was that this episode of her life was almost behind her.

THE BOARDROOM in Philadelphia where Sly and Laura sat with their lawyers to close the sale of Renegade Records to Catrina was as cold as a tomb. And as Laura sat across the table from her mother, prepared to hand her the check for five million as the final surprise, she sensed a mood of conciliation that she hadn't expected. Her mother's eyes, flawlessly made up, looked red-rimmed and glassy, as though she'd been crying. But Laura knew better. Her mother never cried.

"While we're here, Mother," she said, facing her mother more squarely than she ever had in her life, "I have one more piece of business to take care of."

Catrina didn't question her, and her expression remained unwavering.

Reaching into her briefcase, Laura withdrew the five million dollar cashier's check and passed it across the glossy tabletop. "Since you're paying us five million for our parts of the company, that leaves five million remaining in my debt to you. Here it is now."

Catrina's hand trembled as she took the check, stared at it, then laid it back down on the table. After a tense few moments, Catrina regarded the attorneys in the room. "I'd like to speak to my daughter and Mr. Hancock alone," she said. "Please excuse us."

Few people ever questioned the orders of Catrina Rockford, so one by one, the lawyers cleared the room.

Catrina waited until the last one was out and the door had closed behind him, then picked up the check again and stared down at it. "How will you start your new label?" she asked quietly.

Sly clasped his hands in front of him. "How do you know there will be one?"

Catrina gave a bitter smile. "Come now, Sly. You don't think I'm stupid. Your plan was to stick me with something I have no use for, then go and start a carbon copy somewhere else. But you're underestimating me. I have the resources to hire talented people to run Renegade Records to compete with you, and I have a capable team of attorneys who could prove fraud in court when we point out how you rewrote all of your contracts just before selling the company to me." She leaned forward, her eyes cutting Sly. "I could buy any recording company I wanted to, Sly. I could buy Nashville."

"But you still wouldn't have Laura."

Her perfectly shaped nose seemed to redden by degrees, and for a moment, she seemed to hold herself still, as if she might break completely if she made the slightest move. "No, I wouldn't," she said finally. Taking a deep breath, she looked down at the check. "And it occurs to me that the two of you could have bought my share of the company with this five million dollars. In fact, you'd only need two and a half."

"I know you, Mother. That wasn't something you would have considered."

"No, it wasn't," Catrina said, looking down at her hands. "It certainly wasn't. Not then."

She swallowed and turned her assessing eyes back to Laura. "I've given a great deal of thought to how far I could take this, how easily I could destroy you...." Her voice broke, and those rare tears welled in her eyes as she covered her mouth with her hand.

"Why?" Laura asked on a whisper. "Why would you do that?"

Catrina laughed then, softly, and shook her head. "I'd tell myself I was trying to teach you. So that you'd stop making wrong decisions. So that I could—"

"Control me?"

"Mother you," Catrina corrected.

Laura couldn't help the bitter laugh that rose from her throat. "Mother me? By destroying what I love?"

"Yes," Catrina said, and the first tear broke through her lashes and made its way down her cheek. "But you see, I realize now how ludicrous that would be."

Slowly, she picked up the check, then put it in her purse. "I'll accept this check, Laura, but only as payment for the purchase of *my* share of Renegade Records, plus two and a half to fully cover the debt of ten million dollars."

Laura's mouth dropped open, and she stared at Sly, who stared at Catrina with disbelief. "You would do that? Sell me your part of the company and erase my debt?"

Catrina didn't answer for a moment, and finally, she said, "I really have no choice."

Laura's features tightened as the full force of her mother's decision hit her. "Yes, you do, Mother. You have a choice. You've always had a choice."

"Well then, consider this one of the few right ones I've made where you're concerned." She slid her chair back and stood, holding herself as rigid as possible. "I'll have my attorneys draw up the proper papers this afternoon, so we can put this ordeal behind us."

With the regality of the queen of England, Catrina made her way around the table.

"Mother?"

Catrina stopped but didn't look at her daughter.

"I'm still going to marry Sly," Laura said. "And I'll never work for Rockford Enterprises."

"You'll own it one day, Laura," her mother replied. "But I have capable people who can run it." Then she turned back to them, lifting her chin high. "And as for your marriage, I find it difficult to give my blessings. But I can see that he was willing to marry you when you had nothing. I envy that."

Having spoken, she left the room.

Laura and Sly sat motionless, staring at the door, not believing what had just happened. Then slowly, they looked at each other, and smiles crept across their faces. Finally, those smiles broke into laughter, and Laura threw her arms around his neck and he lifted her out of her seat and spun her around.

"Let's go get married," he said. "Right now. Right this minute. While everything feels so good."

Laura was too emotional to speak, but when she took his hand and pulled him out of the room, he knew what the answer would be.

HAVEN CLOSED HER EYES and wailed out the last verse of the song she'd written about prison life, as the inmates of Danbury Federal Correctional Institute came to their feet, shouting and whistling for more. In the front row sat her father, applauding as fervently as any of the others, the tears running down his face.

"And now I'd like to sing you a little song..." She strummed a few chords, then seemed to remember the microphone again. "I wrote for my daddy...." She picked out a few notes, did a little run with her left hand, then strummed again. "The day he was incarcerated."

The room grew so quiet she could hear herself breathing, and she strummed a few more chords. "But before I sing it...I wanted to thank you...for making the first concert of my prison tour such a wonderful experience. I think I've found my haven."

The room erupted again, but soon the sound of her magic quieted them, and she began to weave a spell over all of them as she sang of the man she knew Zane to be, and the fact that when all the layers of fame and success and anger and pain and alcohol and revenge were stripped away, he was still the daddy who used to tuck her in at night, help her say her prayers and tell her never to let that cruel, cold world change her from the person God meant her to be.

As the inmates responded with tears and whistles and cries for more, she got to her feet, slid her stool away and shouted into the mike, "The bottom line is that the only difference between most of you and me is that bottle you once worshiped or that coke you once sold your soul for. And I happen to be one of those who believe that you can find yourself again. It's not too late."

The guards watched, all senses alert, as thunderous applause reverberated throughout the auditorium, but there was nothing to fear. Many of the inmates were crying, and the rest were transfixed by the words she had wrapped around them.

Going to the edge of the stage, Haven hugged her father, kissed him on the cheek, then waved to the rest of the crowd.

Jerry Joe waited in the wings, grinning at the woman he'd fallen in love with. When she came over to him, he hugged her and said, "That sure blows the theory that the more a fan pays for a ticket, the more he'll enjoy the concert."

"The free ones are the ones I like best," Haven told him. "I'm finally doin' somethin' I feel comfortable with."

"You know you won't earn a dime."

"No, but I'll have everything I need."

Settling his arm across her shoulders, Jerry Joe smiled as he walked her out of the prison.

SLY AND LAURA had a glorious wedding ceremony that afternoon in a tiny Lutheran church not far from the attorneys' offices. Their witnesses were the church secretary and the choir director, who sang them a soft duet of "Sweet, Sweet Spirit," then congratulated them as if they'd known them all their lives.

After the ceremony they went to the studio of a photographer recommended by the minister and had a wedding portrait taken—Laura in the white tea-length gown she had purchased only hours before and Sly in the tux he'd brought with him—so that they would forever have a memento of this special day.

Then they called Sly's mother and told her what they had done. Laura listened as his mother laughed out loud and said that eloping was something she had always wanted to do, and she was glad they'd had the nerve.

When they arrived back at the attorneys' offices in their wedding attire, Laura still holding the bouquet they had bought on the way to the church, Catrina failed to acknowledge the event. They signed the necessary papers in relative silence, but once the attorneys had left the room, Laura and Sly stayed behind, looking at Catrina, who stared at them with a porcelain expression that could shatter at any moment.

"I suppose congratulations are in order," Catrina said.

"For the business or the marriage, Mother?"

Catrina gave a deep, laborious sigh. "For both."

Slowly, Laura got up, went around the table, plucked the one pink rose from her white bouquet and handed it to her mother. Catrina's hand trembled as she took it. She looked up at her daughter with misty eyes. Leaning over, Laura pressed a kiss on her cheek. "Thank you, Mama," she whispered.

Catrina sat perfectly still as Laura went back around the table to her husband, gathered up the papers they were taking home and headed for the door.

"You'll be happy, won't you?" Catrina asked suddenly.

"Yes," Laura said. "I'll be happy."

Catrina nodded quietly as they started from the room, but before they left, Laura turned back around. "If I'm ever in Philadelphia, may I come to visit?"

"Of course," her mother said. "And I'll be coming to Nashville."

Laura smiled. "Good."

And as she walked away, she was filled with a hope that she had never felt before, the hope that, someday, Catrina might yet be the mother she needed.

That night, as they walked through the airport to catch their flight back to Nashville, a clown selling balloons got in their way. Laura stopped walking and gazed up at the multicolored balls bobbing above the clown's head. "Have I ever told you that one of my happiest memories as a child involved a helium balloon?"

His eyes swept over her smiling face for a moment, and finally, he pulled out his wallet. "Wait here," he said.

She laughed, knowing he was going to buy her one, and she watched as he spoke quietly to the clown. The clown took the bill Sly offered and handed the entire bunch to Sly.

Laura threw her hand over her mouth as he brought them to her.

"I'll help you," he said with a laugh. "If you hold them by yourself, they might sweep you away and I'll never see you again." Leaning over, he kissed her, a kiss that was long and sweet and full of promise, then handed her the balloons. "Consider them a wedding present. The flight attendants will go crazy, but that's their problem."

"I'm not taking them on the plane," she said. "I have other plans for these."

She took a pen and a small piece of paper out of her purse, then hurriedly scribbled a note and folded it.

Sly watched with an adoring smile, not questioning her. Finally, she looked up and found an exit. "There," she said. "We can go outside there."

She took the balloons in one hand and pulled him along with the other, and in moments they were outside, standing on the tarmac, gazing up into the star-studded sky. She glanced up at the colorful balloons bobbing above her, then carefully tied the note to the ribbon and let them go.

Sly slid his arms around her as they watched the balloons rise quickly into the sky, growing smaller and smaller as they drifted farther away.

"What did the note say?" he asked when the balloons were almost out of sight.

She smiled. "Thank you, God, for Sly."

His embrace tightened around her, and tears came to his eyes as he looked up at the balloons again. A light flared across the sky just before the balloons disappeared completely. "Look," he whispered. "A falling star."

"What do you think that means?"

Sly's voice held a soft chuckle as he turned her around to face him. "I think it means, 'You're welcome.'"

And as he pulled her close and kissed her, Laura felt the thrilling, awe-inspiring peace of knowing that her prayers had finally been answered.

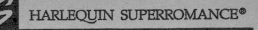

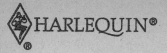 

The proprietors of Weddings, Inc. hope you
have enjoyed visiting Eternity, Massachusetts.
And if you missed any of the exciting Weddings,
Inc. titles, here is your opportunity to complete
your collection:

CHRISTMAS STALKINGS

All wrapped up in spine-tingling packages, here are three books guaranteed to chill your spine…and warm your hearts this holiday season!

#302 THE KID WHO STOLE CHRISTMAS
Linda Stevens

#303 I'LL BE HOME FOR CHRISTMAS
Dawn Stewardson

#304 BEARING GIFTS
Aimée Thurlo

This December, fill your stockings with the "Christmas Stalkings"—for the best in romantic suspense. Only from

HARLEQUIN®

INTRIGUE®

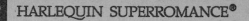

HARLEQUIN SUPERROMANCE®

Pregnant…and on her own!

Her Sister's Baby
by Janice Kay Johnson

Colleen was pregnant with her sister's baby. But it was
Sheila's baby; Colleen had assured her sister of that.
Because Sheila wanted a baby more than anything in the
world. That's why Colleen had volunteered to be a
surrogate mother—*for Sheila.* Not for her brother-in-law,
Michael, although he was the baby's natural father. Then,
tragically, Sheila died—and Michael wanted his child.

Watch for stories in our *Nine Months Later* series.
Available in January,
wherever Harlequin books are sold.

HARLEQUIN SUPERROMANCE®

Reunited!
First Love...Last Love
Stories of lovers reunited.

Next month, watch for **Courting Valerie**, our first **Reunited!** title.

Jay Westcott is obviously the perfect candidate for the job, but Valerie Brettinger isn't sure she wants to work with him. She'd put him out of her mind—and her heart—years ago, when he left to seek his fortune in Chicago. Besides, she doesn't quite trust his motives. Why would a big-shot lawyer like Jay come back to Amsden? And why has he chosen to oppose her on a case that could clearly turn her life upside down?

Courting Valerie by Linda Markowiak
Available in January, wherever Harlequin books are sold.